AN altered light

ALSO BY JENS CHRISTIAN GRØNDAHL

Lucca

Silence in October

jens christian grøndahl

AN altered light

TRANSLATED FROM THE DANISH
BY ANNE BORN

HARCOURT, INC.

Orlando   Austin   New York   San Diego   Toronto   London

www.HarcourtBooks.com

This is a translation of *Et andet lys.*
First published in English in Australia by the Text Publishing Company.

The Literature Committee of the Danish Arts Council provided support
for this translation.

Library of Congress Cataloging-in-Publication Data
Grøndahl, Jens Christian, 1959–
[Andet lys. English]
An altered light/Jens Christian Grøndahl;
translated from the Danish by Anne Born.—1st U.S. ed.
p.   cm.
I. Born, Anne. II. Title.
PT8175.G753A5313 2004
839.8'1374—dc22   2004026550
ISBN 0-15-101043-9
ISBN 978-0-15-101043-1
Text set in Baskerville MT

Printed in the United States of America

First U.S. edition
A C E G I K J H F D B

ACKNOWLEDGMENTS

Special thanks for support and inspiration to
Beatrice Monti, the Santa Maddalena Foundation;
Morten Zeuthen, cellist; Søren Michael Bernth Giessing;
the Israeli embassy in Denmark, and—
as always—my wife, Anne Vad.

A man's road back to himself
is a return from his spiritual exile, for that is what
a personal history amounts to—exile.

SAUL BELLOW
The Actual

AN altered light

I

From Tomorrow to Yesterday

The tree trunks move in time with the rhythm of her rubber soles on the wet path, where the air is still cool after the night rain. The woodland floor is white with anemones; in one place, growing close to the roots of an ancient tree, they make her think of an old, wrinkled hand. She could go on and on without getting tired, without meeting anyone or thinking of anything in particular, and without coming to the edge of the woods. As if the town did not begin just behind the trees, the leafy suburb with its peaceful roads and its houses hidden behind close-trimmed hedges. She doesn't want to think about anything, and almost succeeds; her body is no more than a porous, pulsating machine. The sun breaks through the clouds as she runs back, its light diffused on the gravel drive and the magnolia in front of the kitchen window. His car is no longer parked beside hers, he must have left while she was in the woods.

He hadn't stirred when she rose, and she'd already been in bed when he came home late last night. She lay with her back turned, eyes closed, as he undressed, taking care not to wake her. She leans against one of the pillars of the garage and stretches, before emptying the mailbox and letting herself into the house. She puts the mail on the kitchen table. The little light on the coffeemaker is on; she switches it off. Not so long ago, she would have felt a stab of irritation or a touch of tenderness, depending on her mood. He always forgets to turn off that machine. She puts the kettle on, sprinkles tea leaves into the pot, and goes over to the kitchen window. She observes the magnolia blossoms, already starting to open. They'll have to talk about it, of course, but neither of them seems able to find the right words, the right moment.

She pauses on her way through the sitting room. She stands amid her furniture looking out over the lawn and the pond at the end of the garden. The canopies of the trees are dimly reflected in the shining water. She goes into the bathroom. The shower door is still spotted with little drops. As time went on they have come to make contact during the day only briefly, like passing strangers. But that's the way it has been since the children left home, nothing unusual in that. She takes off her clothes and stands in front of the mirror where a little while ago he stood shaving. She greets her reflection with a wry smile. She has never been able to view herself in a mirror without this moue, as if demonstrating a certain guardedness about what she sees. The dark green eyes and wavy black hair, the angularity of her features. She dyes her hair exactly the color it would have been if she hadn't begun to go gray in her thirties, but that's her only protest against age.

2

Irene Beckman is fifty-six. She is taller than most women of her generation, slim, almost thin. Her dark hair is usually gathered in a ponytail; it bounces after her when she runs, so that at a distance she looks like a young woman. People found her exotic when she was young and beautiful. For decades, Martin had gazed almost devoutly at her unusual features. A gaze that created distance, even when it burned to the touch. Male admiration has always seemed like a subtle form of isolation. The closer they came, the stranger she felt. His stubble is stuck to the inside of the sink; she rinses it away and considers her body. She is satisfied on the whole: women's bodies don't come much better at her age. She turns on the shower, sets it to hot, and steps under the jet. The sharp lines of the cabinet dissolve behind the water running down the glass door.

The thought that everything should remain the same gradually feels as unreal as the thought of a change. What was unimaginable has become real, but she's unable to visualize it. Perhaps it is banality that impedes her mind's eye. The all too common situation is almost more humiliating than the physical or emotional or, for that matter, moral circumstances. All she knows is that there is something in Martin's life called Susanne. She's barely thirty, you can hear that from her voice — and Irene has heard her voice. They didn't sound like two people who'd just met. They sounded as if they already had their shared habits and their own intimate language. She's thought a lot about his carelessness. He has always taken great care except in this one instance.

It was a month or two ago. He must have arrived home just as the telephone rang, and in his haste neglected to switch off the answering machine. They arranged to meet. Presumably, he was with her when Irene came home and played back the day's messages. She erased the tape after she'd listened to their voices a few times, and she did it as if cleaning up after him. She said nothing when he came back

3

late in the evening—newly washed, she thought—as he lay down beside her and gave her a kiss on the cheek.

She has lived through half her life with him, and she has lost
touch with the half he was absent from. She's not normally one to
look back. She can't imagine life without him. He is her friend, her
life's companion. They are as intimate as you would expect to be with
someone you have been so close to, but she doesn't know what she
will say when the time comes. Sometimes she asks herself why he has
said nothing. Their routine is more or less the same, they go out to
dinner on Friday or Saturday, and once or twice he's made the effort
to seduce her when they came home. It never seemed like a diver-
sionary maneuver, but it left her with a feeling of surprise and wonder. He'd gotten quite carried away and had taken her with him, and
that confused and disturbed her.

She puts on her bathrobe, dries her hair, and bends toward the
mirror to make up her face—not much, just a little on the eyelashes
and lips, but she does it defiantly. It has nothing to do with her age,
but it does have something to do with her generation. She had thrown
off her bra only hesitantly and had never gone in for flowing Indian
dresses, but she can still remember the nightgown she wore for years,
sensible cotton in black-and-white stripes. It must have looked like a
prison uniform, as if she'd just escaped; unless it had been marriage
that was the prison. Was it? To be deprived of freedom was the worst
thing you could suffer, but had Martin deprived her of her freedom?
Had she restricted his?

It never occurred to her to question it, but she felt a latent reproach from her women friends—because she found it hard to find
anything to rebel against. She had never been able to believe in a new
society, though she never believed in the existing one. Was it even a
question of belief? Maybe it was because she chose to study law that

4

she came to have such a cool view of the world, unless she'd taken up the law because she was inclined to be skeptical anyway: to see the truth without being ruled by her desires. Early on, that was one of the demands she made of herself, and it still is, more than ever. She didn't mind being overpowered by imagination; it was the tyranny of that power that made her skeptical. She shrank away from the gentle coercion of the new sensibility. Letting yourself go had become a matter of form, and she almost choked with coughing when a bong was passed around—until she plucked up the courage to admit that she felt absolutely no urge to throw off inhibitions.

She opens the closet and looks at Martin's jackets and shirts and her own dresses and blouses. His clothes make her think of Susanne. She pictures Martin in a strange apartment as he takes off his jacket and tie, pale blue shirt, and well-pressed trousers. Will he place them together tidily over the back of a chair? She's sure he'll remember to take off his socks, she taught him that many years ago, but she can't know whether the young woman finds him a touch comical in his sober business suit. Irene cannot visualize her, only the scene of his infidelity—a two-bedroom apartment with IKEA furniture and Matisse posters—and at a pinch her firm young body. It surprises Irene that this conjured-up picture has so little power over her, that it goes no deeper. She feels like a spectator, but the place from which she sees them is the place where her jealousy and pain and rejected female pride should have eaten into her and stung.

The phone rings. She hesitates a moment before sitting down on the edge of the bed and reaching for it. She is sure she'll recognize the voice. Susanne's girlish voice and slightly affected diction. She is annoyed because she picks up the receiver before she has cleared her throat in order to say hello. It's Josephine. Their daughter sounds as if she's standing by a waterfall. As usual, she is incoherent and talks too

5

fast. She is calling from the airport in Frankfurt. Josephine is a stewardess, and Irene is used to being called from every corner of the world. Josephine asks if she can bring a friend home this evening. Of course she can. Irene can't help smiling. She asks if it's anyone she knows. She can hear Josephine is smiling, too, in Frankfurt. Not yet.

They chat for a while before hanging up. Irene stays on the bed drawing patterns with her big toe on the carpet. She's stopped counting the young men Josephine has presented her with. Josephine's way with men reminds her of her way with big cities, and her mother is worried but tries to suppress her motherliness. She gets up and decides on a coffee-brown suit with a tailored jacket and wide trousers.

Martin has left the newspaper on the dining table in the kitchen. She eats a kiwi and sips her tea as she skims through the articles. They've found yet another mass grave on the outskirts of a Bosnian village. She looks at the picture in the newspaper showing forensic workers sorting the partly decomposed remains of bodies and packing them into plastic bags. She looks up at the magnolia outside the kitchen window. For the ten years of the Balkan war, she's read one article after another on the reasons why militia burst into people's homes, dragged them to a mountainside, and shot them like dogs. She has tried to get to the roots of ethnic hostilities, but she is no longer interested in the causes of brutality, only in its reality. She no longer believes the world will ever be better or worse than it is. She's lawyer enough to be skeptical about taking a final stand, but still thinks it is relevant to find out who killed the people whose dismembered remains are on display in the newspaper. Not why, but who.

She notices that the light has grown sharper when she gets outside. She goes back to fetch her sunglasses and catches sight of the notepad beside the telephone where she has jotted down her mother's hospital ward and room number. She promised to visit her after work. How could she have forgotten? She gets into the car and backs out into the road. Her wedding ring clicks against the wheel as she turns the corner. The familiar little sound has accompanied her for so long it feels like a part of her body. Of late she didn't know what to say when Vivian asked how things were going. As if her mother expected something other than a conventional reply to her conventional question. They have never been particularly close, and Irene doesn't want to worry her now. Vivian is getting a new hip, but the thought of the general anesthetic is almost enough to make her want to stick with the wheelchair she's spent the past few months in.

Irene is confident of her mother's sympathy, but she is also sure that Vivian will make light of Martin's infidelity as something inevitable and thus irrelevant. If it's no use talking about unavoidable things, and it isn't, you might as well leave them alone. That's what Vivian thinks. They have hardly ever touched upon the painfully inevitable sides of life, not even when Irene's father left them for a younger woman. But it isn't Martin she really feels like discussing with her mother, it is the strange paralysis she feels in knowing something, yet not being changed by the knowledge.

The sun cast a shaft of light on the road between carefully manicured gardens. She feels privileged to be a part of life out here, where there's plenty of space between houses, and masses of bougainvillea and rhododendron bushes hide the fact that they look so much alike. The privilege resides less in the comfort of their well-padded existence than in the fact that it keeps out the rest of the world. The cruel world she reads about in the papers and sees on television, its wars and massacres and endless hordes of refugees, on foot with their possessions crammed into carts or dying of thirst in the oxygen-depleted air of rusting coffin ships. Her reactions, her sympathy and sometimes anger seem to be out of touch with her life. What can you do? How can you get the proportions right?

She switches on the radio and hears familiar voices and music, Paul McCartney and John Lennon, the sounds of the sixties, of light-heartedness. Has innocence gone out of fashion, or is it only she who has lost it, weighed down by well-nourished melancholy? She drives along the residential road and into the stream of morning traffic on its way into town. The music gives her a stab of nostalgia, a reminder of something lost, but also, she thinks, the memory of another stab, of longing and hunger. A longing without an object, like nostalgia itself, which cannot tell you what it is you have lost, apart from the vague, indefinable quality that is youth. To have the future before you and not be weighed down by knowledge, only by your unenlightened, disoriented restlessness.

She thinks of Martin, a slimmer, softer Martin, and a plump little Josephine and a lanky Peter, her big brother, who at thirty-two is already going bald. She sees her family in thin, fleeting visions in the light above the freeway and the first office buildings, viaducts, and apartment blocks. The same faces, but younger. Suntanned holidays on the grass, in the country, red-cheeked winter Sundays on the toboggan slopes. That kind of fleeting happiness. A small pearl of salt water trickles from the corner of her eye behind her sunglasses.

Good grief, is she sitting here snivelling?

Irene and Martin met in 1961, the year she was an au pair in Paris. She was seventeen, had never been abroad before, and the adventure of being in a foreign city sent any idea of the future into the distance. She had escaped from her conventional home only to land in one at least as conventional, but she had Paris in the bargain and a few precious hours at midday when she roamed around, stood on the back platform of a bus, or sat in the metro with a strange, sinking feeling in her stomach. The family lived in a large apartment on an expansive boulevard. When she felt the need for solitude and the weather was fair, she walked up to Père Lachaise and sat and read on a bench. The world was endless, and Paris and the books united to point out the many ways of endlessness.

At other times she went out walking in the Bois de Vincennes, both perturbed and exhilarated by the thought of getting lost.

She was alone but not lonely, she remembers, merely herself. Her dark hair and pronounced features made her feel at home because no one took any notice of her unless she spoke, at which point her accent revealed that she was not a native. As a child she had wondered about her black hair. Her parents were fair, but her grandfather, she was told, was dark like herself. He came from the Faroes, where many people were dark haired, a legacy of the Portuguese seamen who had gone ashore there over the years. At school Irene had felt different, embarrassed by her difference, and in Paris she was happy to be one of the crowd.

Those were postwar days in Paris. An impoverished place, sootier but also more brilliant and exotic than the city she and Martin visited after they had been married for years, strolling up the Champs Elysées like lost and idle tourists. Back then, it was her town because she was seeing it for the first time and conquering step by step new streets with fresh, alluring corners to turn. She must have covered the equivalent of the distance between Paris and Copenhagen that year, but she remembers surprisingly little. Her Paris is the Paris she later recognized in black-and-white films and photographs, still old-fashioned and yet modern, both more local and more cosmopolitan. It was the Paris of Juliette Greco and Jean-Paul Belmondo, a more innocent, lighthearted place, and it was still long before that notorious spring when for several months the town was on the verge of chaos and revolution.

She had been too early for the revolution. Nor did she want anything to change. She wished that her year in Paris would last forever. She was part of a loosely connected group of au pairs, students, aspiring artists, and perpetual tourists in search of adventure, who met in the cafés and cheap restaurants on the Left Bank. Those who did not live in colleges or with families were constantly on the move around dingy small hotels, and the safest meeting places were the cafés along the Boulevard Saint-Michel.

He had turned up on the edge of her circle, she couldn't remember precisely when. He hardly spoke a word of French and what he lived on was a mystery, but no one bothered to ask. He attached himself to them, and to begin with nobody really noticed him, until his cheerfulness and his small services had made him everyone's friend. He was good-looking with his fair hair and blue eyes, but not in the least attractive to her, and she wouldn't have given his appearance a thought if she hadn't noticed his interest in her. His face was as square as a shoe box, his body firm and muscular, and he spoke and behaved like a street urchin. Neither of these things would have posed a problem, she assured herself, had his obstinate charm not so clearly made her its target and prevented him from grasping her polite rejection of him.

She was in love just then with a young Frenchman with long hair and elegant gestures, the nephew of the woman whose children she looked after. He invited her out to dinner or to concerts, and she kept hoping he would make a pass when they were in the Salle Pleyel or sitting on the iron chairs in the Jardins de Luxembourg, but nothing happened. One evening at dinner, she heard he was to marry a girl from Grenoble.

Summer had come, she was shattered, and when a Swedish friend asked if she would like to come to the Riviera, she jumped at the idea. The girl's boyfriend knew someone whose parents had a villa just outside Nice, and the parents were away. She recalls the heat, the sea, the flat crowns of the pines and the terrace where they sat in the evenings looking out on the chain of lights along the coast. More and more guests arrived at the villa, staying the night in bedrooms and living rooms, and one day Martin turned up with a few friends from the Scandinavian colony in Paris.

He must have talked himself into her life, for the next thing she remembers is walking with him along the Promenade des Anglais. She can't remember how they came to be walking there, just the two of them. He told her about his childhood. His father died when he was little, his mother had married again and had more children, his stepfather did not like him, and he felt unwanted. He told her about his childhood home, about the loneliness and the feeling of being unwanted, but he didn't sound as if he was sorry for himself. He was already a jack of all trades—had been apprenticed to a smith, worked on a conveyor belt, sluiced out a ship's hold. He talked about Liverpool, Porto, and Tangier. A few months earlier he'd signed off in Cherbourg in order to go to Paris, and when he'd spent his pay he took a job washing dishes in a Pigalle nightclub. He told her about all this as if it was nothing special, and his offhand, shy smile did not match the insistent cheerfulness that irritated her so much.

She did not understand herself. Maybe that was why she allowed it to happen. At night for the first time she saw a person who opened himself up completely defenselessly. When he embraced her, she felt more naked than ever before, but at the same time it seemed as if he clung to her slight body, afraid of drowning in the darkness. It alarmed her, and the fear made her cruel. She lay with her back to him, felt his hands, and listened to his whispers, but did not reply. He had come too close, far too quickly. He said he would like to have children with her. She was the first one he had felt like this about. But why her? During the day she avoided him. She didn't want people to notice that there was anything between them, and she saw to it that they were never alone when she lounged in a deck chair in a bikini and sunglasses. She observed his suffering as she chatted easily and nonchalantly with the others, scared of what she had set in motion, ashamed, fascinated, and restless. She felt he wanted something far too dramatic and significant, and it irritated her. Early one morning she packed her bag and left the villa before he woke.

Later on, that summer was turned into something like a marital Genesis, the Promenade des Anglais and the room with the view of the sea, and the pines. She went back to Copenhagen and started to study law, slipped into her old environment and made new friends. She lived in a rented room in one of the streets behind the Royal Theater. For some years she fluttered around, as you do when you have escaped from home to study at university, with nothing but exams to worry about. A liberating, breezy change of air flowed through the town and the times after the cosy, restricted fifties of her childhood. She felt she was hovering like an escaped dragon on the winds of irresponsibility and possibility. She forgot Martin and their flirtation on the Riviera and his ill-timed lovemaking. It was by pure chance that they ran into each other again a few years later, although later on she came to accept the idea that they were meant for each other.

One spring evening she'd gone to Club Montmartre with a young man and another couple to listen to Dexter Gordon. It was a crowded tropical place, and she felt intoxicated although she drank nothing but lemonade. She didn't listen to what the others were saying, completely absorbed by the tall, brown, sweating man in the colored spotlight, playing his saxophone with a virile imagination that lifted the music out of the cramped space, up above the roofs of the town. Suddenly Martin was there at their table. He did not ask permission to sit down and did not seem to notice his rival's expression. He looked funny in his suit, white shirt, and tie. The other guys wore sweaters and desert boots and their hair was longer than his. He shouted over

the music. He wanted to talk to her. She went outside with him because she couldn't have him standing there shouting. He didn't reproach her, did not even seem hurt. He just looked at her. Why had
she left without saying goodbye? She didn't know what to say. He put
his arm through hers, and she let him. As they walked along the pavement, she tried to work out how to shake him off. She never did. He
hadn't forgotten her, and he did not intend to let her vanish again.

He was tireless. He called her day in and day out and waited in
front of the entrance to her apartment. He never gave up although
she did her utmost to discourage him. She let him wait in the hall of
the boarding house after the landlady had knocked and told her she
had a guest. Such a charming young man, the landlady thought.
There were flowers in her room when she came back, and he con-
trived to run into her in the street, always dapper with his side parting and his sky-blue eyes. If she was with someone she laughed at him,
but he merely smiled good-naturedly. He attended business school
and obviously planned to go places, dogged and ambitious as he was,
while all the others were busy dropping out. He smiled at himself in
his peculiar innocence as if not knowing what was so funny, but happy
to contribute to the entertainment.

It might have been so many others, but it was him. She gave in,
exhausted but also relieved, since he would not take no for an answer.
Later on, she asked herself whether she had merely grown resigned
to his unremitting persistence, but she remembers it differently. She
had spent the first twenty years of her life dreaming. Not about anything definite, but rather in a kind of vegetative way. Out of touch
with her surroundings except when, distrait and guarded, she picked
at one possibility or the other with the tips of her fingers. She had not
come close to many men, but enough to feel a strange distaste, not so
much for their infatuation or desire as for her own expectant, half-

averted gaze. Martin inspired something in her, and to start with it resembled envy. She would wish she could want something as strongly as he did. He made her feel inadequate, intensely insignificant, and she wanted with all her heart to be anything but that. She was tired of floating around, and against her will she had come to admire him. She, who had grown up lacking nothing, was brought to envy him, who owned nothing apart from a willpower she had never felt, nor met in anyone else.

They moved out of town, to an apartment in a newly built block close to the suburb where she had spent her childhood. She didn't see the irony of returning, still in her twenties, to the stagnant, bourgeois world she had gone all the way to Paris to escape. Her lower-upper-class background, as she described it to Martin. She was a lawyer, he worked at the bank where he had trained, and where he was promoted to departmental head a few years later. Their neighbors were newlyweds like themselves who had just started a family or were preparing to do so by furnishing bedrooms sensibly, with plenty of closet space. They commuted between town and the well-ordered, optimistic suburb where their children were to grow up. Martin and Irene made friends with some of them, they met on Saturday evenings and sometimes danced to gramophone records in the living rooms amid the practical designer furniture. When she looks back, it seems to her to have all been so naïve. Was that the times, or herself? She cannot tell.

While they were busy getting established, other people their age were actively undermining the establishment. Martin and Irene did not take part in the youth revolution; they were content to watch it from a distance, like the rest of the crowd who disappeared underground each afternoon onto the S train that took them out of town and away from the slightly alarming but fascinating events. They allowed themselves a glance at them, and a whiff of incense and hash in passing, but no more than that. Not until many years later did she realise that she had been in the midst of an immense radical change. While it was happening she had only regarded it as a faint background noise, a flicker at the edge of her field of vision.

She had to ask herself if she was the only one asleep at the time, or whether others, then and at other times had shared her experience. You could imagine a potter in Jerusalem who never realized, as he sat bent over his wheel, that Jesus had been crucified. Or a Parisian cobbler completely unaware of the assault on the Bastille, thinking it was merely street gossip. That was how she had been in '68. Sometimes Josephine and Peter beg her to tell them about that fabulous year, but she never knows where to start or what to say. It was something that happened on television and the radio and in the newspapers. World history was playing itself out dramatically, yes, but it was something you could switch on and off, or add to the pile of papers and magazines beside the sofa.

She was expecting Peter that spring. One mild afternoon she was in a packed streetcar, it had started to rain and she couldn't find a seat. She stood close to a girl her own age; the girl's hair was wet with rain and she wore no bra under her damp, sleeveless blouse. When she reached up to hold onto a strap she revealed a dark tuft of fuzzy hair under her arm. A sweetish smell of sweat wafted into Irene's nostrils, and she didn't know which way to turn. She had suffered from nausea through most of the pregnancy and the pungent presence of the strange girl turned her stomach. For a moment everything went black, and when she raised her head again she was looking straight into a pair of observant brown eyes.

The girl smiled at her, probably because she could see Irene's big stomach under her coat. It was a frank, engaging smile, almost challenging, but something in her gaze touched Irene with a feeling of being inspected, read, and shrewdly summed up. The kind smile and alert eyes told her that the other sympathized with her, but there was a hint of criticism. Not so much for her pregnancy, which naturally restricted her freedom of movement and erotic potential, but for what she was—a nice girl in a raincoat and skirt. Much too nice, much too middle class, helplessly behind the times and pathetically out of step with the swelling wave of liberation.

That was the closest she came to the events of '68.

Martin worked so hard he had no time to raise his nose from the grindstone and consider what he ought to think about the atmosphere of long-haired disobedience and sexed-up curiosity that was spreading, along with the humming feeling that everything could be different from what had gone before. Besides, he already had too much to lose to be attracted by the idea of an entirely new society. Irene's mother was quite satisfied with Martin's ambitious reliability. It irritated Irene that he so obviously enjoyed that. She was irritated because he did not appear to notice the condescending note beneath Vivian's kindness when they visited her at the house in which she'd remained after Irene's father had run off.

In fact, Irene found it hard to come to terms with Martin's enthusiastic desire to please her twittering busybody of a mother, until it dawned on her that he had at long last acquired what he had never had—a family. She knew Vivian would have preferred a young man from their own background, but Martin's earnest industriousness allowed her to forgive his uncertainty in handling cutlery, democrat that she was, in spite of everything. He had guessed her expectations for him and set himself to meet them. In spades. When Irene's father died, it was solely due to Martin that her mother was able to stay on in the villa. All the same, Vivian allowed herself to praise Martin in

17

his absence for how fantastically well he had done for himself, considering his background. Irene was furious, but each time she regretted voicing her rage when she saw Vivian's disorientated smile. Well, but it was fantastic!

He never talked about his ambition, but Irene felt it at all times. She noticed it in his eyes and voice, his firm embrace, his reluctance to talk about the past, and his body, which quivered with energy. She recognized it in the way he jutted his chin and pushed it forward when facing the mirror in the hall to knot his tie each morning. She realized that every single thing he did was a link in his plan to create a life that would compare with her former one. And it was not only to prove himself to the mother of the princess he had won. He wanted to get as far away as possible from his past as a scruffy, unwanted, working-class boy, and she respected him for it. She suppressed her urge to smile at his obsession with material things, for he was as un-snobbish as he was ambitious.

He made her feel secure. He surrounded her with his calm, dogged, almost fanatical adoration, and yes, she fell in love with him. He had unwrapped the blanket she had been swaddled in all her childhood, out of reach, unable to let anyone touch her or stretch out a hand herself to touch anyone or anything.

She became more sharply aware of that when they went to Paris on vacation a few years after Peter was born. Martin had become deputy director of the bank, and they had been able to afford a small terraced house. It was their first trip together and they spent several days going to the old places where they had stayed ten years earlier. She expected the visit to make her feel nostalgic, but nothing like that happened. Just before their departure for home she discovered the reason.

———

They had lunch beneath one of the arcades on the Place de Vosges, then strolled up through the Marais. As they crossed the Place de la République she suddenly thought of the beggar who'd sat on the corner of the square and the Boulevard de Magenta. She hadn't thought of him in all those years. She stopped. Martin looked at her inquiringly, but she said nothing. The beggar had sat right there on the edge of the pavement, his back to the cars and a small metal bowl in front of him. His face was a swollen, reddish, suppurating lump, with cracks where eyes, nostrils, and mouth should have been. You could hear a wheezing, whistling sound from the narrow indents in the lump.

She had only seen him properly once and only for a second or two, before she, like everyone else, had cast down her eyes and hurried on. Afterward, each time she passed the Place de la République she avoided that corner, but at night she often saw him. She gradually realized it was not just disgust or fear that she felt, but shame. Ashamed that she felt no compassion, that her sympathy was delayed and forced.

Irene was an easy prey to that kind of reflection. When she found herself back at the Place de la République, twenty-eight and thinking back to her seventeen-year-old sensitivity, she had to ask herself whether her sheltered childhood, apart from being its fertile soil, had also turned out to be its paradoxical limitation. As a curious au pair on the loose, when she had dared to venture into the seedier districts of Paris, up at Belleville or over behind the Gare du Nord, she saw people who had it hard and whose lives she could not possibly imagine even if she tried. Tough types, who would no doubt shrug their shoulders at a deformed beggar without a face, if they noticed him at all. He was a part of the raw, scabby inventory of their world, and it took a sensitive girl from the northern suburbs of Copenhagen for the beggar's misfortune to gain, so to speak, a consciousness and a conscience through which to make itself felt. But that was no help anyway, for in contrast to the more hard-boiled inhabitants of the poorer districts of Paris, she could not bear the sight of the object of her sensitivity.

In other ways she felt she had escaped from her mother's imprisoning arms and hushed suburb and arrived in the huge, swarming town. Its foreignness made her feel that she was foreign to herself as well.

Her self. Her unknown self.

Ever since she had begun to think about it at the age of thirteen, she knew it existed somewhere in there. She didn't know whether the self lodged in her heart, which according to her biology teacher was nothing more than a muscle, or whether it was somewhere in her brain, which was nothing more than an electrified lump of fat. But the same was true of God, who was said to have his home up in space behind the blue sky. People still believed in Him, even though Gagarin had been up there in his spaceship and later declared triumphantly that there was no God, because he had searched for Him and seen nothing.

If people could go on believing in God after that announcement, she could probably also believe in her own self, although it did not appear in the biology book's plates showing flayed men and women cut in two lengthwise. Even if it was so small that it couldn't be seen through a microscope, she must have a self deep inside her that was wholly her own. If she nourished it and took care of it, one day it would grow bigger and fuller than the little word she took into her mouth every day. It took up so little room, her "I," her little self. It felt so weightless compared with her mother's encompassing "we," so hard to get on with, and it lured and threatened her by turns, according to whether there was something she must do or something she must not do.

Her brother would have understood.

It wasn't until she was fourteen that she discovered she was a twin. It was Henny, her aunt, who gave away the secret without knowing there was a secret to give away. Irene had wondered why Vivian often grew quiet and withdrawn in the days leading up to her birthday. She had been alone one day on a visit to Henny. As they sat looking at old photos, they came across one of Vivian taken when she was pregnant. A young smiling woman, standing at the edge of the sea with such a huge stomach that she had to waddle through the waves with both hands cradling it. Irene was born in July and she couldn't understand why her mother had been so large in April 1944, which was what the faded handwriting under the photograph said. Her brother had been suffocated by the cord, he was dead at birth. When Irene plucked up courage and mentioned him to Vivian some time later, she regretted it at once. Her mother regarded her with a vacant look before she stroked Irene's cheek and went into her room. Since then they had never spoken of him.

Now she had a better understanding of why her mother's "we" had been so hard for her. There was something missing, or rather someone. There was another "we" who had never been declared, and who could have counterbalanced that "we" who was Vivian's alone. The supervising "we" of all the prohibitions and injunctions with which her mother had brought her up, while her father was at work or reading his paper, or later when he was out of the picture altogether. Vivian's "we" grew even more tyrannical after he had left them, and Irene felt like a hostage.

Later she wondered if that was the reason for her being unable to take part in the collective "we" of liberation, of music, dreams, and revolution. She never went to consciousness-raising groups or rock festivals, and never experimented with group sex. There were others

21

who turned their backs on such activities as well, but for her it was not even a question of deciding. When she finally cut herself off from her mother's "we" it had become impossible for her to exchange the one "we" for another, no matter how rebellious or liberated it was.

She thought about her brother when she was alone. Sometimes she imagined him walking beside her on the way to school or in the room where she sat doing homework. She could not picture him, she was unable to imagine what he would have looked like, but she spoke to him in her mind. She never used the word "we," nor did he reply. He became the silent, secret "you" she sent her thoughts to. His almost palpable absence, the empty place at her side that she kept open for him, was linked to the self she felt budding within her. Her innermost self made itself heard with the voice in her that spoke to him and told him her secrets. When she went to Paris for the first time, she stopped thinking about him and talking to him every day. It was as if they had let go of each other to make their own ways separately, and she almost felt she could see him as a dim figure growing smaller behind her, as he raised his hand in farewell.

Ten years later she woke up one night beside Martin in a hotel room over a side street behind the Étoile. She had been standing on a busy street waiting to cross. There was a wide pavement with a balustrade on the other side with a view over the sea. It might have been the Promenade des Anglais, but streetcars were passing, yellow streetcars like the ones in Copenhagen when she was a young child. A black-clad man stood at the balustrade looking out to the horizon, and she waited impatiently for the stream of cars to slacken, for it was her brother standing there. He wasn't dead, he was waiting for her, they had arranged to meet there on the Promenade des Anglais.

She was late and, afraid he would go, she walked out into the traffic. One or two cars braked hard, sounding their horns, a streetcar passed with its strange faces close to her, and when there was a gap, for a moment she couldn't see him. At last she could cross the road and head toward him. He stood with his back to her, but he must have heard her steps for he turned around slowly, and a second before she woke, clammy with sweat and with a stifled cry in her throat, she saw, instead of her brother's unknown face, a suppurating, formlessly swollen lump of flesh with cracks where the eyes, nostrils, and mouth should have been.

Martin slept on; she wanted to wake him but held back. She pressed close to him, listening to the distant traffic. She placed her palm on his chest and felt the faint regular beat of his heart. She thought of little Peter's child's body and his child's eyes, blue and devoid of secrets, eyes only for her, and she felt lonely. For a moment she seemed to be floating in space, like an astronaut on a spacewalk who has lost contact with her ship and is whirling out into nothingness. She thought of how he loved her, the man she lay clinging to, and she grew frightened at the thought—even more frightened than she was at the thought of the endless empty space above the town. She pulled herself still closer to him and he turned in his sleep and drew her into his embrace.

"Irene Beckman..."

As usual, her tone of voice is matter-of-fact, practical. She sits at her desk looking out at the chestnut tree in the courtyard. She could easily have chosen a larger, more impressive office facing the street when she became a partner, but she prefers to be in quieter surroundings, out of the glare of afternoon sun. She likes to look at the branches in winter and the profusion of foliage in summer. She can still take pleasure in picking up a conker from the cobblestones when she has parked her car in the morning, and holding it in her hand like a smooth, hard, childish secret.

There is a pause for a second or two in which she can hear nothing but street noise, as if the call comes from a cell or pay phone.

"My name is Sally Hoppe." The voice is faint but high, almost like a small girl's.

"How can I help you?"

Again a pause full of buses and cars.

"I'm getting a divorce."

Irene can't help smiling at the woman's abrupt reply. At least it is a statement, and she almost says that she is to be divorced too.

"Well, you've come to the right place," she says instead.

"You were recommended to me," says the high voice hurriedly, as if to qualify her inquiry and let Irene know she has not just looked through the yellow pages. She sounds as if she's finding it hard to breathe.

As a rule Irene has been recommended to people. Her reputation as a divorce lawyer has grown with the years, although she had not really sought it. It wasn't her plan to specialize in family law. Originally she wanted to be a defense attorney, but she couldn't come to grips with the idea of having to turn down a case one day because she found her client or his actions too unpleasant, and she knew that day would come. She felt slightly ashamed of that because she thought her imagined reservations signified a lack of professionalism. But in any case, the legal entanglements of family life were easier to face with neutral tolerance than fraud or murder, and gradually the subject began to interest her. The patterns of intimate life, the legal side effects of the misdeeds or disintegration of love.

"It's my husband who wants the divorce," Sally Hoppe goes on in her small voice, slightly hoarse now, either from nervousness or suppressed anger. "He wants to skip the separation period, he's met someone else. They only met a couple of weeks ago. Eleven years of marriage straight down the drain. I am afraid they're planning to get married, he hasn't given a thought to our son...."

Is there an appeal in Sally Hoppe's hectic stream of words? A sisterly demand for sympathy above and beyond the purely businesslike identification with the client? From Sally's explanation she can see the case unfolding. Distorted by emotion, but none the less evident. What about her own? Will that, too, be distorted by mutual recriminations, bitter post-rationalizations and rancorous projections? It's scarcely conceivable. They've never quarrelled in that way. In which way? In a bloody delirium of rejection and self-fulfilling threats. Have they been too honorable or just too nice? Too nice to each other or just too distant?

Sally Hoppe has interrupted her jerky sequence of agitated statements. She is crying. Quiet crying, almost drowned out by the traffic noise. Irene has no idea what to say. When people come to her, as a rule they have more or less curbed their reactions, if only for dignity's sake, and assumed the essential shell of functional urbanity.

"I know it's hard," she says softly, not quite certain whether the other woman can hear her over the street noise.

"Sorry," says Sally Hoppe, sniffing. "Don't worry, I'll pull myself together, I'll get through this somehow."

"I'm sure you will," Irene says hurriedly in the hope that the other woman actually does get a hold of herself so they can get down to business. "What's your husband's name?"

"Thomas Hoppe," she replies, and for a moment sounds as if she will cry again, but she just sniffs.

Irene feels a sudden warmth flood her cheeks. She should have known immediately. What's happened to her?

Clouds have gathered, perhaps it's going to rain. How long ago was it? At least ten years, but it feels like twenty. She has not thought of him for years, he has been nothing more than a vague image passing at the misty edge of consciousness, where futile or demented emotions blend with abandoned expectations. Sally and Thomas. Thomas and Irene. Irene and Martin.

"Now listen...," Irene thinks she sounds far too sympathetic. Faking sensitivity. "Unfortunately I'm unable to take on your case, but I can refer you to one of my colleagues."

Late in the afternoon Irene takes a walk through the center of town. It hasn't rained yet, but the sky is gray blue over the castle islet. A metallic light penetrates the cloud cover, making the façades appear self-illuminated. A light wind causes scraps of paper to rise and spiral between two of the buttresses of the church. She sits on a bench in Nikolaj Square with the massive brick body of the church nave behind her. She watches the passing cyclists, young men in suits with clips round their pant legs, girls with bare legs and flowing hair. A Greenlander lies asleep on a nearby bench with an empty bottle in his arms. She tries to see herself from outside. A well-groomed woman, sitting alone on a bench in one of the city squares as the light fades. She doesn't feel like going home to the quiet house, nor does she want Martin to be there when she arrives. Stillness or silence, she doesn't know which is worse.

She rises and walks along Strøget. She feels the first drops and takes refuge in a clothes shop. There are no other customers. A girl behind the counter is on the telephone and she nods as if they know each other. The girl is very thin, she has a bare midriff in the current fashion and blond streaks in her hair. Irene looks absentmindedly at the clothes, hanging in their color ranges, and takes several dresses into a fitting room. She emerges in one dress then another to look at herself in the large mirror at the center of the shop, her head tilted appraisingly. She meets the girl's eyes in the mirror and for a second she can see what the girl sees. A pampered woman in her fifties, trying to persuade herself she can get away with a low-cut dress. It is pink, almost candy-colored; Irene has never worn that color before,

27

but she buys it anyway. The girl swipes her card. "That color is really good with your hair," she says reassuringly.

Irene smiles, with a touch of irony. There's a world of difference between the fair streaks in the girl's hair and the gray ones that started to appear in her own some twenty-five years ago. The girl must be able to guess she dyes her hair. Outside, the rain descends in swirling threads. The girl escorts her to the glass door and bends down to unlock it. She has a scorpion tattoo on her side. A few figures hurry by under their umbrellas as she fumbles to fit the key in the lock. They stand for a moment in the open doorway, a cold damp gust assails them from the street. "You can stay here while I close the register," says the girl and goes into the shop again. Irene closes her eyes and breathes in the scent of rain.

Thomas Hoppe is getting divorced because he has met someone else. He wants the divorce without trying a separation, although he has known her only a few weeks. For a doubter, he's amazingly resolute, this Thomas. Wonder what he looks like these days? They haven't seen each other since they decided it had to end. He was thirty-one, she was forty-six, it went without saying. Didn't it? She ponders how old the new woman in his life might be—twenty-six?—but stops herself short. She hasn't seen him for ten years, she has hardly given him a thought for the past five, and there always would have been fifteen years between them. That's how life would add up if you could put figures on it, but you can't.

An age difference of fifteen years grows with time, and in a woman's life the speed of that growth reflects the rate of biological depreciation. She knows that very well, and she knew it then too. The fact that one still looks good with dyed hair and can get away with buying a pink, low-necked dress makes no difference. Nor can she claim that the news of Thomas's divorce changes anything. The change happened long ago. It is something that meets her in a form-less, invisible way, like the chilly gust of wind in an open door. A clammy breeze that unexpectedly pierces through her.

Thomas Hoppe is getting divorced, and it has nothing to do with her. Nor does it concern her who has forced him to leave his wife and child so abruptly. The boy must be quite big by now, but it seems Thomas is so taken with this woman that even his beloved son can-not hold him back. She remembers seeing him with the boy, the touching sight, full of tenderness. Tenderness too can be painful, she thinks, and hears Sally Hoppe's high, girlish voice again.

She could gather from her speech that in spite of her little-girl name Sally is a nice young woman from the northern suburbs, much like herself. How old can Sally be? Around forty, like Thomas. A nice woman of forty, unable to call a lawyer without bursting into tears be-cause suddenly the earth has opened beneath her. Thomas cannot possibly have thought through the consequences of his action, or he would not have acted so drastically, if she knows him. But she doesn't, not any more.

The blond-streaked girl smiles through the reflections in the glass as she bends down again to lock the door after her. The wet flagstones of the sidewalk shine in the low sun. It dazzles her under the frayed remnants of cloud cover as she walks back along Strøget. The pedes-trians in front of her are merely dark forms in the backlight. She thinks of Thomas and their time together, but it all seems so hazy, like blurred shadows. She thinks about him, but her thoughts throw no light on the clouded-over past. On the contrary, it seems as if the past shines on her as she walks along the street in the evening sun after the cloudburst, eyes screwed up against the glare.

Is she only visible in the light of her past? A modern lawyer with artificially colored hair who specializes in family law, strolling along

Strøget on the brink of her own divorce, with a shopping bag in her hand containing a slightly too-revealing dress waiting to be hung in the wardrobe with her other impulse purchases. Something is missing in this picture, but what is missing is beginning to take on a regrettable likeness to what she has put behind her, passed by, neglected, or simply lost.

They met in the afternoons at an apartment in town that Thomas had borrowed. She was sure Martin didn't suspect anything. She had not been unfaithful to him before, but it was almost as if she wanted him to find out, she did so little to hide her affair. As if she longed to have it over and done with. Is that how it is for him now? Was that why he hadn't erased Susanne's message on the answering machine? Perhaps it was just a technical mishap, but why is she hoping that his carelessness was conscious? Is it she who is longing again for discovery and confrontation? Why is she waiting, then, instead of telling him she knows what's going on?

There is something contemptible, something spineless about unfaithfulness, thinks Irene, and it is not that she finds it immoral. It is the practical organization of betrayal that seems so distasteful. Not the lie itself but the inventiveness when it comes to organizing the mise-en-scène for burning passion. Practical framework and burning passion, they seem somehow incongruous.

She didn't think that way then.

It has started to rain again. The drops briefly obscure her vision before the wipers sweep them away. The traffic lights ahead glow in the blue-gray weather. She stops at a red light. A man sits in the car beside her, alone, gesticulating with both hands as he speaks. It takes a little while before she notices the thin cord hanging down his cheek. She squints at the clock below the speedometer. The small digital numbers collapse and then form new combinations as she waits behind the wheel.

She's late. No doubt Vivian will be getting impatient. Eager to voice her reproaches, as she does when she waits in her sheltered accommodation with its view of the dark pine trees on the lawn. But today she's not there, and she sees no pine trees, only the town as it looks from above, out her high hospital window. Her operation is scheduled for the day after tomorrow. Irene won't be able to stay long. Josephine and Peter and Sandra are coming to dinner with the children, and she must do some shopping. She tries to think of her mother but her thoughts slide away. She cannot focus on Vivian or the consultant dutifully telling her about the risks of a general anesthetic on people Vivian's age. Freshly shaven and professional, with a cultivated, considerate voice and watchful eyes under his gray, combed-back hair. Nor can she focus on Martin's unfaithfulness. Will he come home for dinner?

Why is she so apathetic?

She wasn't apathetic then, and she felt neither contemptible nor deplorable when she was in her mid-forties and having an affair with a married man half her age. She felt light, almost weightless. Unfaithfulness. That word went out of fashion when she and Martin were young. She recalls one of Martin's colleagues they used to see now and then, a slightly overweight fellow, thinning on top but beautifully groomed in his navy-blue blazer and sailing-club tie. One night he'd turned up wearing a libertine beard, a V-neck sweater, and a silver pendant made of four small, delicately made feet, two with toes turned down flanked by two with toes turned up.

If it had been a cross it would have aroused more attention and no doubt disgust too, despite all the libertinism. Sex was the religion of the time, everyone converted, even Martin's colleague. In the middle of the dinner he bent over her, his breath laden with brie and burgundy, and whispered something to her about a foursome with his wife and Martin. Free love as a social convention, the tyranny of emancipated lust, she thought later had merely been an opportunity for bumbling old lechers.

The man with the broad-minded feet around his neck would never have dared approach her so blatantly even a few years earlier, when he was just a flabby yes-man in his rep tie and blazer. The beard, the necklace, and the sweater were a kind of carnival disguise that allowed him to throw off restraint and let it all hang out, with his dick leading the way. But by then the carnival was the norm, not a departure from it. Irene had never experienced a period more conformist and coercive, not even the much-maligned fifties, when as a teenager she took her first steps into the grown-up world, on stiletto heels with her hair piled up like Audrey Hepburn's. There certainly was something subdued and scared about her first fumblings in the half dark. That was probably the way it had always been when tender young bodies reached out to each other for the first time; but what she remembered from that time more than anything else was a genuine joy seeping out of the gray normality. A flowering and an ecstasy

33

in her contemporaries and in herself as they felt the world opening out to more light and more colors after war, shortages, and fear.

Sincerity and joy—was that to end up in a round of suburban group sex? Merely to show the others how emancipated she was? Talked into it by an unappetizing fool who imposed himself on her with his beard and his membership badge, and with the implication that she would be inhibited and suburban if she refused?

Yes, she was suburban, and no, it didn't make her feel inhibited. She felt free with Martin and the children in the home they'd created for themselves. It was the liberation that seemed intimidating. She can remember her friend Ursula giving her a copy of *The Female Eunuch*. The book sat on her bedside table for weeks before she put it in the bookcase without ever having opened it. As usual, Martin had asked in his amiably interested way if it was an exciting book. There was not much of the phallocrat in her thoughtful husband. It was the time that was bewitched.

To be a witch, that was Ursula's ambition, a witch with no make-up or bra, who left her husband and children and went to consciousness-raising groups to find herself. That was when you could say such things without being laughed at. But they were witches without magic powers, her liberated friends, for the more they emancipated themselves the more they found to complain about. They belonged to the first generation of women who had taken it for granted that they should be educated and earn their own living, and still they felt oppressed. Irene soon grew bored with their weekly covens, where they ran down the men in absentia, hoarse with injustice and cigarette smoke, teeth turned purple from all the Bulgarian wine with which they washed down their humiliation. Nor did she want to go to any consciousness-raising group, she preferred the summer cottage with Martin and the children.

Unfaithfulness. At some point that word had sneaked into the language again, the summer she met Thomas Hoppe in a strange apartment in town. At least a vague idea of peace and order had been reestablished, even though she and Martin, the last couple in their circle of friends, still hadn't got divorced. Why hadn't they divorced a long time ago? Had they stayed together for the sake of the children? Their divorced friends would have considered that the flimsiest of excuses, avowing without exception that happy parents were a prerequisite for happy children. It seemed to her that the opposite was at least as obvious.

Perhaps it was for the children's sake that she stayed with Martin, although Josephine was in ninth grade and Peter had finished college. In any case, it was not for their sake that she threw herself into Thomas's arms. She wasn't thinking of them at all when she lay in his arms. She didn't try to explain her infidelity to herself, nor was her conscience troubled. She knew what she was guilty of but it didn't make her feel guilty. Perhaps it was the dizzy strangeness of lying with Thomas's warm body against her back and feeling the breeze from the open attic windows as she looked out over the rooftops in the evening sunshine.

He'd given her a key. It was odd to walk through town with the key in her handbag on her way to a strange place and an almost strange man. A middle-aged woman gone astray, among the other anonymous figures moving through the town's great grid of directions, destinations and dead ends. She always looked around her, afraid of being recognized, as she let herself into the entrance hall. She liked to get there before him and walk around the apartment or just sit in an armchair and sun herself on the balcony, looking out at the towers of the town. The apartment had three rooms and was furnished in a simple and masculine, almost spartan, style. She made it a habit to buy flowers on her way and arrange them in a vase on the floor beside the bed. Carnations, she remembers. She always bought carnations after she discovered they were Thomas's favorite flowers.

The sparse furniture was old and shabby in a way that was somehow reassuring. The place belonged to a writer; she knew his name but she had never read any of his books. He was published by the firm where Thomas was an editor, and spent much of his time abroad. The walls were covered with bookshelves from floor to ceiling, and on a desk in the middle of the room was an old portable typewriter next to a framed photograph. The girl in the picture was half child, half woman. Her hair was unruly and her eyes shone in her pale, narrow face. The picture had been taken in shadow, with a flash, and you couldn't see whether the background view behind the slim form was of waves or corn. She looked out of the picture with a veiled, dreaming gaze. Irene never tired of studying the unknown girl as she sat with her feet propped against the warm balcony rail, distant, infinitely distant from her own world.

She'd hear him on the stairs, hear the key fitting into the lock. She stayed where she was in the sunlight, eyes closed. He stood still for a little while before approaching her. For a moment he was as impossible to picture as the twin brother she had never met. Then she felt his warm palms on her neck, his fingers gently meeting round her throat and grasping her hair, as she bent her head back and waited for his lips. That was how they met each time.

It seemed most improbable for them to be together here, and it went on seeming like a daydream that had been extended into reality and grown stronger, more risky. Even the way they met had been reckless. She had run him over. One afternoon in early summer when she was heading out of town, the sun blinded her and suddenly she hit a cyclist who was turning out of a side street. There he was with his bike overturned and a gash in his temple. It looked worse than it was, and he was already on his feet when she wrenched herself clear of her paralysis, got out of the car, and approached him through a crowd of pedestrians. His briefcase had fallen off the bike. A girl was gathering up the printed sheets that had scattered all over the bike lane. Irene noticed the child seat fastened to the luggage carrier. An elderly lady had already given him a handkerchief, which was now soaked with blood, but he was in full command, the young man in a black suit, full of apologies, as if it was obvious that he was to blame for the accident.

She drove him to the emergency room. He took the situation calmly, the blood and the cut did not seem to concern him. It was characteristic of him, she discovered later, his detached attitude toward his body and his surroundings. You actually had to run him over to interrupt his train of thought. She was stupefied at her carelessness and insisted on keeping him company in the waiting room. His temple stopped bleeding, and he supported his head thoughtfully in his hands as they sat talking.

He talked and talked, looking at her with his beautiful, deep-set eyes. They were green with a melancholy expression that did not mesh with his otherwise lively, smiling face. They seemed to regard both the unknown woman and himself as if they were strange to his sorrowful gaze. Irene had brought his briefcase, and she helped him restore order to the creased, soiled sheets of uniformly blocked text. It was the proof of a new translation of *Anna Karenina*, he told her. Had she read *Anna Karenina*? Yes, she had, as a young girl, on a bench in the sun in Père Lachaise, in the days when she could remain on her own for hours without feeling lonely or out of touch. She told him about that time, surprised at herself. He launched into a description of Anna, the unhappily married woman, and her initially reluctant,

37

later erring, totally outcast passion, which finally threw her under a locomotive at the station in a provincial Russian town. The nurse seemed almost intrusive when she announced that it was his turn for treatment. Irene waited while his stitches were put in, then drove him home.

If he hadn't left his briefcase in her car, engrossed in interpreting Tolstoy, and if she hadn't forgotten it herself, engrossed in listening, they would never have met again. She called him at the publishing house. The delivery took place at a café. They chatted for a quarter of an hour, and as they sat facing each other, she realized she had been thinking about him; not much, yet more than just fleetingly. She had not told Martin about the accident. She wanted to write a check to cover the repair of his bicycle. He absolutely refused to accept it, it had been entirely his fault. It was an old bike, anyway.

It seemed to her that one explanation canceled out the other. It also seemed to her that he was better looking than she remembered, though he was just as pale and unshaven as the first time they met, his broad-shouldered figure just as awkwardly tense in the black jacket. One of the black-clad young men of the time, but not as supercilious as most of them were. On the contrary, he smiled politely, amusingly shy when she held his gaze. He actually spilled his coffee over the check lying on the table. His distraction made her feel self-confident and controlled, and perhaps because of that she burst out laughing. He looked at her and smiled. When they had shaken hands and gone their separate ways it occurred to her that for a second or two she was falling out of a role.

One afternoon she caught sight of him in a supermarket in town where she sometimes shopped before going home. He stood there immersed in his shopping list with a pained expression, as if he was reading a prison sentence. She stayed on the other side of the freezer, waiting for him to look up. It was the briefest interval, but it was there, before he smiled and smoothed over what she had looked into for a moment. What? She didn't know, but it had been a kind of disclosure, like peeling the bandage off a cut. They exchanged a few pleasantries across the shoals of frozen salmon before going on with their shopping, each aware of the other's movements, smiling when they passed each other with their carts. After she had paid he approached the same check-out. She could have waved and gathered up her bags, but she waited.

They walked together for a while. The familiar streets seemed strange as she moved along next to this unknown, very young man. He had a pack of disposable diapers under his arm, she held it for him when he put his bags down on the pavement to unlock his bicycle. She had used cloth diapers for her babies. She made it into an anecdote, something comically historical, the endless diaper wash, the smell from the big boiling pan. It seemed to amuse him, and she was pleased. They talked about their children, their names, how old they were and so on. She told him Martin, Peter, and Josephine had gone up to the cottage that morning.

You talk about yourself when you don't know what else to say. There is always personal information to call upon, and it's not necessarily because you want to be familiar. You are quite simply in a corner, and it's because of a deeper urge to reach someone—not yet knowing who or what with, which makes it all the more disturbing. They hesitated a moment at a corner before they separated. She stayed there watching him wobble off with his bags on the handlebars and the pack of diapers in the plastic child's seat. He stood on the threshold of experiences from which she had already moved on. He had made her smile with his old-fashioned, unworldly, yet youthfully impulsive manner. She had visualized his life and smiled at it, kindly, almost tenderly, as if they knew each other. But she had also seen herself, and as she drove home in her car she felt strangely wistful.

A few days later, on a Friday, she worked late at the office. She intended to drive up to the cottage when she'd finished. The receptionist had gone home, and she hadn't actually meant to answer the phone when it rang in the outer office. Martin had her direct number. So why did she go out and pick it up? There had been no presentiment, she could just as well have let it go. Thomas had seen the lights on. He had cycled past a little earlier. He spoke quietly, which gave his voice an intimate tone. She might be annoyed with him, he said, but if she had time he would like to see her. She asked why she should be annoyed, but she could tell that her automatic self-assurance was not convincing. They had already crossed a threshold, it had happened across the piles of frozen salmon in the supermarket, when she met his eyes for a second, before the words came to their rescue. Ever since, she had known he wanted something from her, and she had done nothing to bar his way. They arranged to meet in Kongens Have.

She knew what she was doing when she made her way there. If anything she was surprised how easy it felt, her steps light in the blue summer evening. He had kept turning up in her thoughts, or rather behind them, when she was with Martin and the children, or when she sat alone at home.

People still reclined on the lawns with their picnic baskets. He was waiting on a bench by the fountain. Neither of them said anything special as they sat there with self-consciousness between them—the last distance to be traversed. She studied him in the dusk beneath the tree canopies before raising her hand and letting the tips of her fingers brush the scar on his temple. He was neither shy nor awkward when he took her hand.

That was how it began. She looked into herself with his eyes, deeper than she had seen before. There was a power in his gaze and his young, strong body, which infected her with his hunger and made her open herself wide, flushing, hyperaware. She gave herself up, she surrendered to his will, insatiable herself. He could do with her as he liked, and she was enraptured. All she wanted was for him to uproot her completely. When they had made love she lay enclosed by his warm, damp body, looking out at the sunlight on the tiles of the roof ridge and a brick chimney that towered up outside the attic window. There was always a big flock of swifts, and their high-pitched cries above the street filled her with happiness. No, she was happy; the swifts merely restated the theme—that it was happiness; the sated lightness in her limbs; the feeling of the summer breeze deep within the pores of her skin.

She could see him and herself from outside as they lay cheek to cheek, with her folded into his embrace. They resembled each other. His hair was almost black like hers, he had green eyes like hers, and for the briefest, most transparent sliver of a second, he was not her lover but the brother she should have had. Her twin brother, who had been her companion when they came into the world. She dared not turn around for fear of disturbing the brief image of them together in the strange room. She listened to the swifts and the voices in the street.

The thought of her stillborn brother made her lonely again, or was it her happiness? They did not belong together, she and this man. The green eyes in the face that breathed in her hair and pricked her cheek with stubble were not her mirror image. The shrill swifts suddenly made the space around her widen with their circling. That endless space into which she could vanish. His hands embraced her breasts and she heard a faint whistling sound from his lungs as he breathed deeply behind her, and the whistling changed her impression into a different image, a different face. No, not a face, the suppurating, bleeding, formlessly folded flesh where a face should have been, with blind cracks where a pair of eyes should have recognized her. She turned around and pushed her face against his chest, sobbing so he could barely keep hold of her until she composed herself.

Afterward they talked about their lives. He had lost his way, those were his own words, gone astray into a circle. Sometimes she laid a hand on his mouth—what good was it? He had just become a father. He had a son, who lay in his carriage in the front garden of the terrace house he and Sally had bought when they learned she was pregnant. Her parents had lent them money for the down payment. While the little one slept under a fly net stretched over the carriage hood, the promising young editor was telling his somewhat elderly mistress about his wife, who was a dressmaker and had her own shop around the corner from the quiet street where, in a few years, the boy would be able to ride his tricycle in safety.

What did Irene tell him? Can she remember it at all, ten years later? Ten years older than the woman who lay listening to her young lover, whose life was about to start? In a few years he would be the same age as his mistress was then. Did she tell more or less the same story that he now tells the woman who has inspired him to do what he could not then bring himself to do? Break every bond and just go, from one day to the next. From a day that repeated itself and its shifting little variations, to a day when yesterday's hopes for continuity have turned into something of the past. Irene thinks of Sally weeping on the phone this morning, because by breaking up Thomas has dislodged her from a world she had grown accustomed to.

Apart from a chance meeting, she hasn't seen him since the winter after their summer together. It was just before Christmas, by the entrance to a department store, he was pushing his son in a stroller. The little fellow gazed attentively at her from the snug hood of his snowsuit. His father wore a fixed smile, as if they were mere acquaintances. The smile didn't relax and become genuine until they had exchanged a few labored questions and answers and were about to say good-bye and Merry Christmas. Once again there had been a hint of pain in his eyes, but Irene couldn't decide whether it was because they would have to part again or because they had been unlucky enough to run into each other. She inclined to the latter when she recalled his relief as he smiled in farewell to carry on the life that was now his.

She had never believed Thomas would get divorced. She thought often about what he had told her of his life. He had lost himself, he told her, but everything he said suggested the opposite. The tenderness in his voice when he spoke of becoming a father. How he had only come into the world in earnest with the birth of the boy. How the little one bound him and Sally together with their own flesh and blood. The pain, the melancholy when he talked about all he imagined he was about to leave.

He said he had lost his way with Sally, but in reality he was merely enumerating his reasons for staying. Thomas and Sally had known each other for only a month when she became pregnant—but you don't regret a child, he hastened to add.

He explained how different they were, he and Sally. He wasn't sure they would have stayed together had it not been for the child. He spoke with affable self-mockery of his own sad youth and its unhappy infatuations. Suddenly Sally was there with her infectious lightheartedness. It had intoxicated him, her lightheartedness, until the child was born and he discovered how alienated he could feel beside her at night. But he stayed.

43

What did Irene tell him? She can't remember. Did she perhaps tell him a similar story, for the sake of symmetry?

She doesn't think so.

She had arrived at reality in those early years, because she had begun to see it with Martin's wise, vulnerable, insistent eyes. The eyes of the impecunious outcast, the watchful gaze of the underdog.

He had told her of humiliations at work, beatings even, with a resigned smile. If she became indignant because one of his superiors at the bank had treated him arrogantly or made him pay for others' errors, he replied with a shrug. He was like a good-natured boxer who takes his blows and just gets up again, slightly groggy. There was no hint of bluster in him, but she noticed that he had learned early not to leave anything to chance. He had never received something for nothing, and when they were out he always looked around him with a watchful eye. It was in that look that she read the vulnerability beneath his patient slog to create a place for himself in the world. It was the expression of one who is never sure of a welcome.

When he was in fifth grade he ran away from the children's home because he was homesick. It was the end of winter, and bitingly cold, but he walked the whole way. He spent the night in a barn, and it wasn't until the evening of the second day that he reached the town where his mother lived with her new family. The school had called, but his mother didn't seem to be expecting him. Her new husband stayed in the living room with Thomas's half siblings while his mother made him a plate of sandwiches in the kitchen. She seemed embarrassed and walked up and down as if she wanted to make sure the others stayed where they were. That evening his stepfather drove him back to the children's home. Nothing was said during the journey, but on the way something was born in him, a razor-sharp clarity. He told Irene he had felt so alone that it did not occur to him to feel sorry for himself. You're only sorry for yourself if there's a chance that others will be, too. He said it with a smile, as if he were simply stating a fact. She asked if he'd been angry with his mother. He looked at her in amazement. She never heard him speak ill of the family he had said good-bye to so young.

She came to see the world with his indomitable stubbornness and his fear of losing things—things that he had won only because he denied himself the luxury of reproaching the world for what he had not yet wrested from it. Her eyes were opened to the miserly inertia of reality. A naked reality in which you were only rewarded in small, precisely measured portions for your loyalty and willingness. She came to admire his hard work, his common sense and thoroughness and self-discipline as he built up a life to compare with the one she herself had been born into.

While their contemporaries rebelled against bourgeois conventions, he slaved away for his family and their future. While others took things lightly, he took up the reins. While they went off the rails in every direction, he let her know, with a thousand little old-fashioned gallant attentions, that she, and she alone, was his woman. Where others clung to their youth and made a virtue of irresponsibility, he was industrious, adult, and responsible. When he came home and she embraced him at the door, when he played with the children after supper, and when he loomed over her in bed with his large, warm body, she felt herself to be the woman who was his. The only one she could imagine being. When they met she had run away from him, but he'd caught up with her. She gave in to his love, but also to its humble persistence, his naïve belief that it must be her. It was his belief she had finally fallen in love with.

With Martin the future became real. It was no longer a dream. They had embodied it together. She recalls his smile when she was expecting Peter and he could feel the little one moving with his palms on her distended stomach. It was the impatience of the future to become the present. Their future. When she met him he was no one, a sailor who had signed off in Cherbourg and headed for Paris to look around aimlessly, unknown and alone in the world. He was nothing but drive and willpower, but the more he looked at her with those indomitable blue eyes, the more she felt herself to be the girl he loved. Not a refugee who'd jumped on the train for Paris, and not the sister of a dead twin brother. Not the dreaming, introspective ghost sister of childhood, but the girl she had in her heart expected to be. Herself.

When she gave birth to Peter it was as if she gave birth to herself. When she screamed and pushed him out of her body it was as if she broke free from her confined youth. She became an adult. When Martin entered the delivery room and the wrinkled, red munchkin was placed in his arms, it was not only Peter's life but also hers he held in his hands. For the first time ever she could say "we" because it was not a "we" that threatened to suffocate her. Not Vivian's "we" when she was a child, and not her own childish "we," half of which was missing, the stillborn half she had whispered to in the dark. With Martin, she could say "we" with all naturalness. It had become a "we" that opened up to her and embraced her, and which she herself could embrace with her whole being. A husband, two children, a home. A life. Have they really put that behind them? Is the future already the past? How have they come from tomorrow to yesterday?

Unfaithfulness. At some point it had sneaked up on them, on her view of him. Maybe at night while he slept and she lay awake listening to his calm breathing. Maybe when she crept out of bed and sat in the living room, strangely alone in their home in the darkness of night, or when she stood in the doorway of the nursery, watching her children babbling in their sleep. In some way she had discovered that their calm, orderly life was a question of faith; and she realized she had lost it.

She cannot say when, nor could she when she lay talking with Thomas. But she remembers why she laid a hand on his mouth. It was not only that she understood instinctively what was confirmed later on—that he had gone too far when he lay fantasizing about having gone astray, about starting all over again with her children and his little son. There was another reason, too, which made her try to silence him. She was afraid of herself. Afraid of wishing that he would talk himself beyond all bonds.

To begin with, she had wanted no more than those stolen encounters with no treacherous hopes, no thought for what might follow. She was too old to want anything but to lie there as long as it lasted; yet that was no more than a thought. She didn't feel old.

An old hand, wrinkled, clutching the duvet cover, powerless, and greedy. But she is asleep, all greed forgotten, and in sleep she does not feel how powerless she is. Vivian sleeps in her white linen, in her white hospital gown. The clutch of her hand on a corner of the duvet is reminiscent of a baby's reflex-conditioned hold on everything around it. Her features are peaceful and smooth, the furrows in her face merely reflecting what this child has lived through in the course of time.

When Irene gets to the door she realizes she has forgotten to buy flowers. She tiptoes over the linoleum floor and sits down in the armchair by the window. As usual, Vivian is privileged. She has been given a private room, so she can lie in her innocent sleep and forget everything that has occurred to separate her from the child she once was. When the operation is behind her and all has gone well she'll get loads of flowers. And if it doesn't go well? But of course it will.

Irene looks at her mother. She has spent her life tending to the framework of life, absorbing herself in it, beautifying it, ministering to its reliable, orderly changelessness. She was so busy with this framework that it sometimes seemed as if her mother had completely forgotten what was inside the frame. Its content, life's content. But can you distinguish between life and its content? Is life bearable without forms and patterns? The conventional order that so many of Irene's contemporaries were so busy sneering at and overturning, what had replaced it? Confusion, fear, and thoughtlessness are the first words that occur to her as she listens to her mother's labored breathing.

To Vivian, regularity was everything, and she wrapped Irene and her father in an atmosphere of fragrant meals and fragrant cleanliness, fragrant freshly ironed clothes and fragrant fresh flowers in all the vases. But as solicitous as she was, she could be just as uncomprehending, almost confused, if the half-adult Irene tried to share an idea with her, or asked a question with mildly profound implications. She shouldn't puzzle over things so much. Did Vivian herself puzzle over the meaning of it all as she stubbornly maintained the appearance of family life, even when there was no longer any family to take care of? She lived on alone in the house after first her husband and later Irene left her for the magical, boundary-bursting openness of the future, one in the arms of a younger woman, the other along the boulevards of Paris. It was as if she was waiting in the silent house, where the parquetry always shone and the curtains were always newly ironed, but for what? Irene felt a strange discomfort, a strangely impatient pity when she visited Vivian with Martin and the children and allowed her mother to wait on them.

The room is on the top floor of the hospital and from the window there's a wide view over the housing blocks, stretching toward the city center, from which towers and occasional tall buildings rise up beside the harbor and the sound. From the east, twilight is approaching. She glances at her watch, she won't have time to go shopping and cook dinner. Vivian would never have allowed herself to be so unprepared if she knew the family was coming. She would have been busy for hours by now, making soup, a roast, and a dessert. Irene has to smother a sudden irritation with her mother, who's just lying there asleep now that she has come to see her. But the supermarket she usually shops at is open late. They'll have to make do with what the delicatessen has to offer. She feels self-conscious thinking like this, although it's probably Vivian's routine just as much as it is her own.

Vivian is afraid of dying, and there is a risk that she may not wake up once they have used their bag of tricks to lull her into unconsciousness. Wasn't that what the consultant had said, perhaps in slightly different, slightly more polished, medical terms? He reminded her of her father, the engaging consultant with the professional air and the gray, combed-back hair, and it turned out that he and her father had in fact been students together in medical school. She'd felt reassured because he reminded her of her father; she had also felt an instinctive aversion because he was not her father who, in contrast to this man with his well-groomed consultant's appearance, had been eaten up by cancer until only a hollow-cheeked sack was left, with eyes—far too large, far too dark—that haunted her long after they'd buried him. This well-groomed, well-considered replica of her father in his prime had sat behind his immaculately tidy desk with his discreetly sympathetic consultant's air and made it clear that he could not guarantee that Irene would still have a mother after the operation. Even though the risk was small. On the other hand, considering her mother's age, it was his duty...

Irene has to control her silent anger. That's something she's good at. She is sensible. People come to her with their tangled feelings and paralyzed lives because they rely on her common sense. They hang onto it when everything else is desperate, because she can at least fit the splintered framework together and apportion the fragments fairly. Common sense and fairness are like morphine to battered psyches. The thought that, in spite of everything, all will go reasonably and justly when the world is snatched from under your feet. She could easily have helped Sally Hoppe salvage as much as possible from her shipwrecked marriage; indeed, probably more than Irene herself would find reasonable. Actually, deserted women are her specialty. Rejected, defenseless victims of men who have burst through the bounds of family life without warning for the sake of a new sexual adventure. She understands the situation, she knows where to apply pressure to squeeze more and still a little more out of faithless husbands like Thomas, who is no doubt gnawed by guilt just like the others. She could have helped Vivian, too, if it hadn't all happened long before she became a lawyer. She could have cleaned her father out when he decamped. Vivian would have been able to afford an even larger house to furnish and care for.

Her father's new wife was almost twenty years younger than Vivian, and Irene had not seen him for nearly as long. She thinks of Martin and his Susanne. Her father had chosen to obey his desire and flout his duties long before it was fashionable to do so, and she had forgiven him. She managed to forgive him just before cancer began to consume him from within. She nursed him alone toward the end. It got to be too much for his new wife when her husband, once so virile and active, shrivelled up and withered away.

51

Irene's unreasonable anger at the consultant is, of course, just a delayed anger at the father he reminds her of. A misplaced anger provoked by Martin's unfaithfulness, perhaps because it is superficially reminiscent of her father's. But why? Hasn't she forgiven her father? And what does she envisage, at the age of fifty-six? That her mother will go on living forever in the assisted living facility Martin has found for her, looking out at the tall pine trees and waiting for a visit from Irene? Parents die sooner or later, and in the meantime you have had children of your own who will put you in assisted living one day.

As Irene listens to Vivian's breathing, it occurs to her that she has not really talked to her mother for a long time, not for several years. Once it had been Vivian who was distracted and impatient when little Irene pestered her with odd questions or daydreams instead of running out to play. Now the tables are turned. Now she has barely sat down before she is on her way out the door again.

Vivian notices it, too, but it only makes her blunder on more. She can feel Irene is irritable or preoccupied behind her sweet smile. She is aware that her daughter doesn't really listen to her, but she's unable to control her stream of words, and it is Irene who eventually has to stop her by laying a hand on her arm or by simply getting up. Then she falls silent, and Irene doesn't know how she can slip out the door without feeling ashamed. When she comes again a week or two later or just calls to hear how her mother is, it is not always out of a sense of duty. She frequently comes or calls because she is genuinely concerned, to talk to her mother, feel her presence; but not many minutes pass before the feeling fades, replaced by irritation.

Maybe Irene will not succeed. Maybe she won't manage to establish a deeper communication with Vivian, as she did with her father when she took care of him before he died. It was not that they talked a lot. Most of the time he was too drowsy from the morphine, but once or twice she sat by his bed with his hand in hers and looked into the dark eyes grown suddenly large in his emaciated face. It was as if he was looking at death itself; or was it death contemplating her through his eyes?

He talked about the time before she was born, about falling in love with Vivian during the Occupation, about how she had become pregnant before they married so everything had to be arranged in a rush. He smiled as he described how beautiful she had been. For the first time, they talked about her stillborn brother. Vivian had never got over it, and perhaps…he didn't know, it was of no importance now, but perhaps everything would have turned out differently if the boy had lived.

Irene was thankful he didn't go on with his thought experiment. She was also glad that he only talked about her childhood and his meeting with Vivian. She understood that it wasn't to protect himself. It was his way of showing his respect for her origin. By talking about it he let her know it was not a mistake, even though he had behaved later as if he wanted to undo his life. Without being sentimental he managed to show that not only did he love his daughter but also, and which was almost more important, that he had once loved her mother.

The purple dusk has already crept into the room. Vivian's face is indistinct against the white pillow. Perhaps Irene will not show her mother any love. Why does she feel sorry for herself at the thought? Can't she love Vivian more? Has she never been able to?

They have not been close nor has she been dependent on her mother since childhood. And even then? She hid from her mother how in bed at night, she talked to the brother she did not have. Nor must her mother know that she wrote letters to her father. Letters that were never sent because she would not have known where to send them. She was thirteen when her parents separated, and she didn't see her father again until she was thirty-two and it was almost too late. He had not seen her graduate, he had not led her up the aisle, and he had not planted spring bulbs with her children. Vivian had.

Martin persuaded her to seek him out. It was Martin, too, who discovered that he was a consultant at Elsinore Hospital and lived north of the town. She resisted for a long time before she eventually plucked up courage one winter evening, picked up the receiver, and dialed the number Martin had written down. A woman's voice answered. "This is Nina," said the woman unsuspectingly, his new woman, no longer new. Confident and forthcoming like someone who has no doubt about her place in the world and her right to that place. She recognized his voice at once when he came to the telephone. The following Sunday they drove to Elsinore. Martin dropped her off on the coastal road and promised to pick her up an hour later. The children must have been with Vivian that day.

She stood by the wall bordering the road. She was on the verge of thinking better of it. The house was built into the slope and there was a view of the sound and Kullen in Sweden. Martin had been waiting for two hours when she finally joined him. It had not occurred to her to fetch him. The woman who had called herself Nina was not at home. It was just the two of them, Irene and her father. He sat with his back to the view over the snow-covered shore, barely more than a silhouette against the wintry light. He might have been any older man, but he was her father. Now that she had found him she was unsure. For a moment she could not remember any of the questions she'd prepared. Were they at all important? It struck her, more as a feeling than a thought, that the replies might be just as out-of-date.

He had written to her several times over the years. Not fantasy letters like hers, addressed to the night and to sleeplessness, but real letters, which had been returned every time. He'd thought she didn't want anything to do with him. Why hadn't he sought her out? The gray-haired man opposite her shrugged his shoulders and smiled with a bashful expression. He had in fact waited in his car in front of the college when she came out. He'd seen her with her friends, never alone. His courage had failed him, and so the years had passed. He did not have any more children, and did not want them, he didn't want to be an old father. He made it sound like a responsible, considered decision.

She showed him pictures of Peter and Josephine. He touched the shiny surface of the photos with a cautious finger. It seemed like a caress. When she rose to leave he gave her the bundle of letters she had never received. More than a year passed before she would see her mother, and Vivian endured her punishment without protest. Not until her father had died did Irene reach out again, with the express condition that Vivian attend his funeral.

One anger neutralized the other, weighed it and redressed it. In her anger at Vivian she forgot her anger at her father. She did not give it a thought while he was ill. Instead she asked the same question of herself that she'd put to him that Sunday when she found him again. Why had she never thought to visit him? After all, she had been thirteen, hardly a child any more. She was old enough to look him up in the phone book or contact the national registration office or for that matter to phone every hospital in the country to ask if they had a doctor with his name on their books. She also could have asked her mother, who received a substantial sum each month in compensation for his treachery. But she did not ask, and Vivian never uttered a word, either about him or about the divorce.

It was an unspoken pact. The thirteen-year-old Irene crept around the big house in stockinged feet, she remembered to lift chairs instead of pushing them, and she hushed the friends she brought home when her mother retreated to her bedroom to nurse her migraine. Vivian's recurrent attacks enveloped the house in a tense atmosphere of carefulness like a great drawn-in breath. Sometimes Irene was allowed to knock cautiously at the door and serve tea for her in the darkened room, wring out a washcloth in cold water and lay it on her brow. The frail hand that stroked Irene's hair was not only a reward. The vague touch seemed to admonish her.

They were alone, mother and daughter, in the house on the quiet road of old gardens. But it was not a shared loneliness; each was on her own. Vivian with her migraines, Irene with her ghost brother, whispering to him, bent over her homework. It was a welcome interruption of the silence when the cleaning woman roared around with the vacuum cleaner. Mrs. Frölich. It has been a long time since Irene thought of her. She had worked for them as long as Irene could remember, and she was the quiet witness of the misfortune that struck the lady and daughter of the house when the man of the house vanished from their lives from one Friday to the next. Irene didn't know what her mother had said to Mrs. Frölich, she never heard them exchange anything other than practical remarks. Nor did she know what to think about the bar of chocolate she found on her pillow one Friday evening after Mrs. Frölich had been there.

She can still recall her conflicting feelings as she sat on the bed munching Mrs. Frölich's milk chocolate, touched and at the same time discomfited at being the object of their domestic help's discreet sympathy. She hid the chocolate under her bed when her mother came into her room to say goodnight, she didn't understand why. She never said thank you, and yet there was a change. Mrs. Frölich usually took a break before doing the ground floor. She brought her own coffee in a thermos, and Irene fell into the habit of sitting with her in the kitchen. She could not bring herself to refuse when Mrs. Frölich offered her some of her weak coffee. Sometimes Mrs. Frölich brought a cake she had baked. Vivian was seldom at home when she came to clean, and it grew into a kind of break, the weekly coffee time with Mrs. Frölich. Irene spoke more freely with the strange woman than with her mother, and gradually she gave in to the warmth in Mrs. Frölich's eyes.

She was the same age as Vivian, but her heavy body and large face made her seem older. Irene had once heard her parents talking about her at the dinner table. Mrs. Frölich had known better times. She came from what was still known as a good family, and in her time had inherited a small fortune, but her good-for-nothing husband had managed to squander it all before he died of a heart attack. She never had an education and had to provide for herself and her daughter by doing housework. They had been forced to leave their home when her husband died and now lived in a small ground-floor apartment close to the station. The daughter was Irene's age, and Irene said hello every time she met them in the street. Mrs. Frölich talked about her now and then, but only if Irene asked, and always briefly as if she felt it would be presumptuous to go on about the dearest thing in her life. They had seemed so vulnerable, she and her daughter, when Irene saw them in their shabby winter coats, and Mrs. Frölich's daughter would not look Irene in the eye. Maybe she was just shy. When Irene recalled the chocolate Mrs. Frölich had bought her she could feel tears in her eyes, but it wasn't that she felt sorry for herself. She felt ashamed over the cleaner's gesture and her own sympathy when she thought of the ground-floor apartment by the station where Mrs. Frölich tried to maintain a home for her daughter.

Irene and Mrs. Frölich never talked about Vivian or the divorce, yet she avoided telling her mother about their Friday coffee breaks. They made her feel strangely disloyal. Only once did Mrs. Frölich reveal what she thought of Vivian, although it was as much herself she was talking about. One afternoon when Irene was fifteen, Mrs. Frölich asked whether she'd thought about her further education. Irene said she was tired of school. Mrs. Frölich gazed at her earnestly and laid a hand on her arm. They had never made physical contact before. Irene looked down at the hand that was touching her, a broad hand like a man's, with cracked red knuckles. She must promise to get herself educated. A woman should be able to provide for herself, she must not count on being looked after by a man. Irene could see for herself what resulted from just leaving things as they were.

She was frightened by Mrs. Frölich's earnest gaze. Many years later she went to visit her in the ground-floor apartment, where she still lived. It was in December, she had brought a star for the Christmas tree and pictures of Martin and the children. She asked Mrs. Frölich if she could remember what she had once said about getting an education, and remarked playfully that she hadn't known Mrs. Frölich was a feminist. The elderly lady snapped that she was no such thing. She couldn't understand those feminists. "As long as they have an education and a job," she said, "what have they got to complain about?" Her daughter had become a civil engineer and lived in Toronto.

Vivian hardly ever spoke to Irene about the future. She lived incarcerated in the past that Irene's father had closed the door on when he left. As a girl, Irene was alone with her undefined plans for the future. Her only intention was to get away as soon as she could. Away from the silence of the house when Vivian retired to her bedroom and she herself tiptoed around like a mouse. She went riding in the woods several times a week at one of the local riding-schools. They were her happiest hours. She felt comfortable with the horses, the big animals calmed her as she yielded to the rhythm of their movement and at the same time made them yield to her.

She had hardly any friends at that point. Although Vivian was distant and vague as a rule, she could be zealous with her prohibitions and horror stories where boys were concerned, long before any danger was even possible. As it happened, Irene's solitude was her own choice. The boys in her class were silly, and the girls behaved like little ladies. Irene didn't want to be a lady. Vivian was a lady. Irene wanted to be herself, but who was that?

They had hardly any visitors apart from Aunt Henny, who had once revealed what she thought Irene already knew. Henny was a lively woman compared with her sister. It was only with age that Vivian became garrulous, long after Irene had found her father and, later, buried him. When the three of them sat in the greenhouse or out on the lawn under a sunshade, it was like getting a visit from another world. The enthralling world she threw herself into when she was an au pair in that splendid city.

She had reached adulthood before she realized that she had never seen Vivian cry. The weeping had stayed inside her, behind the grief-stricken woman's dignified, unmoving face. Irene had wept for her mother in her place—over her forsakenness, just as much as over her own. Apart from Henny, she was the only person Vivian had left in the world. The world that had gone on around them, without them, and which Irene longed to join.

She felt like a traitor as she waved to Vivian from the window of the sleeping car when the train started to move. There she was, her mother, growing smaller and smaller, waving, alone on the platform until she vanished and Irene sank back in her seat, on her way at last.

"Is it you?"

Vivian has opened her eyes. Irene rises and walks over to the bed. Her mother no longer resembles a child. She sits down on the edge of the bed. Vivian sounds hoarse.

"How long have you been here?"

"Do you want me to turn the light on?"

Irene has already stretched out a hand to light the lamp on the bedside table, but Vivian makes a faint, deprecating movement and she lets her hand sink down on the duvet.

"I should have brought you some flowers."

"Don't worry about that. I've slept so soundly."

"Peter and Sandra are coming to dinner with the children. Josephine's coming too. She is bringing her latest boyfriend."

"Then you don't have time to sit here."

"I didn't mean that…"

Irene strokes her mother's thigh through the duvet. Vivian looks at her.

"How's Martin?"

"I don't know. I mean, well. I think he's well."

"Think?"

Of course Vivian can hear something is going on beneath Irene's harried vagueness.

"I think he's found someone else. No, I know he has."

She's said it now. She hadn't meant to. Irene looks at her mother. She was not going to say anything, at least not until some time had passed, until after Vivian has recovered from the operation. She takes her mother's hand and strokes it.

"What has he told you?"

"He hasn't told me anything."

Irene is annoyed with herself and she can hear the anger in her voice like a cool, distant note. As if it's Vivian she's angry with. She gives her hand a tentative, affectionate squeeze.

"So perhaps it's just…"

"We're getting divorced."

The words feel clear and concrete. It is surprisingly easy to utter them.

"Poor child."

"I am not a…"

Irene interrupts herself in the middle of her reply. She has let go of Vivian's hand. No, she is fifty-six and a half and she should be able to deal with her mother's anxiety. She looks into the worried eyes, each sunk into its net of furrows and folds. She feels the tears again and hastens to wipe them away, using both hands. The movement makes her feel like a little girl although it's Vivian who is little, as she lies in the big bed looking at her timidly.

"It will be all right," Irene smiles at her.

"Do you think so?"

"Of course. They are so clever nowadays."

Vivian looks toward the window.

"Supposing I don't wake up?"

So fear has got the better of her after all. Irene wants to sound casual, but the words seem too hearty as they come, out, "Now stop it, Mom. It's only an anesthetic."

"But the doctor said himself…"

"He has to say that."

"There's so much…," Vivian looks at her again and smiles. "Say hello to the children for me, will you? And Martin."

"I'm not going yet."

"But you have to cook."

"Mom…"

"It's been a long time since I saw Peter and Josephine. I expect they're busy. You're busy too."

"Mom, I'm so sad."

"Now you must be a sensible girl. You are a sensible girl, mind you. And a brave one."

"It's not what you think."

"I've always been very fond of Martin. He's a good man, he's been a good husband to you. You're going through a crisis. But think how many years you've been together. I'm sure he'll come back when he sees how much he's got to lose."

"You don't understand. I don't love him. I haven't loved him for many years; perhaps I never did."

"Never?" Vivian smiles in the dusk. "There's no such thing as never. Nor always. Anyway, that doesn't matter."

"What do you mean?"

"I'd like to go to sleep for a bit."

"But you just slept."

"I sleep so beautifully here. You know, I have always found it so hard to fall asleep. I still wake before sunrise. Listen, be a dear and water my hydrangea, will you? You've still got a key, haven't you?"

"I will, don't worry."

"By the way…"

"Yes?"

"There's something for you in the drawer."

Vivian makes a weary gesture at the bedside table. Irene opens the drawer. She sees a large brown envelope with her name on it, in Vivian's old-fashioned, elegant, but increasingly shaky handwriting.

"What is it?"

"You may open it if things don't go according to plan. Otherwise I ask you not to. Promise?"

"Mom, you're not the first person to get a new hip. These days it's like an assembly line."

"Yes, yes, dear. Will you do as I ask?"

"If you insist…"

Vivian lays her head back on the pillow. Neither of them says anything. When Irene looks at her mother again she sees that Vivian has closed her eyes. Her breathing is peaceful; she is asleep. Irene strokes her leg cautiously under the duvet, as if she is afraid to wake her, but at the same time hoping that Vivian feels the caress in her sleep. She looks at her watch; she needs to get a move on but she lingers a little longer. Yet as she leaves, it feels as if she's running away. She'll come again tomorrow. Tomorrow there will be more time.

There are still a lot of people in the supermarket. Well-dressed, well-groomed suburban people studying the frozen food with a fastidious eye. Well-to-do but hardworking husbands and wives like Martin and Irene, who can afford to live in one of the posh houses out here between the sound and the deer park and drive into town every day, each in their own glossy car. They know quite well that they are privileged, but it's not something that weighs on their conscience. They are aware of the misery and injustice in the world, but their home is here. They don't owe anyone anything, and they pay their taxes with hardly a grumble. They are enlightened, they have a humanistic outlook on things, they know that there's more to life than material possessions. They know the good life demands care, sensitivity, and consideration. They are also full of head-shaking pity for the victims of cruelty and catastrophe and blind, chaotic meaninglessness. All the same, it is with the greatest naturalness and the same sense of equanimity that they fill their baskets and carts with expensive cheeses and choice wines, and no one is more at home among them than Irene.

Irene looks around as she stands at the deli counter waiting to be served. There is Chanel and Gucci everywhere, but they are not hard or unfeeling, the faces she looks into, and why should they be? They are faces like her own, belonging to people whose lives resemble hers. Why then does she feel like an outsider, a strange guest in their world? Is it the thought of Vivian in the hospital bed, her small defenseless form in the twilight? The strange women around her in cashmere and silk have mothers, too, who will die one day, if they're not dead already. Irene tries to concentrate on what she will serve her guests. She'll just be able to get home before they all arrive, Josephine and her new beau, and Peter and Sandra and the children. She looks at the little goat's cheeses rolled in ashes, lying on straw mats under the glass in the refrigerator. Perhaps Martin has already come home.

It felt like a long letter, she thought clutching the envelope as she stood in the hospital foyer waiting for the elevator. She can visualize the tottering handwriting. She can almost hear the voice as she deciphers the feeble, tortuous lines. The whining, helplessly appealing little-girl tone her mother has had for as long as she can remember. As if the world has always been too much for little Vivian, almost literally—as if she carried the whole world on her narrow girl's shoulders. Now she has entered her plea, probably garnished with one or two faint hints of reproach. The martyr, the saint of unrequited love, who throughout Irene's youth tyrannized her to shield her. Irene can't remember anything from the years before her father's departure, save a few misty images of domestic coziness. But if the young Vivian had been only half as whimpering, half as tiresome and almost accusing in her ostentatious caring, half as distant and inaccessible when everything became too much and she had to go and lie down behind a closed door, then Irene can easily understand her father.

He was too sensitive, too considerate, and probably too guilt-ridden to give any hint of why he left, but it wasn't that hard to understand. Nina was a tall, good-looking woman with large breasts and a frank smile, dressed a tad provocatively but without seeming cheap—perhaps because of the candid look and warm smile with which she greeted everyone, even her repressed, rejected stepdaughter. Irene remembers making an effort to meet Nina with equal frankness and friendliness now that the guilt and pain were behind them and she herself was married, the mother of two happy, successful children. She wanted to, but her will was weak. Perhaps it was the thought that she had reached the age Nina was when she met her father. Perhaps it was because she saw her mother, small and deserted in the too-large house, where everything was in its place, newly polished, and dainty, in case anyone should drop in. Anyone? No, Irene. The only one she had left.

But Irene did her best to open up, and they did have a few talks, she and Nina, who was too young to be her mother and too old to be her sister. Out of the corner of her eye she caught her father's grateful glance when he discreetly found something to do while the two of them sat on the sofa and tried to talk themselves into each other's life. Sometimes she went to see them with Martin and the children. Her father experienced himself in the role of grandfather, and the children tried out what it was like to have one. Out of the picture window she could see them on the little beach, Martin with Josephine on his shoulders, her father holding Peter by the hand. She saw her father squat down while he and Peter searched for flat stones. He taught Peter to skip stones while she sat in the house talking to the stranger who had taken Vivian's place. Nina would have liked to have children, but it was too late now. There was no trace of bitterness in her voice, yet all the same Irene recognized that she was holding something back, dammed up, which was evident when Nina took Josephine on her lap and played with the little girl.

They were just getting friendly when Nina slipped out of her father's life, about the same time he fell ill. Irene didn't speak to her at the funeral. Nor did she speak to Vivian. The three lonely women sat in the front pew. There was no gathering afterward. Martin drove Vivian home, Irene and the children took a taxi.

It stopped raining as Irene was pushing her cart across the supermarket parking lot. Beneath the leaden cloud cover, the sky is unnaturally pink. There's a hint of spring in the damp air. She puts her bags in the trunk and slides behind the wheel. Vivian's envelope is on the dashboard. The mere idea of a letter seems pathetic. Because of a hip operation? But why is she still angry? Why is her anger a chess game, constantly being maneuvered into impossible new permutations?

We are getting a divorce.

The words feel neither clear nor concrete anymore as she drives home along the wet roads. Perhaps Vivian is right, maybe it is just a crisis. The word makes it seem so easy to grasp, it doesn't sound right coming from Vivian. Vivian, who hasn't been able to grasp anything for many years. But perhaps she's right, perhaps it is Irene who is making too much of it. Perhaps it is just an affair. Perhaps, perhaps. One can go mad tallying up the proliferation of possibilities. Should she just be a sensible, brave girl? She doesn't feel like a girl anymore, much less a sensible or brave one. But think how many years you have been together. Yes, think about it, far too many years. Vivian is sure he'll come back when he discovers what he's got to lose. Martin is a good man. Yes, but does Irene really want him back? Vivian didn't ask that question. And if she had? I don't love him. I haven't loved him for years. Maybe I never did. Maybe. Is that the truth?

There's no such thing as never, and once it was forever. Was it, perhaps, not forever? Or has it never been forever? Is he on the point of fulfilling her most secret wish? Is he so considerate and thoughtful and responsible as to shoulder the blame for her desire for another life? Is that perhaps what she wants in her heart? Isn't it? Is he about to impose a debt of gratitude on her because he's gentleman enough to take on the role of deceiver in her place? Who's really deceiving whom? Or is it Irene who's deceiving Irene?

I've always been very fond of Martin. There's no such thing as always. Vivian is full of lies. Vivian in her big white bed. A wrinkled, powerless little liar. Vivian has not always been fond of Martin. Not until there was no alternative to liking him. Not until he became head of the bank and Irene's father died and Martin paid the bills so little Vivian could stay in her too-large house, lonely and deserted. Not until then did she start to like him. Her clever, brave, good son-in-law. But Irene distinctly remembers the first time Martin came to the house to be introduced.

She had prepared her mother, briefed her and asked her not to ask about Martin's family. The family he didn't have because he came from a world where the presence of a father or mother is not to be taken for granted. But Vivian has always been forgetful, although there's no such thing as always. There he was, the snotty-nosed orphan, the uncouth proletarian punk, on the edge of Vivian's silk-covered sofa, in a starched shirt and tie, blushing, freshly shaven and trembling with fear of dropping the paper-thin English porcelain cup, while Vivian drilled him mercilessly about his background. He sat there allowing himself to be measured and weighed and humiliated because he loved Irene and had convinced himself that she was the one, and that she would come to love him. That was bravery if you like, and while she grew chalk white with rage and threw Vivian one warning glance after another, she realized she did love him, and that she loved him even more now.

Never doesn't exist. Irene loved Martin once. Never has never been never. Yet, unfaithfulness sneaked in. At one point, in one way or another, in the course of time. How? When? Could Thomas Hoppe explain that? Or Susanne? Probably not. Oh, Susanne, I wish you could never be more than a name. Take my husband or don't take him, but stay away from me; remain a name among so many others.

Martin's car is not in the driveway. That's a relief. He's usually home by now, but nothing is the same today. Irene stays behind the wheel after switching off the ignition. The tree canopies droop with moisture. The sky has faded behind the clouds fragmenting and spreading in the wind. She sits contemplating the house, the flame-shaped magnolia blossoms. It is a contemporary single-story structure, rectangular and painted white, whiter than magnolia. It still looks modern with its straight lines, like a futuristic vision from a more innocent time. Have they already put the future behind them? A blackbird flies past and alights on the letter box by the front door. It hooks its yellow claws around the enamelled edge of the lid. It looks around before taking off again. She can read the name on the small panel on the mailbox, clearly printed in angular letters: BECKMAN.

She took his name. The only thing he had. A name without history, with no affiliation to anyone other than herself. To her and the life, the home, they made together. She refused to accept anything from Vivian, not one silver spoon, not a single heirloom. Martin had been left to himself for as long as he could remember, and she stood with him.

Peter and Josephine were still small when Martin heard one evening that his mother had died. His half brother had phoned. He had not seen his siblings since the time he ran away from the children's home. Two strange, inquisitive children's faces gazing at him from the kitchen doorway before they were shooed into the living room. He had put the receiver down and sat beside her on the sofa. She started to put her arms around him but he pulled away. She was not used to being rejected, but she understood. She asked when the funeral was to be. He said he'd go on his own. She hadn't even suggested going with him, but of course he mustn't go alone. It was one of the few times they almost had a serious argument. He said it was meaningless, there was no reason, she'd never met his mother. Irene insisted, and she insisted on the children going as well.

The funeral took place in the chapel of a hospital outside the provincial town where his mother had lived. He was silent and nervous in the car on the way there. The children quarreled in the back seat. He scolded them, which was rare for him. A week had passed since his half brother phoned, and Irene had noticed no sign of grief in him, only an unusual silence. His stepfather must have died too, as only his two half siblings and a few older people were at the chapel. Afterward, his half sister came up to them, a pale woman with thick glasses. She asked if they would like to come to the neighboring inn. Martin avoided looking at her, ready to deliver an excuse. Irene quickly interjected, of course they would come.

He sat in a corner with Peter and Josephine, his back to the people in the room, which smelled of roasting meat and cigarette smoke. He left it to Irene to talk with the sister and the brother, a bony man in an ill-fitting suit. He looked older than Martin although he must have been ten years younger. Once they were outside and about to get into the car, Martin turned abruptly to Irene. Was she satisfied, then? He was almost shouting. She couldn't remember ever hearing him shout at her. Josephine cried, and he comforted her. On the way home it was Irene who was silent as he tried to amuse them. She was hurt, but also sad that she could not respond to his forced jollity as he sang with the children about a man going to mow a meadow.

In bed that night he begged her to forgive him. She drew him close and held him in her arms as he wept. He said he was ashamed, and she understood. She understood that he was ashamed not because he shouted at her in the children's presence, nor because his shame had prevented him from grieving. They had been one and the same thing, impossible to separate, shame and grief. As she held his large shaking body in her arms, she thought of the time she herself had wept at his side in the hotel room in Paris. Afraid of waking him, afraid of herself, alone with her inexplicable fear.

Irene carries her shopping in and puts the bags on the kitchen table. A magnolia blossom presses a petal against the windowpane. Like a child's nose. The light on the coffeemaker is on. She is sure she switched it off this morning. Someone has been in the house making coffee, the pot on the hot plate is half full. Someone? He must have been home and had a cup of coffee before leaving again. Irene starts unpacking. As usual when she is in distress, she has bought far too much. She opens bottles of red wine and starts to set out the prepared delicacies from the supermarket. Vivian would have reproached her for taking the easy way out. Vivian would never buy prepared food. She would have slaved in the kitchen all afternoon. Irene stops short as she realizes the unreasonably self-oriented turn of her thoughts, but also because she hears a noise far off in the silent house. She doesn't move. She recognizes the sound of running water on tiles. He could

71

have taken a taxi home, of course. Didn't he say a day or two ago that he had to take his car to the garage?

On her way through the house, Irene realizes that she has no idea what to say to the man she has lived with for more than thirty years. She stops in the middle of the living room and looks out the window at the peaceful reflection of the evening sky on the lake. The silence has been going on for a long time, the silence they bracket with passing remarks and still seal with an affectionate kiss. As if for a moment they have forgotten what they both know without saying it. The silence makes her feel like a deceiver. She, the deceived. A deceiver.

Irene goes on into the hallway, stops again. A pair of high-heeled shoes have been kicked off on the carpet and between them a skirt, followed by a blouse. Outside the bathroom door are a bra and a pair of crumpled briefs. The door is ajar, she gives it a push. She makes out the vague outline of a woman's figure behind the glass door of the shower, masked by steam. A slight figure; young. The gushing sound of water stops, the sliding door is pushed aside. It's a second before Josephine smiles. It takes another whole second for Irene to recognize her daughter.

"You frightened me!"

Josephine steps out of the shower. Irene passes her a towel and puts down the toilet seat.

"Sorry about that. Where's Dad?"

Josephine dries herself elaborately. Childishly energetic, Irene thinks, and smiles as she takes a corner of the towel and rubs her daughter's back. Josephine is suntanned although it's springtime. She's brown all over, including her behind.

"He'll be here soon, I expect."

Irene sits down, still shaken. Why didn't she remember Josephine has a key?

"How is he?"

"What do you mean?"

"What do I mean?" Josephine smiles indulgently. "How is he? He has seemed so, I don't know, funny, the last couple of times he called. Is anything wrong?"

"He has a lot on his mind."

You could say that. But what has Josephine noticed? More than she's giving away? Irene has an urge to ask what she means by "funny."

"Peter called a while ago." Josephine hops once or twice to keep her balance as she puts one foot on the edge of the sink. She has long thighs and long legs. "They're late. As usual."

Irene sits and studies her as she dries between her toes. What had she been imagining? Who had she expected to find at the end of the heap of clothes in the corridor? Susanne in the bath? She knows every detail of Josephine's body, her neck, knees, the shape of her hands and feet, and she recognizes herself. Josephine has her body. That's how Irene looked, too, when she was twenty-five. The thought comes to her like a warm, tender wave that for a moment washes over her tension.

"I thought we were going to meet...?"

Irene has stopped trying to keep up with the names of Josephine's boyfriends, there have been so many. But she tries to pretend she knows, until the name pops up in the course of conversation. Josephine is easily offended. It doesn't occur to her that her numerous lovers may be a strain on her mother's memory.

"It's over."

"Already?"

"Yes, and good riddance. He was an idiot."

"He didn't seem to be when you called this morning."

"So what?"

She turns and wraps the towel around her neck. Like a boxer. Irene can see she's spoiling for a fight. Josephine's blue eyes fix on hers. She has pulled her hair back and gathered it into a ponytail. She has Martin's eyes.

"Aren't you sorry?"

"Not especially." She lowers her eyes, opens the medicine cabinet and takes out Irene's foot file and nail scissors. "Why should I be?"

"Maybe because you liked him."

Josephine puts the towel over the edge of the bathtub. "Why are you insisting that I be upset?"

She sits down with one leg raised and starts giving herself a pedicure, chin resting on her bent knee.

"I'm not. You know that."

"Mom! Can't you just stop sticking your nose in?"

Josephine's impatient tone is modified by affectionate tolerance and a reserve that makes Irene feel sad.

"I don't think I ever do."

Why did she say that? Why did she say it that way? Josephine throws her a brief, somber look over her kneecap. Irene looks down at the geometric pattern of the floor tiles. It's been a long time since she has seen her daughter naked. Josephine has shaved her pubic hair so only a little tuft is left. Does she think Irene feels provoked? What does she think her mother's look meant? Her mother, who's been talking to her dutifully about sex since she played with dolls.

"Maybe I should go on the net. One of my girlfriends found her boyfriend on the net. Now she's pregnant."

"The net?"

74

"Yes, you know, the *Internet.*" Josephine knows how to sharpen the most innocuous remark.

"Thanks."

"You write about yourself and attach a photo. That's how you find out if you have common interests."

"Common interests?"

"Yes, for instance if you like skiing or don't like cats. To see if you suit each other, basically."

"Sounds practical." Irene sounds just as sharp. She thinks of Josephine's boyfriends. The nameless crowd of men she has put behind her.

"By the way, I'm off to Beijing tomorrow. They've offered me training for long hauls."

It feels as if Josephine is far away. As if she's talking from the other side of the world. Irene tries to picture her in a hotel lobby in Beijing, smart and long-legged in her flight attendant's uniform with her little suitcase on wheels. Soon she'll probably have a boyfriend on each continent, like a sailor. A Chinese, a Brazilian, and an African, whatever. As if her life will never begin because it consists of nothing but beginnings.

"Aren't you running away from your troubles?"

"Mom, it's my job." Josephine puts her foot on the floor and straightens up with the file in one hand and the nail scissors in the other.

"That's not what I mean." Irene gazes at her brown body and the bleached tips of her hair.

"I know very well what you mean. But I'm not like you. I'm not ready to play happy homemaker yet."

Irene can't escape the notion that suddenly occurs to her. She can't help but find her daughter slightly vulgar.

"Still, that doesn't mean you have to..."

"What?"

Again, the same challenging look. The icy firebreak. Josephine doesn't blink; this is the authority of being young. All the more insuperable because it rests not on contestable experience, but on the indisputable supremacy of youth. And after all, she is quite experienced already, this Josephine.

"All those men...," Irene sighs. "It's as if you mirror yourself in men and get rid of them when you don't like what you see."

"What are you talking about? That sounds like something you've read."

"You can give it a second chance, you know. Stay and fight."

"Like you?"

How much does Josephine know? How much has she noticed, her youthful self-absorption notwithstanding? She still has baby fat around her brain. She can still stand the coldness that makes her mother shiver inside.

"Mom, he was an idiot. Don't you get it? A shitty, charming, lying, ageing idiot. OK?"

She gets up. Irene looks at her. Josephine's breasts are pointing straight into the air.

"It seems as if it's always the men who are the idiots."

"Excuse me? What are you getting at? He could have told me he was married, couldn't he?" She goes out of the bathroom and starts picking her clothes up off the floor. "No wonder he wasn't keen to be introduced to his secret mistress's family."

Irene feels that something else is stirring under the flip comment from the hallway. Something penetrating the voice, bewildered, desperate. She knows she'll be too late to see any trace of it on her daughter's hard face, too late to put an arm around her. She knows her arm will be shrugged off impatiently.

Every time the same game of attraction and repulsion. Come, don't come, understand me, don't interfere. The dance of every mother, every daughter. She doesn't understand her daughter's life, just as Vivian doesn't understand Irene's; and it began at the same age, when they were thirteen years old.

She would like to rise, and go out to Josephine in the hall and embrace her, but she stays there on the toilet seat. It's not just because she knows Josephine would twist away, gently but unmistakably. She knows they care for each other, but often she doesn't know what to say to her daughter.

It's the same with Vivian. All too often she doesn't know what to say to her mother. The silence between two people who love each other.

It began when she was thirteen. It began when Irene's father had found Nina and left Vivian to herself and their daughter, when Vivian started to retreat into herself and pulled Irene with her into a circle of conflicting emotions, a hypnotic circle of sympathy and extortion. Between Josephine and Irene it started when she had said good-bye to Thomas and, in her heart, was on her way back to Martin. On the surface everything was as it had been before, but Josephine must have felt it, too, without knowing what it was.

She didn't understand her daughter, her vulnerability concealed itself behind moodiness. She was so very tolerant and liberal, but that didn't seem to be noted in her favor by their prickly teenage daughter. When she talks to Josephine about her men she is aware of expressing a condemnation that won't own up to itself, and she doesn't even want to be judgmental. Josephine isn't used to criticism from that quarter. From the age of thirteen she could more or less follow her own whim, come home as late as she liked. When Martin grew concerned over her precocity Irene made light of it. That was part of being young. She had to experiment. If they tied her down with prohibitions and rules, as she herself had been tied down by Vivian, it would only drive her further away from them. They couldn't very well barricade her, chain her to the radiator in her room where the young men came and went—some rather mature, from the look of them; older than Peter, too old to be their sons. Mature young male creatures you risked meeting in their underpants in the morning.

Where were you, Irene Beckman?

What did you do when you came home from your trysts with a strange man? You fell into the repetitious, everyday rhythm, circling in the family's gentle, sleepwalking orbit, but something inside you had torn itself free. A small, wild moon of desire and longing and unrest. A part of you had escaped from your "we" and Josephine felt it, in her way, just as Martin felt it when he reached out for you in the dark.

She feels giddy as she gets up to follow Josephine. She can't have drunk enough water today. She has a vision. It is not a pleasant one, let alone a revelation. She clutches the sink for support as she looks at herself in the mirror. She sees Martin in a strange bed, bending over a strange young woman.

Martin, what are you doing? Do you think you've found an escape route? A way out of one life and into another? It is more likely a blind alley. Yes, I know exactly what you're thinking. I know what everyone will think. I am a vindictive, fifty-six-year-old woman keeping menopause at bay with hormone pills, grinding her teeth with rage at nature's blind lack of fairness. For you are still virile, indeed, you've never looked better, even if your healthy color stems from high blood pressure and the bottle of wine you drink every night. But you certainly look good, and you are irresistible in a suit. So authoritative, so sure of yourself, and then you still have those hungry, boyish blue eyes. You're still attractive, while I am a middle-aged woman, pathetically trying to look twenty years younger and spending too much money on low-cut dresses in edgy colors, which I'll never have the courage to wear.

Yes, I am angry, but not at you. My anger's the pawn on the board, relentlessly pushed into this or that impossible new permutation. Even I, the divorce lawyer to whom nothing human is alien; even I, with my experience, cannot see how in the whole raging hell I'll get this game sorted out.

Now you'll understand more clearly why I wasn't so keen to act for Sally Hoppe. Yet another discarded female in her forties. Discarded by that same Thomas I was once ready to discard my Martin for. My life's sin of omission?

I'm sure you won't believe me. No one will. I know what I look and sound like.

The gravel in the drive crunches under tires, but there is no sound of an engine. Irene pauses on the threshold of the dining room. Josephine is setting the table. She has set it for seven. It's a long, rustic table, made of walnut, and Martin loves to sit at the head pouring himself a taste before he serves the others. Josephine folds the flowered paper napkins in triangles and puts them on the plates. The printed design on the napkins is a reproduction of a Persian faience dish. The small flowers and delicate, symmetrically branched stems fall into a pattern that seems at once logical and natural.

There is a self-forgetful, childishly pedantic meticulousness about her movements which makes Irene think of the seven-year-old

Josephine back when she began to be helpful. How often they worked together, helping each other while waiting for Father to come home. A less complicated time, she thinks, even though it was so busy, so full of big and small problems. Days and evenings that followed a pattern of minimal change through the years as the children grew. The calm, imperceptible growth of a life's pattern.

A car door slams outside. Josephine looks up. Twenty-five-year-old Josephine, who has just ended an affair with a married man. Maybe he has told Susanne he is married; maybe not until now. Maybe she's clapped her thighs together and thrown him out. Maybe Father has come home with his mission unaccomplished. The two women stand motionless listening to the steps advancing across the gravel.

The rain rises in yellow clouds behind the cars in the lamplight above the ring road. She drives fast, does not know where. She knows what she's putting behind her. Irene and Martin Beckman. Their life.

Irene Beckman is to be divorced, just like Sally Hoppe. That's all she knows. It is no longer her life. There is no "we." Only her unknown self. And the road ahead. There are other cars with people in them, alone or together, perhaps alone together, not many at this hour, and there is the wheel in her hands. The freeway heading southwest.

"Now that we are together…"

He'd been drinking. He'd had a few drinks before he arrived, florid and smiling, with kindly blue eyes, so familiar. She has never given it a thought, the possibility that he might be the one to make the break. Faithful, considerate Martin. He kissed her on the cheek before going into the bedroom to change. He even remembered to ask after Vivian. Their eyes met briefly.

You don't know each other. You think you do, but you don't. You have merely grown accustomed to each other, but the initial wonderment is still there. A pair of blue eyes, impossible to see through. The will and faith or doubt of someone else. The initial wonderment is no longer wondrous, it has become something like insufficiency, something you hide beneath familiar habits. Habits that join us and yet obscure the early, original wonderment.

Who are you? What do you hold inside you, and what will you do with it? Where will you go? Is it too cramped, or is there too much room around all that your will and faith and doubt are pregnant with?

"Now that we are together, all of us..."

Peter and Sandra arrived a little later with the twins. She could hear them outside as they jumped out of the car, Emil and Amalie, impatient after sitting still in their car seats. They jumped at her like squirrels, and for a moment she didn't know what to do with all that love. She squeezed her eyes, the light shone so brightly from their four dark ones. She embraced them, kissed their soft nut-colored cheeks, and ruffled their inky black hair.

She and Martin had gone with Peter and Sandra to the airport, right out to where the plane from Bombay landed, on the morning when they met their twins. The door in the shining fuselage was opened at last by two shy women in saris, each with a red spot on her forehead. She could not help linking the two caste marks with the two babies. Like two seals, two secret greetings from another world. The twins had been found one morning outside an orphanage in Kerala, no one knew where they came from. Two small unwanted creatures left on a doorstep, where a nun found them and carried them inside. Martin put an arm round Irene's shoulders and pulled her close while

Peter and Sandra were each given a little human parcel. The tears streamed freely down their new grandfather's cheeks, and Irene kissed him and tasted salt mixed with the scent of aftershave.

Peter and Sandra had done the right thing. For years, they had tried to have a child. And when they realized that the act of love had become an act of will, hard and persistent work, they called a halt to the artificial fertilization techniques. One night they watched a television report from the Indian slums and each knew what the other was thinking. If their will had managed to wrench itself free of all the romantic seductive veils, all the blurred and silently significant moods of falling in love, if now only will was left, raw, crude, and frustrated, they might as well decide to bestow the love they had stored up on one or two of the world's orphans.

The framework was already in place. Peter was thriving as a furniture designer, with his own studio and a growing clientele. They had been sensible when they bought the house, a rather dull suburban affair in a nondescript silver wedding district; but there was a garden and fresh air and a quiet road where a child could skip and ride a tricycle. Other young families had begun to move in on the heels of the previous, largely working-class inhabitants. The setting was complete, only the contents were missing. Until one day a twin perambulator was parked under the pear tree in the garden, and in it lay two small unknown babies who had travelled from the other side of the Earth to find their names and parents. They would pick pears one day, not mangoes.

"Now that we are together, all of us, there is something…"

Irene sat contemplating the others, Emil and Amalie, Peter and Sandra. Steady, sensible Peter, who devotes himself to life's framework. Not just their own but everyone else's, too, as he designs the furniture we sit in and lie on when we make love or quarrel. When we are full of faith, or doubt if there is any enduring, weighty meaning in it all. The furniture that will accommodate us when we learn that we are going to be mothers or fathers; when we receive news of a death, or just sit over coffee and watch the nightly transmissions of atrocities and infamy in the world. Peter can deal with it, he knows how to clear a corner in this chaotic, volatile world. Listening to his sister, who was talking about Beijing, he affectionately stroked Sandra's hand. Sensible, good-natured Sandra with the reddish brown curls and freckles that make her look like a child. She isn't a child; thin, fine lines are already showing in the corners of her eyes; life has begun to print its lasting marks. The life they have made for themselves, full of love and purpose.

To Vivian's immense satisfaction, Sandra chose to give up her job and stay at home to look after the babies. Irene herself had gone back to work as soon as Peter and Josephine were old enough for nursery school. It's a different world now, but there is a serenity about her daughter-in-law when she is caring for her foundlings from Kerala. A naturalness—in other women the result of nine months of hormone eruptions—which the sight of the Indian mites at the airport aroused in less than a second. Apparently there is nothing in the world she would rather do than care for them. Two children, a house, a home. She once told Irene that the twins had freed her from herself and all the egocentric anxieties of her youth. Although Irene never dreamed of giving up work to raise her family, she understands Sandra better than she understands her frustrated, roving daughter. She understands her, but she understands her at a distance. She can see herself in Sandra, but it is a different Irene she sees, in another time. She has never told them that she, too, is a twin. That she has lived with the feeling of being watched over by an invisible shadow.

"Now that we are together, all of us, there is something I would like to tell you."

Martin sat at the head of the table as usual, between Sandra and Josephine. He had changed his white shirt and tie for a navy blue polo shirt and an old cardigan, but he did not seem relaxed at all. There was something hard and angular about his kindly, blue eyes. Everyone fell silent. Donald Duck could be heard in the adjoining living room—Emil and Amalie were watching the Cartoon Network. The others looked at Martin, disoriented at first, not by his words so much as by his tone. Irene could see from his face that he had drunk more than usual. The way he stared at them. She was probably the only one who could see it, but she saw something else as well. Fear. He avoided looking at her as he talked.

"It will probably come as a surprise to you..."

"Have you been given a golden handshake?" Josephine smiled her cheeky smile, which he had never been able to resist. "Are the two of you moving to the south of France? Are you going to be an olive farmer with a mustache and a beret?"

Sweet, cocky Josephine. Peter took Sandra's hand and smiled tentatively, his eyes wandering from Martin to Irene. Sandra leaned back in her chair and straightened the napkin on her lap. A logical, natural pattern.

"Perhaps even as a shock..."

Martin, you're not going to. That's not the way you should do this, is it? Where's your selflessness? Your respect? Where have you gone, Martin? Who is this man sitting in your place at the head of the table in your polo shirt and favorite cardigan?

"The thing is, I have met another woman, and I have decided that I want to live with her."

The remnants of Josephine's smile had not yet left her face before a sob burst from her throat.

Sandra leaned further back and looked away. Peter's face was a motionless mask; he stared at the stranger at the end of the table.

That's what it is, he's met another woman. He wants to go and live with her. He's decided on it. He desires to. Is it his desire he's decided on? Or does he just want to make a decision? Get it over with. Their silent, well-groomed, comfortable hell of an unresolved situation.

She is crying, cheeky, sharp Josephine. This girl who doesn't believe in sticking at it, who goes her own way, can't bear for us to fall apart. She who doesn't want to see anything other than the flickering inconstancy of it all.

And Peter. He has turned white. He suddenly seems to be twenty-five years older. Your image. The man who does the right thing, full of tenderness and solicitude. He looks at me and there is darkness in his eyes.

"What's her name?"

Josephine sniffed and dried her eyes, her voice cracking, but she had stopped crying.

Peter knocked over his glass as he struck the table with a fist.

"Bastard!"

Sandra laid a hand on his shoulder. He shook it off as he stood up. The chair screeched on the floor. The twins sat up on the sofa. Sandra went to them. Peter took a step toward Martin.

"You stupid bastard! Stupid filthy bastard!"

Martin leaned back and looked up at his son. Josephine started to cry again. Irene rose and went into the hall. Peter caught up with her on the drive. She opened her car door.

"Where are you going?"

Irene looked at him. "I don't really know." She smiled slightly and got into the car.

"Come home with us. You can stay with us tonight. As long as you like."

"No, thank you, Peter. It's sweet of you but I'd rather be alone."

She started the car and backed out of the driveway. The beams of light moved up his body and struck his face.

She's been driving for an hour when the rain stops. The road is thinning out in the fog. She drives more slowly, breathes more calmly now.

Just before the Great Belt Bridge she pulls into a gas station. As she stands by the pump, her eyes light on Vivian's envelope. It is still there on the dashboard where she left it earlier in the evening. She goes inside to pay. A stout young man looks at her from behind the counter. She picks up a bottle of mineral water and reaches for a bar of chocolate from one of the shelves. She doesn't usually eat chocolate. The young attendant is pale, and his pallor is increased by the sharp overhead lighting and his white shirt. The shirt is too small, it strains around his broad torso. His face is too small. He looks as if someone has blown him up. If you let a little air out of him he would look quite good, like a child, an unprotected child with unfinished features in his padded face. A solitary child you can't get hold of and protect because he has grown too big and shapeless.

She asks for a pack of cigarettes. She hasn't smoked for years. While the attendant rings up her purchases with his plump fingers she lets her eyes run over the covers of the glossy magazines under the counter. There is a whole shelf of pornographic magazines. Some of the girls cup their hands around their large breasts with gentle, protective gestures. They gaze up at her with a startled air, as if surprised at a private moment, as if their breasts are their children, small newborn twins which they nurse holding a protective hand around their naked heads.

She gets into the car. A short distance ahead she can glimpse the lit pylons of the bridge through the fog. She reaches out for Vivian's envelope and opens it. Inside is a letter, folded once in the middle around an old exercise book bound in worn brown cardboard. On the back of the notebook the multiplication tables from one to ten are printed in columns of neat figures. She turns it over and recognizes the intricate handwriting, but it is a younger hand that has covered the printed lines on the front cover with ink:

Lago Maggiore
May 1948

She leafs through the exercise book. A young hand, without the hesitations of age; assured, firm. The ink has faded to a paler, watery blue shade. She compares the steady writing with the letter, undated, written with a ballpoint pen, shaky. She pictures Vivian's hand as she reads, its prominent, dark veins. Its grip of a fold in the duvet cover, wrinkled, weak.

Dearest Irene,

When you read this it will be too late for us to talk. I have not been a particularly good mother, but there's nothing to be done about that now. Some people are good at it, others... [illegible].

I don't intend to defend myself. I don't understand why we bother so much about childhood. It takes up so little time. Think of all those years when one is not a child or young anymore. You have been grown up for so long, my dear. So much has gone well for you. That is my greatest joy.

Through the years I have been on the verge of giving you this little book several times. I probably should have done it long ago, but I didn't, because I was afraid it would do more harm than good. I was a coward, too. My cowardice has always... [illegible].

As I said, I shall not ask your forgiveness, but perhaps you will understand me better. You are sure to be both angry and upset by it, but at least you will have those feelings for the right reasons. Though I think you would rather... [illegible]... and will probably... [illegible]. Take care of yourself and Martin. I will think of you as long as I can.

With very much love,
Your mother

Irene puts the letter and the notebook back in the envelope. She starts the car and looks at the digital clock in the corner of the dashboard. For a moment it shows only four small, angled, verdigris-green zeros, the last two separated from the first ones by a flashing colon. Then the last zero is replaced by a vertical, segmented line. It is no longer the same day. Tomorrow has changed into yesterday.

There is hardly any traffic on the bridge. The steel girders and the taut wires stream to meet her in a pattern of vibrating repetition, like a gateway that repeats itself inward in perspective. As if each second is merely an entrance to the next one.

Lago Maggiore
May 1948
My dear little girl. I can see you from the window up here. You're toddling along the terrace holding Franca's hand. You are wearing your wool coat, the one with the velvet collar. It can still be cool here, it is so high up. You stop to look at the flowers in the

big pots and the view across the lake. Franca lifts you up and points to the mountains on the other side. The lake is so smooth and shining that the mountains are reflected in it. You can't understand what she says, but I can't either. She is only a year or two younger than I am. She looks after you for a few hours every day so I can rest. Late in the afternoon the three of us go for a walk along the path beside the lake shore. The lake is a dark solid blue at the end of the day when the sun has set behind the mountains. We are here alone.

I have been sent here to recuperate, they say my nerves are weak, but you are with me, my little star. I can hear your clear voice. You can't talk to each other, but you get along well. You pick a flower from one of the pots and offer it to her, and she bends down to take it. Now you disappear from sight. I wonder if you will remember Franca and the flowers and the mountains and the lake?

I don't know where to begin. I think I will start with a day five years ago. An autumn day in Copenhagen, 1943. The National Radio Orchestra is rehearsing. Mahler's Fifth Symphony. I often play it on the record player when I try to think through that day.

The orchestra has come to the Scherzo, the waltz-like passage for strings. In the cello group there is a young man, younger than his colleagues, in his mid-twenties. His name is Samuel, and he has been a member of the orchestra for about a year. He was taken on just after he passed his examination at the Academy of Music; they have high hopes for him. Samuel gives himself over completely to the soaring waltz-like theme. He doesn't see that another young man has sneaked into the auditorium. It's not until the brass and tympani interrupt the strings that Samuel lowers his bow, and then he catches sight of the young man, who has taken a seat in the front row. Samuel nods to him, no doubt wondering how his friend managed to get in.

He doesn't look down there during the rest of the rehearsal. He is entirely absorbed by the music and it makes him forget everything else. He forgets the war and the German soldiers, the air raid sirens, the rumors and fears. He also forgets his parents and his sister in the small apartment in the side street, over his father's shop, the worries at the dinner table, his parents' low-voiced discussion, his little sister playing with her doll, understanding nothing.

The family came to Denmark while Samuel was still growing up. He doesn't remember much of Leningrad, but he can remember the floes on the Neva in springtime, the huge blocks of ice turning slowly on their way under the bridge near the Winter Palace. When you talk to him it is clear he comes from another country, but not when he plays his cello. When he plays it doesn't matter where he came from, the music is the same, and it is wonderful.

During a break in the rehearsal, Samuel and the other young man go into the foyer. They look different, those two. Samuel is slight and not very tall. His face is pale and narrow, dominated by his nose and large dark eyes. His friend's hair is golden, it keeps falling over one of his ice-blue eyes. He is tall, suntanned, and broad shouldered with strong arms under his shirt sleeves, which he has rolled up above his elbows although it is mid-October.

As a matter of fact, it is not only their appearance that makes them so different, nor the gap in their ages. Samuel's friend is a few years younger. He has never been outside Denmark apart from a skiing trip to Norway before the Occupation, and he has no understanding at all of music—he's a medical student who

91

spends most of his spare time in the warmer months at the university rowing club. He looks serious as he stands whispering to Samuel, who listens equally earnestly, looking down at his shabby shoes.

When the break is over, Samuel takes his place in the orchestra. The conductor mounts the dais and addresses a few words to the musicians. Then he lifts his baton and the strings start up, accompanied by the harp, breathlessly quiet and lingering at first, with the opening bars of the Adagietto from Mahler's Fifth. Samuel sinks into himself as the music gradually increases in fullness and intensity. His whole being is in motion, and the music is a kind of parting.

This is the second time in his life that he is saying farewell to a place, and the music echoes in his memory as he sits in the streetcar with his instrument case and looks out at the town where he has lived while becoming a young man, the streets and the squares so familiar to him, the shops he knows. He sees people cycling along, and you would think it was all pleasant and at peace, although a state of emergency has been declared, the government has resigned, and no one knows what will happen next.

He finds his parents waiting for him at home. They have already packed. His little sister cries and asks too many questions they don't know how to answer. One of the neighbors' wives is there, too; Samuel's mother talks to her quietly, and a key changes hands. Samuel tells them there is something he has to do. His father gets angry, normally his voice is never raised, but Samuel is obstinate, and soon he goes out again.

Late that evening, his friend stands on the quay of one of the small harbors north of town. It is a clear night and there is a multitude of stars. A cutter lies beside the quay. Below deck are

Samuel's family and one or two other families. His cello case is with the suitcases. They cannot understand what has happened to him, it is long after the appointed time. They whisper below deck but otherwise nothing is heard except the gentle lapping of water against the wharf.

Samuel's friend peers at the coastal road where the darkened houses look deserted. At last he sees the vague outline of a figure on a bicycle approaching. The friend greets Samuel with a sign, and they manage a quick handshake before he boards the cutter, which casts off and glides out of the harbor, out to the sound, setting a course for the Swedish coast. Samuel stays at the stern looking back until the fisherman lays a hand on his shoulder and points to the open hatchway and stepladder leading below deck. When Samuel has gone below, the hatch is closed.

That is how I imagine it, and that was more or less what Samuel's friend told me. But I have never told him that I was the one Samuel had been visiting.

It's light when Irene wakes. A pale spring sunshine, harsh and clear, penetrates the thin curtains and reflects dully from the gray, convex television screen. You can see the marks of the cloth used to clean it. She has fallen asleep in her clothes. There is a brief swishing sound each time a car drives past on the freeway. She can hear voices outside on the sidewalk, a man and a woman speaking German. A keychain clatters against a door as it's being locked. The voices fade. She undresses and goes into the bathroom. She stops for a moment and looks at her naked body in the mirror.

Irene Beckman, fifty-six.

As usual, it is a mystery how the tap in the shower works. Why can't the manufacturers make up their minds once and for all? She jumps out with a half-smothered groan when she is hit by the icy cold jet. Then she manages to adjust the water temperature and lets the heat sink into her bones.

After drying herself, she fastens the towel firmly over her breast, piles up the pillows against the headboard, and settles herself in bed. She takes the notebook out of the brown envelope on the bedside table, lights a cigarette, opens the book, and continues. The nicotine enters her blood and Irene feels a dizzy lightness. Now and then, she raises her eyes and looks at the shadows in the folds of the curtains.

Luckily I was alone at home when Samuel came. Mom and Dad were at the theater with Henny, and the maid had left out some sandwiches for me in the kitchen. I was sitting at the kitchen table when I caught sight of him outside the window. We shared the sandwiches and talked. I could feel something was wrong, but he wouldn't tell me what it was. He wanted us to sit out in the garden but I was afraid the neighbors would see us. My parents didn't like me being with Samuel. Nor did his parents.

We went up to my room. He held onto my hand while he told me that he and his parents had to go. It was impossible to know when we would see each other again. I can recall that I cried, both because he had to leave and because he terrified me with his solemn voice. He had tears in his eyes. He told me he loved me. He had said it before but that night he said it in such a mournful way. He asked if I would wait for him. I didn't know how to answer, but when I looked into his dark, unhappy eyes, I said yes. I said yes although neither of us could know how long I would have to go on waiting.

He hadn't been to our home many times. My parents thought he was too old for me, but I didn't think that was the reason for their not liking him. He often gave me tickets to the National Radio concerts. He was so handsome, sitting there among the other musicians, and I never grew tired of watching his face as he played, entirely lost in the music.

Samuel was different from the other young men I knew. He was serious and sensitive, and although he talked with an accent he had words for so many things I didn't know how to express. He was already a grown man, and he made me feel like a grown woman, not just a schoolgirl with nothing but fun and games in my head.

He was my first real love, Irene. I felt I could talk to him about things I couldn't discuss with anyone else. He never laughed at me, and he never made me feel stupid even though he knew so much. He told me about music and books, the Greek philosophers, and natural history. Sometimes I questioned him about his religion, and he did reply, but he didn't believe in God, neither the god of his parents nor any other. I didn't know whether I believed in God myself. I still don't know, but if I did believe in God, surely I would know. Samuel would say that if one could not say yes, one had already said no. I often think about that.

He could be so tough when he argued with me, but if he saw me getting frightened or confused he hastened to smile and kiss my forehead. One of his favorite subjects was the future. We used to meet in the Botanical Gardens on Sundays. We sat outside the greenhouse on a bench in the sun.

He wanted to go to America. He never tired of talking about America. He could describe New York as if he had been there. When the war was over he would go there and join one of the big orchestras, and I would come with him. Our children would be born Americans, for there it made no difference who you were and where you came from, only if you were determined.

There was so much determination in Samuel. I had never thought as far ahead as the question of children. I was in love with him but I didn't know whether he was the man of my dreams. How could I know that? Samuel would have said that if he was I would know it. He himself was sure, and I only know that because he said so and shared his dream of our future together with me. I know because I could see and feel it in him. He didn't care about our parents, even though he was very fond of his mother and father, and even though they expected him to marry one of their own.

One day shortly before he went to Sweden, my mother came into my room. She was trying to make me see reason, as she put it. Like children play best together, she said. I asked her if all children weren't alike, but she just smiled and looked at me sadly, stroking my cheek. In my heart I did not feel Samuel and I were alike, but it was not on account of his religion, nor because he was older than I. I did not feel equal to him because he was so much cleverer, and because he had a much stronger will. I was in love but I was also all at sea.

He suggested we lie down for a while. We lay side by side on my bed as the evening crept in. I don't know how long we stayed like that. Part of the time we talked, part of the time we just lay there looking into each other's eyes. He caressed me so gently, and his eyes were so sad. We had never been together like that before. He said he had never loved anyone as he loved me. He asked if I loved him, and I said I did. He grew bolder, and I did not put up much resistance although I thought I probably should have. I felt what it was he wanted. He said he would take good care. It was the first time I had been with anyone that way.

He didn't want to leave. He wanted to stay with me, and it was only with difficulty that I got him out the door. He was already late. I went with him to the garden gate, and we kissed for the last time. When he mounted his bicycle he asked me again if I would wait, and again I said yes, mostly to get him to go, for time was getting short. He turned around several times and almost fell off his bike, and I couldn't help smiling although I was crying.

A day or two later Samuel's friend came to invite me out. It happened several times, we went to the cinema and he walked me home afterward. We got on well and it turned out we had a lot in common. Our parents knew each other, so it was strange that I had not seen more of him, and I thought I had found a good friend. For he was Samuel's friend, and I thought of Samuel all the time.

I thought about him night and day. I thought about the year we had met, almost secretly. And about our last evening. I had no one to talk to about Samuel. Henny had sided with Mom and Dad, I was alone a lot, and it was a relief to be invited out and forget my gloomy thoughts.

At first, I did not think there was more to it than friendship, until one evening when we were waiting at a trolley stop and he suddenly asked if he could kiss me. I didn't know whether Samuel had told him about me, but they were friends, after all. I realized suddenly that he had turned up in my life just as Samuel had left it. I could have asked him what kind of friend he was, but I didn't. Instead I made a hasty decision and gave him the kiss he had asked for.

I was frightened. I didn't know what to do, I just knew that something unusual was happening. I dared not go to our own doctor, so I found one at the other end of town, and the doctor confirmed what I feared. What was I to do? I had no one to talk to. I did not even dare to confide in Henny.

Samuel's friend and I saw more and more of each other, and shortly after the evening at the trolley stop he invited me home. He was alone in the house, as I had been on the evening I parted from Samuel. He had lighted candles and brought a bottle of his father's wine up from the cellar. He was sweet and gentle, but of course I understood what he wanted, and I gave way. I did not even ask him to take care. He asked if it was the first time for me, and I lied.

He suspected nothing, later on I was sure of that. We began to appear in public as an official couple, and I noticed when we were with other people how much he was respected. Sometimes I did not hear from him for several days, and when he did turn up again he never explained what he had been doing. Naturally I wondered if he had found someone else, but gradually it dawned on me that he was involved in something important. There was so much going on one didn't know about in those years, and so much one must not talk about.

When I dared not wait any longer I cycled over to my new love and told him what the doctor had said. He just looked at me, then ran out into the garden. I stayed in his parents' living room, and he soon reappeared with a bouquet of his mother's roses. He kneeled by the sofa where I sat and asked if I would marry him.

I was two months pregnant when the wedding took place. We moved into a small apartment in town, near the metropolitan hospital where he was interning. His father provided the apartment for us. By winter I had grown big, and was expecting twins.

Yes, my dear, you should have had a brother, but he did not

live. They took him away before I could get a glimpse of him. I thought Samuel had been wrong about God. I thought that there must be a God after all, and this was God's punishment for deserting my beloved. But there you lay, my little girl, in my arms. God had chosen to punish me and to give me the greatest gift at one and the same time. We avoided any mention of your brother. Your father tried to protect me from his sorrow, to wipe it out with the joy of having you, and I let him. For I was protecting him, too.

I am protecting you both. Neither of you shall know the truth as long as I live. But I have to keep it somewhere. That is why I'm writing this. I shall never forget his face, when he saw you for the first time. He became your father, Irene. I had tears in my eyes when he came home from the hospital and lifted you up and you laughed in your gurgling way. I think we shall be happy. I think we can be. We have buried your brother in our hearts, and I bury my secret in mine. When I come to the end of my story I will forget and only look ahead. I will forget the war and Samuel and your brother. We will try to be happy, and I will do my best, my little one.

It is hard for me at times to hold onto the world around me. I seem to be drifting away, into the dark. That is why we are here. I have been hospitalized several times. They gave me electric shock treatment. They think something is wrong with my mind, for of course I cannot tell them why I get so dark inside that I don't know who I am or what to do with myself. The consultant at home says I need rest. He says I can't tolerate sudden upsets. He gives me medicine. I would rather take medicine than have electric shocks, but the drugs make me so lethargic that I can't care for you properly. It's as if I vanish into a gray cloud that pins down my arms and legs.

You are my consolation, my little treasure, but you can also make me tremble when you smile and look at me with your clear open eyes. You are my crime and my gift of grace, and I can hardly grasp that idea. Sometimes I fear going to pieces at the mere thought of it.

I only saw Samuel once more. It was on a Sunday in late summer, a few months after the Liberation. Your father and I went for a walk with you in your stroller, in the Botanical Gardens. Samuel sat on a bench outside the greenhouse, where he and I had so often sat. It was as if he knew we would pass by. He stood up and moved over to the balustrade as we walked along the path below. I had promised to wait for him, but I had not kept my word. I don't know whether your father saw him, but he made no sign of doing so. Samuel stood watching us as we strolled by along with the other people out for their Sunday walk.

Last winter I heard he might have gone to Palestine. Now they have their own country, his people, who have been through so much. I hope he is alive and well down there, even though there is so much strife. I hope he will meet a woman and have children with her and be happy.

When I met his gaze for a brief moment, there by the greenhouse, I realized he still loved me, and that it was as he had said. That I was the love of his life. Was he mine? I don't know anymore.

You are my love, Irene. Only you can save my life, and you don't know it. You will not know it until the day I am no longer here. I wonder how life will have turned out, when you read these lines many years from now? Will you forgive or condemn me? I will not be there to receive your forgiveness or your condemnation, and that is probably for the best.

Evening has fallen over the lake. It gets so dark at the end of the day, and you can no longer see the villages on the other side. The mountains over there are dark and unvarying, as if they had been cut out of dark blue paper. I can hear you in the hall, Franca is talking to you in her language, and you answer her in ours. In a moment you will come in and life will go on. Now I will close this notebook, hide it away and forget about it. Forget everything.

II

A strange sense of freedom

The low sun is shining on the façades to the east. Vivian lies watching the news. She holds up the remote and lowers the volume when Irene comes in and sits down on the edge of the bed. The two women gaze at the afternoon sky as images move inaudibly on the screen. The usual young Palestinians throwing stones at Israeli soldiers in armored troop carriers. Shaky images, dust and smoke. Scarred concrete houses with flat roofs, laundry, and television antennae in the glaring sunlight. Irene is holding Vivian's hand.

"Martin's moved out."

She looks up at the screen. A street corner in Jerusalem or Tel Aviv. A bomb has shattered an entire building. Broken walls, rescue workers, and the wounded. Ambulances, military police. She wonders whether Samuel is still alive. If he's living his life in Jerusalem or Tel Aviv, an old man, long retired. Is he alone or with someone else? A woman he's spent most of his life with? A son or daughter who's never learned the foreign languages Samuel learned to speak? Perhaps he's watching the same pictures on television. Perhaps he sees the ice floes on the Neva in spring. Perhaps he sometimes thinks of the girl in Copenhagen who promised to wait for him. Perhaps he's dead.

"It's probably for the best."

Vivian's voice is still muffled with sleep. She has lost weight, her eyes are more sunken, and the vein in her left temple stands out more. It looks like a worm under her thin skin.

"Do you think so?"

"I've never been sure he was the right man for you. Give me a sip of juice, will you?"

"But Mom, a week ago you said just the opposite."

Irene hands her the glass from the bedside table. The brown envelope is still beside the flower vase.

"Did I?" Vivian slurps a mouthful of juice.

Irene takes the glass from her. Vivian's head sinks back onto the pillow. "I've never really understood you." She looks out at the sky. "You can be so..."

"So what?"

"I don't know...," She looks at Irene. "They say I will go home soon. Have you remembered to water my hydrangea?"

"Yes, Mom."

"I've been thinking about your father lately. We weren't suited for each other, either."

Irene looks at her. Vivian looks out at the clouds. It's a trap. She's not so confused after all. She's trying to find out if Irene has read the notebook.

103

"You got on well enough as long as it lasted," says Irene.

She rises and kisses her mother's forehead. Vivian's hydrangea must have died long ago. Irene hasn't been to the apartment since Vivian was admitted to hospital. She walks toward the door.

"Give my love to Martin and the children."

She turns. "I will."

Irene has visited Vivian every day for the past week. She'll be sprinting with the best of them when she gets used to the new hip, that's what the consultant says. Irene took the brown envelope with her the day after the operation. She put it down on Vivian's duvet, with a big bouquet of flowers. Vivian touched the roses and the envelope lightly. Irene had glued the envelope shut again, thinking that opening it had been like opening the wrong door and quickly shutting it again. A door in the corridor of a hotel by Lago Maggiore that you happen to open, revealing a strange room occupied by strangers, who turn and look at you in surprise.

It has nothing to do with her. They will never speak of what Vivian wrote in the notebook, in her schoolgirl handwriting, one spring long ago beside Lago Maggiore.

The nurse came in with the flowers in a vase and put it on the bedside table. Irene held her mother's hand as they looked silently out the window and at the tightly bunched petals of the roses. The flowers and the mountains and the lake. Irene remembers them only vaguely, like something she once saw in a picture. She cannot remember the young woman who took care of her. Franca. Nor the young woman who watched them from her window when she looked up from the notebook she'd been writing her secret in, just so she'd have somewhere to keep it.

Irene stroked the loose, wrinkled skin of Vivian's hand as she pictured the young woman living through wartime with two children in her womb. She imagined her joy and fear, her innocence and deceit. How they had blended into an indefinable, nameless emotion, which sucked her into its darkness from time to time.

She also imagined the young intern at the Municipal Hospital. She saw him come home and catch sight of his young wife at the window. She saw him embrace Vivian from behind as they looked down at the street, where people cycled past as if everything was normal. As if there were no war, and everything between the two people up there had not been paralyzed from the start by the loneliness of suppression.

She thinks about Samuel. She can't visualize him. His image dissolves into the autumn night, in the stern of a cutter with its lights extinguished. The closest she gets is her own reflection.

She spent the morning in her motel room, lying on the bed listening to the traffic on the freeway. When she had read through Vivian's notebook again she went into the bathroom. She stood in front of the mirror for a long time trying to isolate the features Samuel had left her. She couldn't work out whether she was the stranger or the woman in the mirror who returned her gaze.

She regarded her black hair and pronounced dark eyebrows, the dark eyes, distinctive nose, and sharply defined, protruding jaw. She began to think about Vivian's maritime story of a Faroese relation with Portuguese ancestors. Why not? Every time she was on the brink of forming an impression of Samuel he eluded her, and she bent forward as if the mirror was a window into what was hidden by the cascade of years. But there was nothing behind the image, only the image itself.

After she'd dressed and paid for the room, she drove the last few kilometers out to the North Sea. She left the car in a parking lot behind the dunes. There was drizzle in the air and the sand was heavy on the path through the marram grass. She was wearing the same pumps as the day before, and she staggered up the last row of dunes before the beach. Everything around her was gray, the overcast sky, the sea that dissolved into a fog bank, and the broad beach beneath her. There was an onshore wind, and the great breakers foamed as they chased each other shoreward. She caught sight of a small, dark figure walking along the edge of the surf. By the time she was down on the beach it had vanished. As she stood watching the waves break and recede she realized that she, too, would be no more than an anonymous, insect-like figure to anyone who saw her from up on the dunes.

She recalled the black-and-white photo she had once seen of her mother, standing bare-legged at the edge of the shore one day in the spring of 1944, smiling and pregnant in her summer dress. A high-spirited, carefree moment, two happy eyes fixed on Irene as if she is greeting the future with simple joy. It made her think of those snap-shots in the newspaper of people who have been murdered. They al-ways smile with the same trusting face, as if nothing bad can happen to them, and for a moment you feel that the evil emanates from your own eyes, full of cruel knowledge. As if you can't know their fate without doing violence to the expectant innocence shining from their eyes.

As she walked along the shore she thought of everything that sep-arated her from the distant summer day when Vivian stood smiling at the photographer. Was it the young doctor who took that picture in the first year of their marriage? Ignorant of the darkness lurking behind her happy eyes, the despair that would intrude like a threat-ening shadow underneath the calm exterior. A monster that could suddenly burst up to gasp for air, and with that breath rob her of hers.

Irene walked for an hour in the din of the crashing waves without meeting anyone. On her way she passed the ruins of German defense works half covered in sand. They'd been here since the Occupation, alien bodies of armed concrete, and they had become part of the landscape. They were much the same age as she was, but she'd never connected her life with the war. It belonged to a remote past that merely brushed the start of her life with its foreign soldiers, air-raid sirens, and basement bomb shelters. It was Vivian's world, not Irene's; she'd only heard about it, and Vivian had been determined to forget it, like everyone else. They hadn't discussed the war at home and she had no idea that her father had taken part in the Resistance.

As a child she'd seen pictures of bombed German towns, wastelands of annihilation with gutted buildings where ragged human beings tried to reestablish their lives. They were pictures from a world in which she had no part. There had been hardly any ruins in the town where she'd grown up. The war had left behind no more than a few bunkers in the parks and the sound of sirens from the rooftops every Wednesday at twelve o'clock. Life had gone on almost as if nothing had happened, lighthearted and innocent. The war had been a passing storm, and luckily no lightning had struck.

Samuel could have ended up one of those doomed, tonsured figures in prison clothing, but he'd escaped that fate, he and his cello, thanks to the friend who immediately took his place and became father to his child. Shouldn't he be glad to have been shipped off to safety? After all, it was unlikely that anything would have come of their relationship. Like children play best, and Vivian had done what she could to forget him, just as she'd tried to forget the war.

If you can't say yes, you've already said no.

On her way back to Copenhagen, Irene thought about what Samuel had said to Vivian. He must have been a stiff-necked young man, demanding and self-conscious and certainly more than a little self-important. Irene could not think of him other than as a young man, although he must be well over seventy if he was still alive.

But even on that evening Vivian's yes was already a no. His uncompromising willpower was just as strange to her as his birthplace, where the ice floes bobbed in the river in the spring sunshine. Maybe Vivian has never been able to say yes to anything or anyone. Had she said yes to Samuel's rescuer and successor? Actually, no. It was neither genuine nor wholehearted, that yes that was later to be betrayed. Her second yes had been as unsound as the first one, and she herself could not stand by it. Again and again when she became lost in her inner self, where no one could reach her, it revealed its weakness.

If you can't stick by your yes, shouldn't you have said no?

Irene's reply to Martin had been as weak as Vivian's, and now he was left with his guilt in precisely the same way as her father, who was not even her father. Poor Martin, she thought, as she drove with the other cars along the freeway to Copenhagen. His will had been as strong as Samuel's. He, too, had believed he could create his life by sheer determination and, unlike Samuel, life had agreed with him. She should never have let him catch up with her, but he dazzled them both with his willpower. When did he begin to waver in the void that opened up between them? When did his will give up? Irene doesn't know how long they've circled around each other in the tracks of the life that was once theirs.

When she arrived back home she found a scrap of paper on the kitchen table. She recognized his clumsy handwriting. The kitchen was tidy and he'd even remembered to switch off the coffeemaker before he left.

Dear Irene,

I don't know where you are as I write this, but I hope everything's OK with you. It all turned out differently than I had intended. I am no good at this. I know I have hurt you deeply, and I can only hope that one day you will be able to forgive me. I suggest a divorce without an intervening separation. My lawyer will contact you, or yours. If you want me for anything you are welcome to call me at the office. There will be no problem about division of property. You can have everything.

Take care,

Martin

PS: Ursula just called. I told her how it is. She wants you to call her.

Martin, it's not easy for you. Meticulous, upright Martin. In the midst of all this manic chaos you are as solicitous as ever, at least where material things are concerned. Yes, I will call Ursula, thank you for the message. And thank you for the house as well. I think I will sell it. The children can share the proceeds. Wouldn't that be like us? Dear, sweet Martin, how I wish I could hold you right now, and take your familiar face between my hands. For you know you're right. It's all utterly different from anything you, who are so good and so conscientious, have ever thought or could conceive of in your wildest imagination.

I'm the one who asks forgiveness. I'm the one who's lied, and I've hurt myself more deeply than you have ever been remotely close to doing. But you mustn't tell me to take care. You can't ask that. Give yourself to Susanne, enjoy her youth. Let go of that ugly conscience; but don't soothe it with the idea that I'm going to be fine. Do you understand? Go your own way, it's time you did, but don't look back.

And try not to reassure yourself that you've left me reasonably intact, for you have no idea what you were dealing with.

The magnolia blossoms had opened. Some had dropped their petals on the grass between the house wall and the drive. She went into the living room, stopped at the desk by the large window, and watched the faint vibrations in the lake's silvery reflection of the gray clouds.

Less than twenty-four hours had passed, yet everything had completely changed. She listened to Peter's anxious voice without hearing what he said. The custodian of family values, the trustee of consideration and care, already going bald and ever so serious and sincere. Ursula had left the next message. She, too, sounded worried, but beneath her sympathetic words there was a hint of reproach, perhaps because Irene had not confided in her old friend. Peter had rung again, he said something about a search for her if she didn't call back soon. The last message was from Martin. He asked for a sign of life, as he put it, then he paused as if he wanted to say something more. There was a noise in the background, a pneumatic drill. Apparently construction work was under way in Susanne's street. Martin cleared his throat and put down the phone. What were they all imagining? That she'd walked into the sea?

She went into the bedroom, undressed, and opened the big wardrobe that covered one wall. It was empty where his suits and shirts had hung. The sight of the empty shelves and bare, shiny rails woke her from something like mild anesthesia, but it wasn't feeling she awoke to.

Reality was what she awoke to, but a reality she never could have imagined. She gazed dumbly at the shelves. Oregon pine. A cabinetmaker had made the wardrobe specifically for their bedroom when they moved in. Irene had designed it herself. She pulled the slid-

110

ing door closed and let her hand sweep its rust-colored veins. It still gave off the scent of wood, so many years later. The smell of Oregon pine forests. Could you hide yourself there? Hide yourself and forget. Standing quite still among the tall red trunks.

She doesn't want to know what she was never supposed to know. It wasn't for this that she leaned out of the compartment window as a young girl and waved goodbye to her mother on the platform and saw her disappear, relieved, at last on her way out and away. Far away from everything she knew, everything that had enclosed her. This wasn't why she lost herself in the wandering forest of Parisian boulevards with a dizzy feeling that something was waking inside her. She hadn't met a man, left him, and finally given in to his will—made his will hers—in order to be told many years later that the bonds she'd torn off and freed herself from were false. That her freedom and the life she'd chosen were not hers but someone else's. Someone she didn't know and would never come to know. Another man's daughter.

In the long run she had been unable to say no to the man who wanted so fervently to possess her and to do so much with her, and if she could not say no it was because she had already said yes to their life. Her self. Their life. One thing spun itself into the other in a logical, natural pattern, but in some way, at some point in time, she must have lost the thread.

Nor does she accept the sympathy that has enveloped her for the past week. She spared Vivian, who still believed it was merely a crisis, but otherwise she announced to everyone what had happened. She probably came across as being blunt, but that was preferable to letting their friends find out about it indirectly. She couldn't have borne their hesitant glances, their uncertainty as to whether they should talk about what they knew.

Her assistant, a neat, attractive girl in her early thirties, became teary and dropped her face into her hands, as if she'd been told of a death. Irene almost feels that she has to comfort the girl, who's recently married with a little son. Divorce is the most ordinary thing in the world, and it's their trade, but she can see how this otherwise efficient girl, with her suit and her stylish hair, is finding it difficult to keep fear and sympathy apart. Perhaps it's always like this, perhaps the sympathetic sigh is always a sigh of relief as well. She feels quite sorry for the girl, struggling so bravely to combine her career dreams with her idea of herself as caring mother and competitive sex kitten all rolled into one.

Irene keeps to herself, often not even answering the telephone. She sits in the living room smoking and watching television. Every morning she goes for a run in the woods before going to work. If anyone offers a comforting remark she brushes it off, brusquely at times, although she immediately corrects herself so that others won't think she is merely trying to mask the pain. She feels terrorized by the expectations of what she must feel, but also by her own attempts to fend them off. She is being suffocated by sympathy. Ursula, who phones her constantly and cannot understand why she won't come and cry on her shoulder. Peter, who finally came to fetch her one evening and forcibly took her into his and Sandra's care.

She didn't know what to say to them. She read a bedtime story to the twins before dinner, and as she sat with her grandchildren and their soft toys she avoided looking up at Peter and Sandra, who stood in the doorway observing her bravery with self-satisfied smiles. It was almost unbearable, but she controlled herself and completed the story. When she looked up again the sentimental parents had luckily withdrawn. Emil was dozing off and she lifted him up onto the top bunk.

Amalie lay gazing at her with dark eyes. They smiled at each other and Irene sat for a while cuddling her feet, before she switched off the nightlight and kissed her cheek.

When she went down Peter was outside grilling a fish. He's remodeled the kitchen, knocked through a wall into the dining room. He's such a handyman. Sandra poured her a glass of wine. The door to the terrace was open, and Peter talked obsessively about the sunroom they were planning to build. He'd already obtained zoning permission. It would have old-fashioned mullion windows, he explained. He'd found a carpenter who knew how to make them with thermal panes so one could sit out there even in winter. Irene avoided Sandra's eyes as she listened to Peter and kept him going with her questions. She liked Sandra well enough, but she couldn't stand her daughter-in-law's affectionate, anxious gaze. She wanted a cigarette but resisted the craving. She hadn't smoked since Peter was a little boy and she knew he would read too much into it.

Josephine arrived soon afterward, straight from the airport. She was still in her stewardess's uniform. She kissed Irene on both cheeks, a bit coquettishly. Irene asked her about Beijing. They chatted on until Irene put down her knife and fork and asked if any of them had spoken to Martin. She didn't say "Dad" as she used to, but otherwise she did her best to sound casual.

Silence fell. Peter studied the fish bones on his plate. Sandra rose and went to the fridge. Josephine cleared her throat, she'd seen him the day after...the event still had no name. Sandra opened another bottle of wine. Josephine said she'd met Susanne, who was actually very sweet. Irene said she was sure she was. Peter looked angrily at his sister. Sandra came back with the wine and sat down. She looked down at her hands. Peter would have nothing to do with them. He tried to say it with contempt. Irene smiled but knew she shouldn't. She could see that much on her son's face. She told him to behave like a grown-up. She wished she'd said it in a more friendly tone.

She shrugged and felt for the pack of cigarettes in her bag. She told them she'd decided to sell the house. Peter rose abruptly. Why did she want to sell it? He was almost shouting. Irene lit a cigarette. Her voice was calm. He picked up a lemon from the kitchen table. After all, it was their childhood home. He looked at her, tossing the lemon from hand to hand. Sandra burst out laughing. He'd actually left home some time ago, hadn't he! The sarcasm made him blush. He was on the verge of tears.

It was the house, thought Irene. It was the thought of her selling the house that made him crack. The framework of their life. It had to remain the same after he himself had grown out of it and made his own home. What caused his reaction was neither his mother's feelings, nor his father's, but the terror of seeing them step out of their roles as custodians of his thirty-year-old, prematurely balding nostalgia. He was like Martin, and like his father he cared for the framework of life; and yet he still resembled the little boy he no longer was, the little boy who had admired his father so fervently.

Peter came and sat down at the table. How long had she known about it? When had he told her? The evening before, said Irene as she asked herself why she'd lied. The truth seemed to her to be shameful in a vague, incomprehensible way, as if she had become Martin's accomplice. Josephine turned to her. She didn't understand. Martin had told her he hadn't said anything. He hadn't been able to get himself to say it.

Peter shifted his gaze from Josephine to Irene. Did that mean...? How could anyone be such a coward?

There was amazement and disgust in his face, and Irene felt stricken. It hadn't come as any surprise, she said quietly. She felt it sounded as if she was defending Martin, and suddenly she wished she could defend him against their furious son. She said she'd had a hunch. There was no need to judge him. These things happened.

She put down her napkin beside her plate and rose. Peter just sat looking at her. Josephine got up to hug her. Sandra went out with her. "I'm sure you'll be absolutely fine," she said, as Irene put on her coat. Irene touched her cheek. Darkness had fallen outside. She went out to her car. Sandra stood in the doorway, just a silhouette against the light in the hall. She waved. Irene waved back.

The shadows of the cars are long and narrow, and the sunlight burns through the windows at the end of the Lakes. She still has more than an hour before she has to be at Ursula's. She accepted the dinner invitation, even though she didn't feel like going. Ursula said she needed to see people. She has no desire to see people. She has no desire to sit at Ursula's table surrounded by her peers, experienced people, cultured like herself, embraced by their sympathy and respect for how "absolutely fine" she is. It was no use walling herself up, Ursula had said. Why not? Irene had wanted to ask. Ursula said she must hold on to her life. What life? If Irene had asked that, it wouldn't have been out of bitterness or sorrow. She'd have asked the question out of sincere astonishment. An astonishment so deep that she can't see to the bottom of it.

She parks in a side street and sits down at a sidewalk café facing the lake. The water is a glowing expanse of reflections beyond the trees along the shore. The traffic is busy. She would have been home by now. In a short while Martin would have parked his car beside hers in the drive. She can hear the crunch of the gravel under the tires as his car glides into the garage, one of the familiar sounds of her life. He would kiss her lips and go into the bedroom to change into something casual. They'd sit with a drink in the living room, facing each other from their respective sofas, Martin with his feet on the arm as they took turns recounting the day's events.

They weren't short of topics. There was always something or other, their work, some practical thing to be done, vacation plans, invitations, that kind of thing. They might also discuss politics and make a point of disagreeing, for the sake of discussion. The silence was in the pauses, remarkably smooth, where they would lose their foothold for a moment. The sort of pauses where you seem to see yourselves from outside, discovering with a flash of insight that you have imagined a place from which your life is visible as a finite whole. But where could that be?

After the children had left home they got into the habit of eating late. They spent the hours before they went into the kitchen stretched out with their tinkling glasses of whiskey. Martin had begun to take an interest in cooking in recent years, he brought home one cookbook after another—Italian, Thai, Turkish—and they had gradually eaten their way around the world. They enjoyed being together in the kitchen trying out a new dish, but before they started on it they lay chatting or reading the paper. That was the time when the children or Vivian would call, and while one held the phone the other would gesticulate, whisper aloud, or produce little notes. Usually it was a welcome interruption when Peter or Josephine called, but they probably didn't find their life any more tedious than others of their age; quite likely less so.

The years could have gone on passing like this quite easily. Why not? People admired them. If ever there was a pair who stuck together it was Irene and Martin. Their friends have been genuinely shocked when they called to invite her out or to express their concern so that it wouldn't be their fault if Irene was left alone feeling like a leper. They're so dismayed that she has to ask herself whether she and Martin were the only ones flying the flag for the old order.

Once they've eaten she'll smile and say she's tired. While he cleans up in the kitchen she'll go to bed with a book, and when he comes up an hour later she'll have fallen asleep, or nearly. This is the precarious moment of the evening, but they've accustomed themselves to it and found ways to get past it. Soon afterward he'll put out his light, stroke her back and kiss her cheek before rolling over and retreating affably under the duvet. Very occasionally he'll make a move, cautious and timid, something that irritates her intensely, so that she has to overcome both her irritation and her general disinclination if she decides to accede to the diffident questioning of his hands. In the past, they didn't turn the light out. She recalls the contrast—how alive she felt then as he stood naked at the end of the bed, the soft light shining on the smooth skin of his erection. She had not been very experienced when they became lovers. She learned about her own desire in partnership with him. But in some way or another, at some moment or another...

As the intervals grew longer and longer, the two of them became more awkward when it finally did happen. If it was summertime they could glimpse each other's faces dimly in the blue light from outside. She imagined he saw the same thing in her eyes that she saw in his:

the same shyness, the same almost apologetic attempt to play their part in the theater of sexuality. At first, it had been the most natural thing in the world. She tried to rekindle her desire, to feel once more the titillating, prickling wildfire that had spread over her skin whenever he touched her, lowered his large body over her, unrestrained in his passion, and covered her, enclosed her, closed himself around her; and she in turn enfolded herself around his piercing hunger. But at some point he became aware that, for her, there was a conscious attempt to resuscitate something. As time went by she stopped hiding it; and then one wonderful day he experienced something he had thought was lost to him. Something by the name of Susanne. And who could begrudge him that?

Irene closes her eyes in the sun. She listens to the talk at the café tables around her. Mostly women half her age. Several of them have a stroller parked at their side. There is prestige in children, Irene thinks, looking at the stylish vehicles. Was it like that in her time? She listens to their cocky tones and affected turns of phrase, the particular jargon of a generation, a little strange and yet so familiar. They are about thirty, and on top of the world. They've acquired their education, found a job, a man, and a child; life has begun but is still before them, still like a game. They can't take themselves really seriously yet, cheerfully surprised as they are to find themselves in the situation their mothers were in as young women. They've collected their chicks from crèche, and now they sit here chatting about their jobs and children and men.

It's their break, this afternoon hour at an outdoor café in the sun before each goes home to her busy, hopeful little world, and they touch each other carefully with their irony and laughter as if to assure themselves they're traveling together. That they're not alone in being surprised and looking forward to everything that awaits them. They go together, a complete little fleet that has set sail and delightedly feels the force of the wind now that they're out in deep water, out of their parents' safe harbor. In a few years, several of them will be divorced and on their own with a child or two, and they know it. They hear about it all the time, but none of them believes it will happen to her. Irene thinks of Josephine, her flying daughter who hasn't reported yet to the flotilla of young families. She thinks of Peter and Sandra and their happily anxious considerations about a garden room and choice of school, about whether Emil is slightly nearsighted, whether Amalie will need braces. On their way to happiness and fulfillment. And yet perhaps they will never be happier than they are now, at the start of the journey.

To her surprise, Irene notices there are tears in her eyes. She takes her sunglasses from her bag so as to better observe the young mothers and small kicking toddlers. She feels sudden relief at not having to go home to those silent rooms and get used to the fact that Martin won't be coming. Where has he gone? Josephine knows, she's already visited her father and his new love. Irene could have wormed out of Josephine quite discreetly what she's like and what sort of home she has, but the lightness in her tone would have seemed studied. It would have sounded as if she was afraid of giving something away that she didn't want to.

Maybe Susanne lives not far from where Irene is sitting. Maybe she lives on the other side of the lakes in the old working-class district that has become so fashionable. Once the stairways smelled of paraffin and washing fluttered in the dark, narrow courtyards; now, the corner shops and tobacconists have given way to upscale cafés and boutiques, and antique shops specializing in orange and brown vintage furniture from the seventies. Maybe Martin has gone to live with her in one of these renovated tenements in a side street, where other young people have moved in with their espresso machines and retro kitsch. Irene tries to picture them in an apartment like this, but what is her vantage point supposed to be? How is she to find the place from which his new life can be seen as a finite whole? She'll need something to prop her up if her imagination is to place her at eye level with the unknown.

Scaffolding. Maybe they've put up scaffolding in front of her façade. They might be putting new windows in the building, thermal panes with old-fashioned mullions. Irene looks around her before climbing the ladders linking the narrow platforms of the scaffolding, careful not to tear her tights on a coupling between the steel pipes. Susanne's window is open and she has no curtains, young and unconventional as she is. There she lies on the double bed, naked, her face hidden beneath her folded arms. She hasn't shaved her armpits. Martin is kneeling on one of the polished boards at the foot of the bed with his back to the window. He must have just come home from the bank, he's still got his suit on.

Home? Yes, this is his home now, a sparsely furnished but chic apartment without carpets or curtains. He is embracing her spread thighs and burying his face between them. He's good at it, better than Irene can remember, but it's been a long time. Susanne's writhing and moaning. Then she sits up in bed and pulls him to her, and under their impatient scuffling the suit, the shirt and tie, socks, and underpants slip down onto the floor in a pile. Irene recognizes the tie, she bought it for him recently. Fascinated, she watches the bodies weave themselves together. She's amazed at Martin's intensity. She finds it a touch comical, too, but it doesn't make her feel superior. Slightly comical, but moving, the undammed passion he unleashes on the young woman.

Afterward, he sinks down exhausted, his flushed face resting on her stomach. She half sits up and plays with his hair.

"Martin?"

He looks up, thunderstruck, as he recognizes Irene's voice and catches sight of her outside the window.

"Sorry to interrupt. I just wanted to see how you are."

Susanne shrinks back in the bed and creeps under the duvet. Martin sits up on the edge and pulls on his underpants feverishly. Irene can't help smiling at his modesty.

"May I come in for a moment?"

Martin and Susanne both nod without looking at each other. Irene straddles the windowsill.

"I haven't come to make a scene, you mustn't think that."

Her friendly tone helps them relax a little. Martin looks down at the yellow nails of his big toes. How many details like that does Susanne have to ignore? His slightly drooping paunch. The hairs in his ears. Susanne glances into the adjoining room. She's lovely, sitting there with rumpled hair, huddled under the duvet like a child. Irene is sure there's nothing wicked in her.

"I just thought we should say good-bye to each other properly."

Martin looks at her again with a guilty expression. Susanne gets up from the bed.

"I'll go and make coffee," she offers.

Irene sits down beside Martin on the edge of the bed. He looks down at the floor again.

"She seems like a sweet girl. Why didn't you just tell me? Were you afraid to?"

Martin nods. She lifts a hand to stroke his cheek, but lets it drop on her lap again. She looks around.

"This is lovely."

He nods again.

"We'll move when we find something bigger," he says. "How about you?"

"I'm moving, too."

"If there's anything I can do to help…"

She smiles. "Thank you."

They're silent for a while. Now and then their eyes meet.

"Are you very much in love?" she asks pleasantly.

"I think so," he says.

"Martin, what kind of answer is that? If you can't say yes, it's because the answer is no."

He looks terrified.

"I'm not saying that because I want you back," she goes on. "I don't." She doesn't know how to interpret his look. Regret? "You should have done it long ago," she says. "You mustn't feel bad about it, do you hear? I'm not who you think I am."

She gets up. Susanne comes in with a pot of coffee and three cups on a tray. She's put on a bathrobe and tied up her hair in a loose bun. Irene smiles at her.

"It was good to meet you."

"Would you like a cup of coffee?"

"Just a little one, then."

Irene is surprised at herself, but why shouldn't she have a cup of coffee with her successor? Martin gathers up his clothes. Irene and Susanne sit together on the bed. He goes into the next room and gets dressed. Susanne pours out the coffee.

"You must forgive me for asking so directly," says Irene, "but did you insist, or was this his own decision?"

Susanne looks at her. Martin sits on a chair next door and bends over to tie his shoelaces.

"His own."

"So you must have been quite surprised."

Susanne smiles. A lock of hair falls down, Irene strokes it away from her face. She can see Martin through the open door. He's standing in front of the window, hands in his pockets. She lets her hand brush Susanne's cheek and neck before it creeps down to the belt of her robe.

"May I?"

Susanne shrugs, and Irene loosens the belt so the robe slides open. Susanne leans back as Irene studies her.

"What is he to you?"

Susanne looks up at the ceiling. "A man," she replies.

"What else?"

"He knows what he wants."

"Yes, he does." Irene brushes the young woman's breasts and stomach with the back of her hand. "And do you know what you want?"

Susanne doesn't answer.

"You are lovely," Irene says quietly, stroking Susanne's smooth skin. "Are you going to have children?"

Susanne glances up at her over her nipples. "I haven't thought about that. He's, you know...," she interrupts herself as she looks at Martin.

"When you decide to leave him," Irene says, "do it quickly. Promise?"

Susanne nods.

Irene rises and walks to the window. She throws a last glance at the bed, then she climbs out onto the scaffolding.

"One gets accustomed to life as it is." He has a pleasant voice, and he's not stupid. "It gradually blends into the world one's been used to..."

He leans back in his seat as the streetlights stream toward her and slide over the windshield. It's after midnight, and Irene is in a stranger's car on the way out of town. It's not at all what she had in mind, but she's drunk too much to drive. Ursula has been pouring Valpolicella into her all evening, and the stranger insisted on taking her home. She would have preferred to call a taxi, but he kept urging her in his inoffensive way. It would have been too pointed to reject his offer, particularly when he claimed it wouldn't take him out of his way. Ursula insisted, too, less quietly, in fact pretty vociferously, thanks also to the Valpolicella. Finally Irene gave in, mostly to shut Ursula up. It felt like a setup, a well-meaning setup.

"What may have begun as pure coincidence acquires substance with time…"

The stranger's name is Bertel. He, too, is divorced, a lawyer like herself; his field is human rights. In other words, a small-L liberal, and good-looking to boot with his curly hair and appropriately casual olive-green tweed jacket. A divorced, well-groomed, attractive liberal. He'd like to go to bed with her if she's interested—he has, rather charmingly, made that clear during the course of the evening—but he's stayed at a respectful distance. He's behaved beautifully; there's even an amused glint in his eye in case for some reason she's put off by his straightforward intentions.

"That's why it actually is the end of the world when you get divorced…."

She couldn't count the number of times she and Martin have taken the same route, one or other of them behind the wheel, after a dinner like this evening's. The route is unchanged; the apartment blocks and office buildings along the freeway, the residential districts further out, and the house one is going home to, alone with someone or another. You think the world has changed, but it's only your own connection with it that's shifted slightly. The infrastructure remains intact when the heart breaks. Perhaps we should value that, although it seems like an earthquake, and even though the broken heart can feel betrayed by the unmarked endurance of its surroundings. It isn't the end of the world, and it's not even adding insult to injury that the world refrains from coming to an end with your ideas and attachments.

"Behind the world you thought you knew another one appears, a world you don't know, and in which you have no idea who you are…."

Is her heart broken?

She doesn't know, certainly not now, comfortably dulled by Ursula's

Valpolicella, which has come to rest like a soft, oily film between her self and everything a self can relate to. Her unknown self has never seemed more unknown to her. Her heart. Perhaps it wasn't an earthquake after all, perhaps a smaller tremor could have done the job. Recent events just may have led her to discover a fracture hidden for many years, an invisible crack, made apparent by the pull of opposing forces.

Opposing forces. A man who is no longer her husband. A father who is no longer her father. An unknown father, maybe dead, maybe still alive. A strange man, sitting beside her and talking to her although she's not listening.

"But you depend on people anyhow, no matter how coincidental it is who you meet...."

Strange, strange, strange to sit here, on the way home in the company of someone you don't know. You do in fact belong together whether you follow your strongest impulse or are simply carried along. You're inseparable from the life you live and from the person you live it with. You have children, and what was a momentary fusion turns into a bond of flesh and blood, united in the children.

"Of course, the others depend on you as well...."

Wasn't that what Vivian hoped for as a young woman, when she sat overlooking Lago Maggiore and consigned her secret to the silent oblivion of a school exercise book? How brave and determined young Vivian was. Why should a single false step at the start prevent her from finding her way through life, finding the way to her life? Nevertheless she did go to pieces, torn in two by opposing forces. Reduced to fragments by the dissonance between the truth won and the truth she had concealed. They touched each other, her truths, along a hidden fracture where darkness and loneliness gradually opened up and pulled her down.

"The world's full of wild hopes. It's just very rare for them to join hands, isn't it?"

He turns toward her when they stop at a red light. She returns his gaze. An engaging, totally strange gaze. Even the faint scent of after-shave is foreign. She doesn't know that brand, and she doesn't know this man, who looks at her while he's talking to her, honestly and straightforwardly interested. Indomitably hopeful as he sits talking about his divorce in polite abstractions. Then, fortunately, the light changes and he drives on. They've reached her suburb, she gives him directions. Soon he'll stand in front of her house and she'll turn to him and smile and say thank you for your company, it was lovely to meet you.

Lovely? Maybe "a pleasure" would suffice. Thank you for the company, Bertel. It was a pleasure meeting you, good of you to let me know I'm still an attractive woman, one an attractive man might want to go to bed with, seeing that we're both separated. See you!

Of course, she could invite him in and offer him a whiskey, take her clothes off and spread her legs while he looks at her with his liberal gaze. Isn't a good fuck exactly what she needs? Wasn't that what Ursula had in mind when she called to invite her to dinner, just a few friends, all very casual, as she put it? A brisk, hearty—and very casual—fuck to put the whole thing into perspective.

It was a beautiful evening and she enjoyed the walk beneath the trees in their new foliage. She hesitated in front of the door to the apartment before ringing the bell. She could hear the other guests as she went up the staircase with its carved paneling and brightly polished brass. Ursula stood in the doorway waiting for her. Her resonant laughter drowned out the social chorus and the jazz record she'd put on to welcome her guests.

128

She smiled fondly when she saw Irene. She'd put her steel-gray hair up in a soft knot secured by two lacquered chopsticks and she wore a long embroidered kaftan that effectively hid her pear-shaped figure. As usual, her too-empathetic expression was framed with heavy eye shadow. Ursula always looks as if she uses Magic Markers when she's putting on makeup: red for her mouth, black for her eyes, and green for her heavy eyelids. She's given to generous arm movements. Maybe that's why she feels most comfortable in loose, oriental clothing.

Martin didn't like her. He felt intimidated by her unconventionality, and Irene had fallen into the habit of seeing her friend alone. That suited Ursula perfectly; she returned Martin's dislike, but for reasons of her own. Ursula saw in Martin nothing but a bourgeois oaf with whom she couldn't possibly have anything in common. How Irene could be married to him was beyond her. Irene was hurt on Martin's behalf, but she couldn't very well show it or rush to his defense. She'd been unwise enough to confide her affair with Thomas Hoppe to Ursula. Ever since, Ursula had made it clear that in her view Irene was living a lie.

According to Ursula, that was just about the worst thing one could do. While the affair was going on she had indicated several times in no uncertain terms that in her opinion Irene ought to leave Martin. She herself had left a husband and young children to train, at a relatively late age, as a psychotherapist and install herself in the large aristocratic apartment furnished with oriental antiques. This was where she received her clients and a succession of lovers. Irene had the impression that the latter were replaced much more frequently than the distressed souls who came to weep on her shoulder at a fee that seemed astronomical when you considered that Ursula's only expense was Kleenex.

It was Martin who characterized her like this, in a rare fit of sarcasm, but Irene just smiled without responding. She understood why Martin must be alarmed by her anarchist friend, but she was fascinated. Ursula was alone because she wished to be alone. The world came to her and she decided how much of it she would allow inside her door. She even answered the phone only when she felt like it. Why should people receive her attention just because they took it into their heads to call? Wasn't the telephone the epitome of social coercion? Irene had thought of her friend during the past few weeks, sitting alone in the silent house and letting it ring while she gazed out of the window.

Ursula introduced her to the assembled company with an affectionate hand under her arm. They stood sipping their drinks in a corner room with Chinese cupboards, chairs, and chaise lounges. From the bay window you could glimpse the lakes. Although it was warm outside, Ursula had lit the wood-burning stove, a tall affair in the Swedish style. Irene smiled and held out her hand. She didn't know any of them, but she was used to that. There were always new faces at Ursula's parties; people passed through her life and were soon replaced by others. Irene had the impression that she herself was one of the few recurring figures in a fluctuating circle of professional acquaintances and casual contacts, media personalities and shady barflies; friendships and love affairs quickly ignited and extinguished with equal speed.

There was something unrestrained about Ursula's social life, and something lonely. Racy and frank, she could make herself at home in any circle with the greatest of ease, but she wasn't part of any particular group. She openly admitted this. Irene didn't know anyone else who had so resolutely cut off every inherited or conventionally binding commitment in order to go her own sweet way and shape her life according to her whims. Nor did she know anyone prepared like Ursula to take the consequences of the life she had chosen. She respected her headstrong friend for her matter-of-fact approach. If she was lonely, that was the price she'd chosen to pay, and she didn't complain. When she left her children she had to deal with their anger for years, but she just waited until they decided to forgive her and started, gradually, to come back of their own accord. She still could have found herself a new husband but at the time she wasn't interested, and later she became too eccentric for anyone to risk considering her seriously. She made do with her gentlemen-in-waiting, as she called them.

At first, Irene thought the tweedy human rights lawyer was Ursula's latest find. She and Bertel worked for the same organization and had met each other during a tour of refugee camps in the Balkans. Ursula had interviewed a group of Muslim women who had been raped during the ethnic cleansing. He explained this over drinks, when they were alone together. He talked of the establishment of the International Criminal Court and of the historic prospect of national law yielding to conventions based on the universality of human rights. A breakthrough in our concept of law; or rather, a realization of the philosophical potential in that concept, he said, as he rescued an errant drop with a cultured movement of his tongue.

She nodded, how interesting. It did actually interest her, but she was unable to listen. How humiliating. Could she really not look past her own navel? How typically feminine. She regretted having put on her new pink dress, it was really too low cut and she thought she must resemble someone she'd hate to be. A mature, divorced woman quivering with brave defiance.

Bertel seemed to appreciate her new acquisition, in spite of all the refugee camps in the Balkans. But it was only when he said he'd been looking forward to meeting her that Ursula's intentions dawned on Irene. Ursula had told him about her, he said with an exploratory glance, immediately softened with a smile. Only positive things… As they talked she realized he was flirting, discreetly, sympathetically— and yet unmistakably. What had Ursula told him?

Among the other guests was an artist with long gray hair. Irene thought she'd heard his name before. He became the center of attention when they sat down to dinner, a male counterpart to Ursula. He'd painted the large piece in the dining room, a hefty abstract thing with loud colors and dramatic gestures. He was with a younger woman in tight leather pants. She sat with her hand on his thigh while he held forth. The talk was of the Balkans, of the Serbs' paranoid self-obsession and the criminal hesitation of the West. Irene didn't join in the conversation. She was amazed that they could sit drinking Valpolicella and expounding about genocide and mass graves with such swaggering bravado. But what had she expected? Were they supposed to don sackcloth and ashes before discussing the horrors of the world outside Ursula's oriental chambers? Shouldn't they be talking of divorces and Chinese antiques?

They had finished the first course, and Irene took advantage of the pause. They met in the long hallway. Ursula came along it with a haunch of venison in black currant sauce. Irene asked if she could help with anything. Ursula asked how she was. She said she was fine. Irene didn't know where to turn in the narrow passage, or how to avoid her friend's probing glance. Of course it was all quite strange. Ursula nodded. Stop nodding like that, Irene felt like yelling. Instead she stroked Ursula's plump upper arm through the loose sleeve and went on along the corridor, thinking she'd just used Ursula's own gesture on her, maybe to forestall a similar gentle touch.

In the bathroom she splashed her face with cold water, then stood for a long time observing a stray drop crawling down her mirrored face. Irene Beckman. The mirror made her look as if she was crying. Her mascara had run slightly, she dried it with a corner of the hand towel. The door to Ursula's bedroom was ajar. The bed was unmade, and on the floor were piles of newspapers and books—novels, biographies, books on psychology. On top of one of the piles lay a vibrator. She picked it up. It was quite a whopper, bigger than anything of the kind she'd ever held, skin-colored and with a textured surface. She pressed the button beside the battery cover and couldn't help smiling at the snarling sound and the tingling feeling on her palm.

Perhaps she ought to get one as a replacement for Martin. Wasn't this thing a necessity in a modern woman's life? She switched off the rotating gadget and put it down. Was she being a prude? Why else should she feel she had touched something grotesque and vaguely degrading? She'd been modest when she was young, but with Martin she'd put modesty behind her. She'd learned to look at her own desire and that of others in broad, sensible daylight; and to follow the liberated, fearless mood of the times. And yet here she was suppressing a giggle at the sight of Ursula's dildo.

She felt her cheeks flooding with heat, not because of the stolen glimpse into her friend's private life, but because of her own giggling embarrassment. It seemed both anachronistic and immature. Even Vivian might well have had one of these in her drawer over the years. Irene looked at the lonely prosthesis on the bedside table, as if its owner had detached it and left it there. A prosthesis was what it was, after all—a substitute, something to be used in the absence of something else.

When she returned to the dinner table, the painter's muse was telling a story. She looked as if she lived in a solarium, her face a leather mask. Now he was the one who rested a hand on her thigh.

She was talking about a friend who'd just been ditched by her husband. One day he told her he'd met someone else. He'd decided to leave. Just like that! He couldn't have given it that much thought, though, having known his lover for only a couple of weeks. Sally hadn't had the least suspicion. Their son had come home with his skateboard and just managed to say hi to his father before he vanished out of their lives. The little boy had been a real child of love. Sally and Thomas had only known each other a month when she pulled the plug on her pills.

She'd really believed they were meant for each other. She'd gone completely to pieces. She'd thought they were getting on perfectly, better than ever. They'd just been on the most fantastic Easter vacation to Venice, said Leather Mask, just the two of them, really romantic. Even their sex life was better than ever before, and then he just took off with a woman he didn't even know. He even had the nerve to claim he loved her. How could you say you loved someone after two weeks? He'd played that trick once or twice before, suddenly falling madly in love and feeling as if he had to leave his wife and child; but each time he'd gone back to her, and each time she'd forgiven him. Sally was far too nice, but Leather Mask had told her not to even think about taking him back this time. She'd totally collapsed. She really thought they'd worked through their problems. That he was more mature and aware of his ambivalence and his two-minute obsessions. But it was typical of him to try to overproblematize the relationship in some way. In fact, he was a wimp who could obviously only compensate for his own feebleness by behaving like a shit.

It was one thing to ruin Sally's life like that, but how could you let your son down at a point when the kid most needed a male role model? He'd already had trouble keeping up at school, but no one could really be surprised if he was becoming dysfunctional. On the other hand, he was an incredible support to his mother; he was a real man there. Unlike his travesty of a father, who didn't have the stamina to buckle down for the long haul and keep his mouth shut, if he couldn't keep his pants zipped in the meantime. Of course he might still back down like the other times.

He'd always been a dreamer, got his warped, romantic ideas about love from the novels he always had his nose buried in. He'd only learned about real life because Sally understood how to keep him grounded. He'd have been nothing without her. But it almost seemed as if he was afraid of backing down, the way he burned his bridges. He could at least have waited a bit. Just as they'd waited...

Leather Mask stroked her painter's long gray hair. He hadn't just cut and run. They'd met secretly for almost two years before he told his wife. Before he was sure about what he was doing. He'd shown that consideration. But Thomas had not only stuck the knife in and then not hung around to help her process her grief, he'd also demanded a divorce. What a fucking sadist. As if it wasn't enough to fuck her over so callously, he could hardly wait to put her head in the noose.

Leather Mask tossed her head to shake off a stray lock of her carefully styled hair, but it looked as if it was Irene she was shaking her head at. Wasn't she a divorce lawyer? It was as if Irene suddenly became the object for all the other woman's solarium-tanned disgust. Could you demand a divorce, just like that?

She smiled forbearingly at Irene's dazed expression. Her smile carved deep furrows in her face. It was probably meant to be a lay person's expectant smile, with due respect for the professional, but it came off looking like the smile of someone waiting expectantly for a dim-witted child. Irene held her glass in two fingers and twirled it slowly around as she replied. Well, yes, you could. If there was a written declaration of consummated infidelity, signed by the third party.

Leather Mask leaned back in her chair. No doubt the bitch had already signed. She'd seen them together, Thomas and the new one. It was sickening, how foolish he looked. He looked like the village idiot. But she clearly had him wrapped round her little finger. It was obvious she'd been the one who'd insisted on his divorce so that they could get married. She'd probably taken pains to get pregnant. Anyway, that was what Sally was afraid of.

Actually, she felt sorry for him. The new woman was a poet or something like that. One of those exotic beauties, and by all accounts a nympho. Leather Mask had heard about her. It didn't seem to be the first time she'd scored a married man, it was obviously a game to her. Around town they were saying she was better at licking dicks than writing poems. But then Thomas was a publisher, that was presumably a bonus. And a poet with big tits was more than he could resist. But from what she'd heard it didn't take long for the men to run off screaming.

Leather Mask had also heard that the poet had had a relationship with another writer published by Thomas's house. She was something of a starfucker, the story went. Well, she wouldn't mention any names, but there were rumors of a well-known author. Three times her age. Married, of course. She mostly chose older men. Probably some sort of daddy thing going on there. Poor Thomas! It was his turn now, wife and child or no wife and child. She was obviously tired of the more mature models.

Leather Mask emptied her glass and pursed her lips. It was one thing to drop the wife after eleven years, just because you met someone else, but to leave your son...

As Irene sits next to Bertel watching the familiar suburban streets rushing forward to meet her, she wonders what she might have said.

She feels she should have come to Thomas's defense. She was on the point of doing so when it dawned on her who it was they were talking about, but she said nothing.

Even their sex life had never been better.

That, of course, is more than she can say for herself and Martin. She visualizes the words. Sex life. She sees Ursula's vibrator on the bedside table, the little button beside the battery cover. Working life. Family life. Sex life. All neatly framed. The framework of life. They'd even been to Venice, just the two of them, really romantic. Even romance has its box and frame. She visualizes the Rialto Bridge. Despite one's ironic reservations, the Rialto Bridge is arguably an ideal frame in which to set a kiss, even after eleven years. Especially after eleven years. How can you say you love someone after fourteen days? Irene still doesn't know how to answer, but she would like to have answered. Ambivalence. The smoothness of that word makes your thoughts slide off it. Relationship overproblematization. She's never heard that word before. Stamina. Grief processing. She tries to visualize a grief processor, in a boilersuit made of black velvet. The words that Leather Mask spouted sounded like something from the fat psychology books in the pile beneath Ursula's dildo. The kind of words you can switch on and insert in your ear. Dysfunctional. Irene hears the snarling, stiff-necked sound of the plastic orgasm prosthesis.

What about herself? Hasn't she just spent the past week overproblematizing her own ambivalence to the point of total dysfunctionality? Instead of rolling up her sleeves and getting on with the grief process? She can feel Ursula's Valpolicella muddling her thoughts. Had it been just a question of seizing the day, the crucial two minutes? A question of stamina? She tries to visualize Thomas, Thomas in Venice. She's walking beside him along one of the canals, they are hand-in-hand, looking at the moss-green water and the marble lace-work of the façades.

How can you say you love someone after two weeks? Irene has no idea, but Sally must know, having gotten pregnant after a month's acquaintance. That was one thing she could have said in answer to Sally's friend. But she kept quiet. She might also have asked Leather Mask which was worse: to deceive your wife for two years, or to take the leap into your love after only a couple of minutes—eyes open or closed according to how courageous you are—and then accept the consequences. But she kept quiet. She did so when she discovered that Ursula had been observing her as Leather Mask went on talking, hoarse with red wine, cigarettes, and righteous indignation.

Leather Mask looked at her again. Rumor had it she'd been deserted herself—for a younger woman, no less. She must know what it was like to be ditched.

Irene looked at Ursula, but her friend merely returned her gaze with affectionate understanding and equally affectionate expectation. If Irene's eyes were telling her that she felt betrayed, that she could do without Ursula initiating others into her private life and making it the object of social entertainment, on a par with Bosnia's violated women and the rejected Sally Hoppe, if that was what she was trying to tell Ursula, it was a message that was totally lost.

Ursula had no knowledge of the gray zone, the air lock between inner and outer, in which most other people spend their lives. The soft, gradual crossing between confinement and exposure, where you might be lucky enough to avoid both if you keep yourself in motion. This, then, was the price of freedom.

It had occurred to Irene more than once that her friend would have been totally insufferable if she had not possessed a phenomenal ability to win the trust of others. Ursula was a good listener, surpris-

138

ingly, and she knew how to spot the weak points in her confidant's fortifications, so that a single innocent but well-placed question brought the walls crashing down. That was how she had made Irene confide the affair with Thomas Hoppe to her, and it was presumably the reason she was one of the most sought-after therapists in town. One might have feared that the more timid and introverted examples of humanity would flee at the sight of her painted clown face, but instead they came flocking. Ursula the clown was also a priestess in the secular confessional of psychotherapy.

That was how she listened as Leather Mask sat reducing Thomas Hoppe to a helpless voodoo doll for her avenging female solidarity. And that was how she listened in the silence that followed while everyone waited for Irene to explain what it was like to be ditched by your husband for a woman who, according to reliable sources, could easily be her daughter.

Come now, Irene. What are you waiting for? They all wish you well. No one here would hesitate to include you in their understanding and sympathy. After all, you and Sally are in the same boat. Good lord, that affair of ten years ago, no one's going to blame you for that now. No one can expect to go through life without someone on the side. Besides, he slunk back to his family with his tail nicely between his legs, didn't he? It isn't your fault he's run off and cut his ties to everything he and Sally had built up. He hasn't declared undying love to you after no more than a couple of weeks. You're not the one who's turned his head and wound him around your little finger, that wimp of a dreamer, with no stamina, no heart.

And aren't you a tad too old for all that anyway, Irene? For luring men astray? Men want youthful flesh between the sheets, it's how they are, the bastards. But there's no reason why they should get off scot free. At least you can give vent to your bile, your inner foaming fury. Are your feelings too refined for that? What do you actually get out of your sensitivity, Irene, your ambivalent, distanced forgiveness?

Have a glass of red wine. Knock it back, it'll do you good. And just give some thought to the fact that you only started to fantasize about Thomas again after you found out Martin's got someone else. You're not a bit better than the others. The heart's an opportunist, whether it breaks or endures. Don't be too delicate to talk about Martin. There's enough there. Even the way he came out with it, the coward. With your children as hostages and the Provençal refectory table as a buffer zone. He didn't dare tell you when you were alone. Tell us about it. Tell us about his sneaking cowardice. And tell us something about Susanne, the little whore. A bank manager, and a reasonably well-preserved one, too—it's the jackpot for a tart like that. Coming into your life and stealing your husband, just because he fits her tight young cunt. Just because you don't wet your pants every time he gets a hard-on.

Irene was silent.

Her silence was getting quite embarrassing for everyone, except for Ursula of course. She just sat there letting the quietness thicken, observing Irene with her empathetic gaze, underlined by thick mascara.

Bertel came to her rescue. He'd been watching her, too, while Leather Mask stuck her pins into Thomas until he was bristling like a hedgehog. When the others began to fidget uneasily he revealed his chivalrous side, Irene thinks, as her road comes to meet them. He gives her a sideways glance, apparently afraid to ask why she is smiling. He, too, has fallen silent. They are approaching her house, and the moment when he'll find out whether he's made a fruitless journey.

He put down his cutlery, cleared his throat and said he could certainly understand if it was hard for her to talk about it. He himself was newly divorced, and besides...We usually say it takes two to make a divorce, and he didn't mention this to suggest in any way that Irene didn't have good reason to be angry with her husband—or rather, her future ex, if you could put it that way. It was the nature of the thing that he couldn't know anything about Thomas and Sally's private life, but as a wise man once said, everyone has their reasons; he could certainly attest to that. Nor should one believe everything one hears....He'd turned to Leather Mask. As far as he knows, she's had no personal acquaintance with Thomas's new—well, what should we call it?—partner....

He stops the car in front of the house. Neither of them has spoken for a while. She turns to him.

"Thank you for the lift."

"Any time."

He smiles, and if he was expecting more he's hiding it well. She gets out and is about to slam the door when she bends forward to make eye contact instead.

"Can you drive if I offer you a whiskey?"

He shrugs, amused.

"You'd better park in the driveway."

She stands at the front door guiding him. She wonders what he sees in the beam of his headlights. An attractive woman of his own age in a slightly too-pink, slightly too-low-cut dress. A divorced woman who wants to while away her loneliness in his company and spend a night exchanging mature caresses and abstractions. A kindred spirit. She's already regretting her decision as the sound of car tires on gravel dies away and the headlights are switched off.

The tree trunks around her move in time with her breathing; she is one with the rhythm, everything else is merely a passing show. As if no matter how far she runs the woods won't come to an end. She follows her usual route, first along the bridle path, then along a narrow path leading through the undergrowth. For years she has run every morning, in a firm ritual that measures the gradual change in everything else. By following the same trail, she notices the small changes in the seasons, as now when spring is turning into summer. The wood anemones are already over, and the new foliage of the trees is no longer the same fresh and curling light green.

The woods have remained the same, or nearly so, in their closed circle of seasons, while she herself and the others grew older, until they left home. First the children, then Martin. Gradually they've moved away from each other, affectionately, tenderly, and inevitably.

She seldom meets anyone, only a single rider who comes trotting toward her. She observes the rippling play of muscles under the smooth skin and recalls the feeling of being carried along, raised above the earth on a wave of bones. It is long ago, but suddenly she clearly remembers the smells in the stable, horse droppings and leather, the ringing clatter of harness and hooves on cobblestones. The contact, the silent intimacy with the wise animal, so much larger than her without being the least bit frightening.

A recollection crops up of something she once read. Everything must change in order to remain the same. That's what she believed, but the opposite is true. Everything remained the same so as to suddenly change completely. Everything is so changed, so changeable now, even her thoughts and feelings. The night has left a brittle, crackling sweetness in her body, as she runs along, eased into a new morning, a different time, porous and strangely open.

Bertel was a gentle lover, but not timid or shy, the way Martin had gradually become as his hands and kisses learned to anticipate her evasions. Bertel knew what he wanted, like a practiced dancer allowing you to give yourself up and let him lead, embrace, and swing you, sure he will not let go. It was strange, but not as strange as she had thought it would be, not as lonely. They were alone together, but not on their own. It was strange to make love with a strange man in the bed and the house she knows so well—but it is quite as much the house and the bed which have come to seem like a strange place.

To begin with, it was slightly awkward as they sat apart from each other on separate sofas, each with a drink, exactly as she and Martin used to sit. She even felt guilty—how absurd—at sitting opposite Bertel and imagining what he looked like with no clothes on. They talked quite candidly about life and marriage. She felt guilty at the idea of him sitting in Martin's place, although not with his feet up, and she remembered suddenly that she had not felt a scrap of guilt when she'd given herself to Thomas Hoppe.

She put down her glass, stretched out her arms on the back of the sofa and looked him in the eye, making him stop in mid-sentence. She couldn't decide whether she was giving herself up to Ursula's intriguing intervention or if she'd taken the bait in protest, since not to do so would seem too obstinate, too much of a clumsy admission that she really was destitute. She had not the least idea of what she was doing, but it made her feel dissolute, to slam her glass down on the table, lean back with outspread arms, and ask Bertel if he felt like making love.

She knew perfectly well he did. He said so with a smile—not exactly self-assured, but not like someone who feels trapped. He had addressed her then in a subdued, intimate tone, as if they already knew each other. It was she who was bashful when they went into the bedroom and started to undress, quite prosaically, as if it were the most natural thing in the world to have a strange man taking off his clothes and laying them on the chair where Martin used to leave his. The small fit of irrational guilt soon passed, but after he'd got down to his underpants there were a few difficult moments in the transition from floor to bed that she managed to carry off only through sheer determination to complete her inebriated, ill-considered enterprise.

He felt that and he was kind. He took his time and let her look at his body just as it was, with the beginnings of a paunch and slightly drooping shoulders; not in the least distracted himself by her sagging breasts. It might have been much worse. If she'd forgotten that in fact she had preserved something of her girlish charm, that she was still long-limbed and slim, he reminded her of it with his investigating, gently lingering caresses. She asked him not to turn off the light; she let him look at her, and she looked at him and did her best to remember how one goes about it.

She found she could safely leave everything to him and simply allow herself to be led and carried away. He was dependable and experienced enough not to seem single-minded. She was about to let herself go when she happened to look him in the face and suddenly gave an involuntary giggle. It was his solemn air, almost devout, that struck her as risible. As if it were a sacred act! Swiftly she passed a caressing hand over his forehead—in apology, but also to cover his eyes and stroke away his discomfort.

She closed her eyes as he moved on top of her. As she felt his breath and stubble on her throat, his weight and the glowing, distending feeling as he filled her out with his thrusts, she visualized again what she had imagined earlier in the day, eyes closed behind her sunglasses, from the pavement beside the lakes. She stood once more on her ladder, looking in through a window at Susanne and Martin making love. Martin, who for years had craved his wife unavailingly until he gave up and found another woman. In dull, heavy thrusts she was struck for the first time by something that felt painfully like rejection because he had not gone on desiring her.

She opened her eyes again to escape the image of Martin between Susanne's legs, wrenching herself away from the thought that she was holding a substitute in the vicelike grip of her knees; and as she looked into Bertel's straining face he came, with an ostentatious cry of ecstasy. She grabbed hold of his head and pushed him down, afraid he would look at her and realize what she was thinking, and he obediently buried his face between her thighs.

She looked up at the ceiling, at the serrated spot of light from the pleated shade of the bedside lamp. She stared into the dull yellow sunburst as he urged her on, and it worked. Her body was no more than a porous, pulsating, accelerating, overheated machine, and eventually it took off. At last she was released from the morass of thoughts as if hovering for a long moment, dazzled by the sun, on glowing wings which melted and sent her out into a free, dizzying, breathless fall.

Afterward, she felt surprised at herself. She relaxed in his embrace as if she had always done so. He talked about his daughter, she told him about Peter and Josephine, and while they exchanged their stories, she knew it would never happen again. She made that clear when he was about to get into his car. She had gone outside with him, stood shivering in the cool morning air, arms crossed over her bathrobe. He said he would call her. She shook her head. He looked at her. No? She smiled. No. He hesitated for a second before he shrugged his shoulders, smiling in reply, and got behind the wheel. She waved as he reversed and stayed there while he changed gear. She waved again. He waved back and disappeared out of her life. She stood for a while looking at the withered magnolia petals on the grass. Then she went inside and began to clear away breakfast.

She made breakfast for him as she had done so often for Martin. They sat facing each other, he fully dressed, she in her bathrobe. Quite intimate, really. Once a man and a woman have been to bed together, a certain intimacy follows. Not while it's happening, but afterward.

During this kind of unexpected breakfast you have to make a quick decision, and if you can't say yes it's because you have already said no. If you do say yes, you are on the way to an uncertain beginning, especially if you're no longer young. You feel your way forward hesitantly, as if you have an infinite amount of time.

The doorbell rang. Was it Bertel perhaps, come back? Was he as stubborn as Martin had been in his time? Was he the type who wouldn't accept that it had to be no if you couldn't say yes, OK, immediately? Or was it Martin? Had he been sitting in his car a couple of houses away and seen an unknown man come out of what was once his property, followed by his soon-to-be ex-wife waving good-bye and then standing there on the grass? Was he having regrets? Had he found that he wasn't so addicted to young flesh between the sheets, that in the long run he could live without his good old, well-tried wife? As she waited for a few moments, a saucer in her hand, Irene realized she missed him. His familiar body, his familiar sounds. His calm voice and affectionate blue eyes, his loving care, his will and belief. His caresses at night, which she had too seldom made an effort to respond to.

She leaned over the sink to look out of the window. A young man stood at the front door in a dark suit, white shirt, and tie. He looked like one of those people who want to sell you a Bible, and she had already decided not to go to the door when she remembered that she'd made an appointment the day before with a real estate agent. She went and opened the door. He smiled politely. Irene Beckman? She threw her arms out as if she was not absolutely sure.

"Make yourself at home," she said, and went into the bedroom to put on her running gear. He was in the living room with his head in the fireplace when she returned. She told him to close the door when he left. He had soot on his ear. He would send an outline of the sale notice. When she went outside her gaze fell on the mailbox with the label in its small window: BECKMAN. She broke a nail as she struggled with the label but out it came. She threw it into the trash and ran off along the road.

Soon she will have taken her last morning run. Everything has changed already. Only her office, the view of the chestnut tree in the courtyard, her secretary, her partners, and her trainee with the career hair and scruples, will remain as a stable framework for the impermanence. Job and family, the scales of everyday, that score has long since been settled, but only now is she taking notice. Since the morning when she arrived home from her impromptu trip to the North Sea she has spent more time at the office than usual. She prefers to stay late, even when she doesn't have to, glad to be alone and at work. The legal pinpricks of other families are soothing, and she is reassured to find her professional acumen intact. Irene Beckman is still to be reckoned with while the rest of her life becomes history. More than ever, she appreciates sitting in her quiet office with a division of assets or an order for child support, sometimes gazing absently into the shadows and wrinkled leaves of the tree outside.

As she reached the edge of the woods she wondered what the real estate agent would see on his tour of the house. What he would be able to read of their life from their furniture and their possessions. Not much, probably. She recalled a television program they'd watched together in which an advertising agent had visited various homes and described the absent occupants through their inventory. It amused Martin, but she was irritated by the smooth soothsayer. Things get in the way, she said. They shine too brightly, and cast into shadow all the other things that might be there to see. He didn't understand what she meant, and she gave up trying to explain.

But things do get in the way. Not only the objects you surround yourself with. Surroundings get in the way, too, she has often thought of that, ever since her childhood. At eight she was struck by a terrifying suspicion that inner and outer walls were demonic pieces of scenery hiding an abyss. That her parents were not really her parents but fiendishly clever actors who deceived her and lulled her into a false sense of security with all the reliable repetitions of everyday routine.

As a small girl she had already sensed that not all was as it seemed. It was not only the closed door of the bedroom where her mother retired with her headaches; not only the door of her own

148

room, which she insisted be left open so that she could make sure, in the crack of light, that the stage sets were not taken down for the night. She actually spied on them. She slipped out of bed and crept down the hall to the stairs. She kept watch on the man in the living room who smoked a pipe and read the newspaper. The woman who sat with a book on her lap gazing out the window. While she observed them from her hiding place she wondered if that was how they spent their time after hours, the actors. She listened to their prosaic conversation, but she couldn't hear whether they were still acting or not. Whether it was just the talk of colleagues brought together by chance, any man and woman.

In time, her suspicions grew more metaphysical. As a sixteen-year-old she no longer believed her surroundings to be stage sets, but like so many youngsters she developed her own moral sensitivity to perspective. She had not yet discovered that others her age had similar thoughts, but she had the same indignant sense of a discrepancy in the conception of near and far. Her secure surroundings barred her immediate outlook with its trivial events, while the great world was like white noise in the background, on the radio, vague shadows on the grainy pictures in the papers. She read and listened to reports of war and starvation, about the struggle of impoverished peoples against oppression, about horrors and catastrophes and the atomic threat, and it revolted her that no one in her circle took any interest in the fact that the world was in flames. It disgusted her that her friends could agonize about some boy who wouldn't have anything to do with them or a dress they couldn't afford while people in other places were dying of hunger or being blown to bits.

But it wasn't just compassion for her deserted mother and her universal compassion for the sufferings of the world that made her feel confined. It was also a deeper, indefinable feeling of not being in contact with reality. An unfathomable comprehensive reality, which she longed for in the bus on the way to school or the railway car into town. Her longing made her feel ashamed, linked as it was to something as superficial as boredom, but she was unable to escape its torpor. It covered her like sticky dust when she leaned her forehead against the window of the bus or train and watched the bland suburbs pass by. The real world was waiting for her somewhere behind those houses and streets.

She was dizzy with joy over every little thing she saw when she stood for the first time on the back platform of a Parisian bus, free at last, far from everything she knew—until she discovered that the promised reality always flies off when you approach it. Every crack in the restrictive barriers of her surroundings only opened onto new obstacles, new restrictions for the gaze that longed to penetrate the unknown. When was she most truly in Paris? When she sat outside Les Deux Magots or strolled across Île Saint Louis? No, she had already arrived when she was lying in the sleeping car from Copenhagen; and when she arrived she had already parted from the goal of her dreams.

She learned to adapt. She found a place for her dreams in her adult perspective, where that which is close gets in the way of that which is far away, and where everyone sees the world from their own vantage point, blinded by the familiar horizon of their surroundings. The only thing remaining, an unpleasant afterimage in the shadows of her mind, was the beggar on the Place de la République, with the shapeless, suppurating knot of flesh where his face should have been.

She ended up with her own life, as everyone ends up with a life—more or less favored, with a more or less equal distribution of happiness and pain. She has been lucky, she thinks, on her way through the woods.

It occurs to her that she has lived her life in a dream. Not her own dream, but that of the anonymous poverty-stricken millions who dream of a life bolstered by security. She has lived that life, but this morning it's as if she has woken from the dream. She pictures her house, pictures the young agent moving from one room to another as he calculates its current value. She sees her house through his eyes. The house where the middle-aged woman in jogging gear has lived with her husband and their children.

She slows her pace and stops.

The black eyes gaze at her without blinking. The leaves and the shadows of the branches almost conceal the animal. It is a doe, and she stands motionless like an image surrounded by leaves that tremble in the breeze. A second or two passes, then she bends her knees; there is a thump on the forest floor as she takes off and vanishes with long, lithe leaps among the tree trunks.

As Irene runs out of the woods and back along the quiet roads she thinks of Vivian in her hospital bed waiting for breakfast. Maybe she looks at the view and asks herself if he's dead now, the young man with the cello who disappeared across the sound one autumn night. Her former husband has been reduced to earth and bones in the churchyard without ever having discovered that he was not the father of Irene. And Martin? Maybe he's in his office, thinking of her with shame or relief, or both.

She sees Martin at his desk. He looks out the window. The unremarkable view. The same every day through seasons and years. It's as if he feels her thinking about him. He turns around in his chair with an inquiring look.

"Martin, what are you thinking of?"

He smiles. "It's been a long time since you asked me that."

"I know. Everything's a long time ago."

"I was thinking we are all on our way."

If she could reach him now, she would stroke his face. "We can't bear it, can we?"

"What?"

"Not being on our way."

"Now stop that, Irene. You know you can't bear the thought of arriving either."

"Can't I?"

"No, because what comes next?"

Now she is the one to smile. "Yes, what comes next?"

He shrugs his shoulders and waves before bending over the papers on his desk.

He recalls a morning the previous summer. The sea was calm, the sun not yet risen. They had been to a party in a neighbor's garden. As they walked home along the quiet roads they could still hear the music far away, behind the summer cottages between the shore and the plantation. They decided to take a dip before going to bed. Irene pictures the two of them. Sally's body is pale and dim against the green depths. They swim apart from each other, neither speaks. The rings on the water join together as they spread.

He talks of the stillness between them. Irene visualizes the gray light that seems to come from nowhere. The smooth, calm, pale colors of the water, the faded timbers of a breakwater, black below, covered with seaweed and mussel shells. He describes the feeling, re-curring over the years, but completely clear and plain to him in the flat light, the feeling of being bound together and yet separated, having grown together and yet being unable to reach each other's innermost self.

The feeling had been there the whole time under the surface, but mostly he'd been able to ignore it, sitting there behind the shining reflections of everything that was happening. In any case, it's in the past now, and who could ever catalog all the choices they might have made, let alone their implications? But that doesn't mean they couldn't be recorded somewhere. All your sins of omission along with your dismay at having betrayed others...

In his case the split is still there, but it's no longer a hidden fracture within him. It is the division between a life that was his and one that hasn't yet become his. He would like to be able to say that he knows what he's doing, but who is he to know? Yesterday's man, or tomorrow's? He is neither one nor the other. The past already fades, but it does so more slowly than it takes the future to arrive.

You forget a lot about a person whom you have not seen for many years. One of the things Irene had forgotten was Thomas Hoppe's apologetic smile. It's accompanied by a snort of laughter that emerges through his nose in the same way as the smoke from his cigarette. She had also forgotten how much he smoked. The snort and the smile make it seem as if he wants to cancel what he has just said, or at least make light of it. He doesn't seem uncertain, he is just not sure whether he has said what he wanted to say; and besides, he is polite, doesn't care to talk about himself. Is it out of politeness though? She doesn't know, but he is polite, correct, obliging, and a little old-fashioned.

It's hard to believe he is fifteen years younger than she is, and it was the same before. He seemed like a precocious child, but that's changed. He says he has always been the age he is now. It was his body that limped along behind, he smiles apologetically. He is forty-one, and it suits him, he says, not to be young any longer. He was no good at being young. He smiles again, and she thinks he seems young when he says that. She recognizes the young man from that time, he smiles at her through the marked features of a much older man. You do not know yourself.

He falls silent. The pauses embarrass them. The abyss of conversation, where once their caresses built a bridge. Now the words merely sink into silence like coins in a wishing well. There are moments when she thinks they are talking instead of touching. She doesn't know if he feels the same way. You don't know each other. She wouldn't dream of asking, but there is no physical contact between them, not a kiss on the cheek, not even a handshake.

It felt remarkable not to at least kiss each other's cheek or extend a hand when they met. But a handshake would have been too formal, a kiss on the cheek too much. She believes he thinks the same thing, but doesn't ask. Now what do you call that? A tacit agreement. Their mutual lack of touch as they take turns speaking. Those are the terms for meeting someone you had not expected to see again. As if he were a ghost. There are moments, like now, in the pauses, when she has to suppress an urge to stretch out a hand, even if only to stroke his face lightly. She admits it, the urge to touch, and she suppresses it. Is she frightened he might run away screaming?

She admitted it to herself, her urge, even when she saw him waiting at the place they'd agreed on. She pushed it away as she sat down opposite him. She regretted she'd called him, afraid of what he was thinking, as if he could read her thoughts. Lucky they don't know each other.

They arranged to have lunch at the Langelinie Pavilion. She told her secretary she'd be out for the rest of the day. She doesn't usually go out like this, but the secretary didn't seem at all surprised. It was Irene who surprised herself by stepping out of her daily routine. She has no appointments for the afternoon, and there are no letters or telephone calls that couldn't wait until tomorrow. Nevertheless, it felt like something forbidden when she left, just as it had before. He had already arrived and was sitting at a table on the terrace with its view over the harbor.

There's not a cloud in the sky, and the air is soft. Summer has come. He smiles. Yes...she thinks this is the sort of place where you meet your lover, slightly out of the way. In fact they'd never met at a restaurant, both of them terrified they'd be seen by someone they knew. He still looks good; better, in fact. He's one of those men who look better as they become worn. Perhaps he's right, perhaps being young didn't suit him. But she remembers clearly how she had to touch him when they met, and let him touch her. She can't explain why. Maybe his face was reason enough, his broad face and the odd way his body is put together. His torso, slightly too short for the long legs, broad without being bulky. His pale skin and dark hair, the green eyes, the languid line of his mouth. She has to remind herself constantly that what she feels on seeing him again is a recollection.

The waiter pours their wine and replaces the bottle in the ice bucket. She watches a ferryboat passing through the harbor. When she phoned she told him about her forthcoming divorce. He said he was glad she'd called. He asked if she was busy. He's alone and completely devastated by guilt and love. Another snort of laughter. Tatiana has been in Stockholm for a few days visiting her mother. Her name is Tatiana. He's going to meet her at the airport in a couple of hours. Was that why he suggested they should meet so soon?

They haven't seen each other for many years and being together again is so unexpected that neither of them can think of anything ordinary to say. Nothing is ordinary any more for either of them. She talks about herself and Martin, but in brief desultory snatches. She doesn't mention Vivian, or what was in the notebook from Lago Maggiore. While she talks she realizes that she hasn't come to confide in him or tell him her story; she has come to put it behind her. Only now does she realize it. She has simply come to see him. See what has become of him since that summer, and maybe catch a glimpse of what he saw at that time, when they made love and lay watching the sky above the rooftops. She knows they didn't see the same thing, but she had to see him again to know for sure.

He has never felt this naked, he says. His skin has been peeled off, his social skin. But of course she's in the midst of it herself. He says it with his apologetic smile, as if doubting whether he is expressing himself accurately. Whether he isn't presenting his emotional life a touch melodramatically. A divorce isn't the end of the world, the sun goes on shining and the ferries still depart on time.

"I keep on going back to that morning," he says. "We're swimming side by side in the cold water without saying anything. She's so close and yet so distant."

"I know what you mean." Irene meets his eyes.

She has no idea.

He looks at her again.

"The life you've lived feels heavier than all your dreams," he says.

"Oh, yes."

"Is it just that you grow older?"

"Are you asking me?"

"Sorry."

Now she's the one to avert her gaze.

Fifteen years. After all, there are fifteen years between them. He is still young, whether he likes it or not. He doesn't sound as if he does. It seems as if his age weighs him down, and at the same time he sounds like one who can't do without the burden.

He can't remember what he was thinking as they swam together that morning. Together and yet each on their own. He remembers it solely as a picture, but when he looks at it again, he never comes to the same conclusion. He thinks one thing, then another. Sometimes he asks himself why he left her. At other times he asks himself how he could have spent so many years with her. But he can't think the two thoughts at the same time. He's in pieces, and one half cannot recognize the other.

But the smile is the same. The self-mocking smile.

He talks about his life. Their life. A logical, natural pattern. Self-fulfilling. Recognizable. He doesn't know if it's Sally he misses, at moments so painful he feels he's about to stop breathing. The one she is. Or if it's just their life.

Just?

He can't distinguish. She and he, the boy, their home. The quiet, daily tenderness and the melancholy on Sundays, when they have nothing to do but be together. The familiar things and familiar routines, the familiar view from the windows. The habits that veiled his original wonder so he could only hazily manage to distinguish himself from the life that had become his. The world as he knew it. It is an image he describes, immovable, firmly framed, his family portrait.

He says Tatiana is sure she saw him once. That he was the person she passed in the street one night some years ago, a man in his thirties, still young, but with an old expression. She remembers it because she could not forget the wildness of his eyes. A look of longing and desperation.

Irene recalls what he told her once after they had made love. How he could fantasize about the woman and the child, the closeness of their life, as he lay falling in love with his words about it, simultaneously dreaming of forsaking it. But he is wrong. Life becomes a thing of the past more quickly than the future takes to arrive. That's why you are so hesitant, so terrified, of taking the leap from yesterday into tomorrow.

As she listens to him talk about his life, Irene realizes that he is not after all the man she met one afternoon ten years ago. He really has grown older, and he has reached the point she was at during that summer when she lay in his arms and envisaged a different life. The age difference is the same, but another difference has appeared. He has found the courage that failed them both—leaving her, at any rate, with only the consolation of how maturely and reasonably she ended the relationship. But the same undercurrent has drawn her, the same need for contact, which eventually drove him to put his shoulder to the frame and make that desperate effort to break out of his own picture. He can't recognize himself; he can only look back with wonder and regret at the broken fragments.

They don't talk about that summer. To speak of it would be like touching. They must keep afloat, together, yet divided by the years that have passed and the years that would always have been between them. She wonders what he sees when he meets her eyes. Does he compare her changed face with his recollection of the face he once held between his hands? Does he think, yes, she would be bound to look like this?

She was the one who ended the affair. She was too old for him, old enough to be the one who made the break. Clear and levelheaded as Irene Beckman can be, in spite of all the crisp sweetness. He would have made the decision himself one day, scared at the thought of seeing her getting older, feeling the age difference grow from an interesting shift to a chasm they could only have straddled by grim determination.

Because they still have not touched upon their old affair it is hard for Irene to see her place in the story he's telling. She's not in the picture. Maybe he has told Tatiana that he had had an affair long ago with a woman fifteen years older than himself, but that is another story, which Irene will never get to hear.

He looks across at the wharf and the oil tanks further out.

"When Magnus was five, he said something I've been thinking about lately. 'Inside, you are alone,' he said, 'and outside you are with others.'" He looks at her again. "I forgot to ask him if there's a door between inside and outside."

"We'd better hope for his sake there is."

He looks down and pushes the breadcrumbs around on the tablecloth.

"It was like being walled up in myself. The first years with Sally and Magnus...I did think I'd come home. That was how it felt to begin with. Until I discovered I'd built our home around my innermost chamber, without thinking about whether there was an entrance." He laughs through his nose. "I'm probably losing myself in my own metaphor. But when I was about to explain to Magnus why I was leaving, I couldn't think of anything except to repeat to him what he'd said as a five year old."

He smiles as his eyes start to fill. From shame or self-pity? A modern father is a sentimental father, Irene thinks. Her own Peter comes to mind, continually citing the words of wisdom in Emil and Amalie's prattle. The children are the definitive authority in his life. And good for them—but sometimes it's almost as if he's bragging about the hours he spends on his knees among the Legos with his kids. Surely he must get bored now and then? But if she were to drop a hint to that effect she would sense immediately the indignation beneath his pious joy.

160

And here's Thomas getting sappy. It didn't stop him from walking out. This is nothing but an afterthought for the sake of decency in the wake of his brutal resolution. The brimming eyes merely testify to the conscience that held him back for years and which he has finally violated.

"I'm not suited to infidelity. The fearful business of secrecy. Having to check yourself the whole time. I'm no good at lying, and I couldn't bear to see Sally smiling at me when I came back from seeing Tatiana."

"You must have been sure of it all the same."

"When I did it, yes. Just as I was when Sally told me after a month that she was pregnant. The doubt doesn't come until later. Not doubting what I've done; doubting myself instead. Do you understand?"

"No."

"If only the word soul hadn't gone out of fashion...."

"Soul?"

"You can barely get yourself to utter it, can you? Not without ironic scare quotes."

He draws quote marks in the air with an exaggerated gesture, as if he wants not only to emphasize his own irony, but also to make an ironic comment on it. Irene has seen Josephine do that when she wanted to safeguard herself against the crass and intrusive assumption that she was speaking from the heart. She watches yet another ferryboat go past between Thomas's quotation-marking fingers. At least it has no doubts about where it's going. He lets his hands sink down on his lap.

"It's like a cumbersome heirloom, the soul; you don't know what to do with it. It's not, what do they call it now, 'compatible.' But I think it was his own five-year-old soul Magnus was trying to place when he said you're alone inside." He twists his languid mouth into a wry grimace. "You know, the soul's irremediable loneliness and so forth..."

"You're forgetting your quotation marks."

"I've left them to Sally along with the furniture. She was always so ironical about my penchant for intellectualizing. She wasn't alone in that. In my circle, the girls were in charge of the practicalities while the men were the smartasses. When we went out or had people for dinner the men always ended up sitting at one end of the table while the women sat at the other. We discussed literature and politics, they talked about children. We might as well have retired to some gentleman's study with wingback chairs and brandy in snifters. We were so goddamn intellectual, but I don't think you could really have called us bohemian. A bunch of pompous yuppies in their thirties, each with a philosophy of life, and all insured to the hilt. I can get quite feminist when I think of it, but it didn't bother Sally."

Thomas is warming up. He lights a fresh cigarette and exhales. He's talking faster and there isn't much doubt in his voice now, as he sits there piling up his barricades of sarcasm.

"Maybe she liked you."

"Perhaps. But there is something alarming about women's will. When nature came calling she went like a lamb; she was pregnant in about five seconds flat to the poor jerk she'd offloaded her love onto."

Irene cocks her head but he goes on, oblivious. He is not being fair either to Sally or to his life, and she can see he knows it himself but he nevertheless persists. Something in him is urging him on, and he can't resist it. He raises his glass and drinks, snaps his mouth shut and looks her in the eye.

"You're the ones who really rule the world. Your will is so much stronger because it gives birth. It creates facts. And it convinces you that love, too, can be reproduced. Of course, one loves one's child, simply because it's there, and love for the child shines on the woman who bore it. But in the long run it turns out to be a faint reflection, if you don't...if there isn't..."

He stops short. Is he blushing, or is it just the spring sunshine burnishing his cheeks?

"So Tatiana's saved your soul, then?"

She regrets her teasing tone. It might almost sound as if she were jealous, but he doesn't seem to notice her irony.

"Well, I'd started to think there was something wrong with me, when I lay awake at night beside Sally. After she'd fallen asleep and I lay thinking of my perfect life. When I was asking myself if I hadn't gone astray all those years earlier, when I was young and ran into her one evening. A girl among so many others, an evening out of all the other evenings."

Irene is content to listen while he talks himself out of one life and into another.

"I've started to believe that things do coalesce. Only we can't see it, because we're either too blind or too farsighted."

Irene smiles.

"You can probably find a connection in any chaos if you have the imagination. It's so tempting to see warnings in retrospect."

This is the lawyer speaking, she can hear it herself, but something in her resists his eagerness to make passion align itself with the soul's magic formula. As if he was merely obeying its deep urgency and not—as he'd realize if he were honest about it—the other way around. Using the soul as a fancy euphemism for desire. How do you deal with something as banal as desire, Thomas? The visceral excitement of a strange woman? How many of the pure of heart do you think have been lured into lascivious thoughts by the lovely face, the

163

delectable youth of a woman's body? Soul is such a facile word. Like a good-luck charm.

"Do you remember the apartment I borrowed in town?"

She nods and raises her glass. Is there a place for her in his story after all?

"It belonged to Herbert Verhoeven, the writer. But do you also remember the framed photograph on his desk? A black-and-white photo of a girl?"

She watches a ferryboat pass through the dewy, straw-yellow hemisphere of her wine glass. It swells up and shrinks back again as it sails on through the harbor.

Thomas met Tatiana at Herbert Verhoeven's funeral. Before then they had only heard of each other. A month later she turned up at the publishing house with a manuscript Herbert had been working on when he died. A handful of typed, unnumbered pages from their trip to Belgrade during the student demonstrations in the winter of '97.

Herbert would have been eighty on his next birthday, but Thomas had never seriously thought he would die. There was so much life in the restless and curious, eternally suntanned turbine of a man. Herbert radiated a warmth that was felt by everyone who came near him when he held hands, men as well as women, or took their arm in a friendly grasp, smiling with the whole keyboard of his bridgework. It was the charm that his enemies found unforgivable—and they had always outnumbered his friends. His life seemed like a whirlwind of women and controversies, but for decades on end he sat in the eye of the storm, working six hours a day. "I write in the morning," he once said. "Then I go out and make my mistakes."

Herbert made his debut shortly after the war with a collection of short stories in high modernist style, but since then he had concentrated on journalism. His books on contemporary political subjects had provoked what he called the pietists of the cultural elite. He had nothing but ridicule for intellectuals who preferred to cut corners with reality. Like so many of his generation, he had been attracted by communism, but the pact between Hitler and Stalin scuttled his belief. He was imprisoned with the other communists, escaped, and joined the Resistance. Later he was arrested by the Gestapo and sent to a camp in Germany. There was some doubt as to how long he'd withstood torture, a doubt he never escaped.

Herbert became a loner at a time when it was all about joining in, belonging, declaring one's conviction and fidelity. He abhorred the idea of a unifying, redemptive creed. Eleven years after the Occupation he was a foreign correspondent stationed in Hungary when Soviet troops entered the country. He did not confine himself to writing home. His last report from Budapest was not without heroic swagger in its description of himself, lying on the top floor of a building with a group of rebels, shooting at the Russian tanks.

Deep down, he was the solitary type. He had few male friends and preferred the company of women. To Herbert, the most natural way of being with a woman was to go to bed with her, and that was the usual outcome; but what he needed just as much was their sympathy, and he was always a loyal and thoughtful friend to the women he'd "had something to do with."

He had stayed in his marriage. He lived with Emma, the cool sphinx who held his life together, for almost forty years. She could still arouse attention with her aquiline nose and regal hairstyle, and she had not stopped loving him even if she hid it behind her unapproach-able façade. No one who had seen him lead her onto a dance floor could doubt that he was the man in her life. One almost forgot she was not the only woman in his, considerate and courteous as he was. When Thomas met him Herbert and Emma hadn't shared a bed for decades. She had inherited a house on Funen where they lived through those years, and where she brought up their children while he traveled the world.

Verhoeven was not his family name, but rather the name of a comrade in the concentration camp who had died in his arms. It be-came his nom de plume. He had a message and it wasn't one he had evolved himself. He wrote to bear witness, not to present a different world, but it would be half a lifetime before he finally told his own story. It was Thomas who persuaded him to write his memoirs. Not until he read the manuscript did he realize that his friend's roguish warmth and need for physical contact were the expression of un-quenchable amazement in someone who has been to hell and back.

He was skin and bones when he was driven northward in one of the white buses. "I decided on life even though I didn't have anything to keep it in," he said, laughing hoarsely. He had been lucky; sturdier men than he had succumbed. The experience left him with an un-failing lust for life and an appetite for sharp clothes. He seldom ap-peared in public without a suit and tie. It was a question of dignity; his elegance was both a defense and a statement in itself, and he saw no contradiction between his sympathy for the oppressed and his taste for handmade English shoes. Tatiana described how he would wear a tailored overcoat to demonstrations in the gray streets of Belgrade.

"I have lived my life on borrowed time," he said one afternoon as he sat in Thomas's office going over the final proofs. "You wouldn't un-derstand that. You shouldn't, either." His voice was almost a whisper.

"You see, there are no witnesses. Not even those of us who can say we were there. The witnesses are gone. No one can bear witness to what they witnessed before they disappeared."

Thomas meets Irene's eyes as he repeats his friend's words. Again she is struck by the fact that he's still young, in spite of himself. They are both young compared with Herbert. Neither of them is in contact with the story he had to tell.

Irene thinks of her unknown father who escaped when he, too, was intended to vanish, and it occurs to her that Thomas talks of Herbert Verhoeven as one would speak of one's father. With the same warmth that resembles pride, as if he had a stake in what he is telling. Irene knows nothing about Thomas's father, they never talked about their families. It wasn't his past, or hers, they were meeting to share. Nor was it the future; but all the same, they must have sought out each other to get away from what they knew and what lay behind them. As if neither of them could bring themselves to be what they'd turned into.

Did Thomas look for a father in Herbert Verhoeven? Did he try, in his friendship with the older man, to replace a father? It may sound like that, and maybe that's a way of establishing a family, too.

Perhaps after all it isn't a father he sought in Herbert; perhaps to his surprise he merely found a friend. And she? Is she about to search for a father? Having thought she'd buried her father long ago. What can a father have to say about her today that she hasn't already worked out with greater precision for herself?

Thomas became a father about the time he met Herbert. He'd been a reader for the publishing house for years before he was offered an editorial position. He had dreamed of writing and had struggled fruitlessly with a novel, but he was relieved, he says, when he locked his attempts in a drawer. It gave him the feeling of growing up. He had a wife and a small son to come home to, his life had substance

168

and a direction. Maybe it was true that he'd been no good at being young. He'd been shy and uncertain with girls. If he'd only known what Herbert had once confided to him, citing the biography of Casanova: "Whether the answer is yes or no, they're glad to have been asked."

Irene can't help smiling, and she is just about to laugh when Thomas blushes at his friend's slyness. She lifts the bottle out of the cooler and refills his glass.

"Here's to Casanova!"

He drinks the toast with her, slightly flustered, and she asks herself whether it was the rake's proverbial wisdom that had given Thomas the courage, one summer evening, to make a date with her on a bench in the King's Garden. She doesn't think so. She doesn't remember it as a seduction, his lingering gaze, her hand that reached out to his face in the silence between them. It just had more to say about them, that silence, than anything they knew.

When Herbert was in town Thomas often went to see him in the attic apartment where he worked and spent time with his successive mistresses. "Have they given you the day off?" Herbert would say with a disarming smile. "I must say you've got your life running on rails. You're almost as straight as the Trans-Siberian—sleepers as far as the eye can see."

Thomas couldn't understand what Herbert saw in him. Herbert was everything Thomas wasn't. All they had in common was that both of them, when young, had realized their limitations and given up on becoming real authors. Herbert's irony was as lighthearted as ever, but Thomas sensed how vulnerable he was. After so many years his friend would still bow to the idea that it is more exalted to write about oneself than about the rest of the world. But of course Thomas didn't write at all. So why had Herbert chosen him to be his confidant?

"You're the perfect reader," he replied when Thomas got around to asking. "You know that imagination isn't an alternative to reality. On the contrary, you possess a surplus of reality, even if people don't think so. It will make you suffer. Present circumstances will never be enough. You'll always be hungry for more."

Is he avoiding her eyes? No, he has just turned around to catch the waiter's eye. He comes over to their table. Thomas asks for the bill and turns to her again. He tells her about Tatiana. Fantasizing, thinks Irene. That's another way of labeling your secret, homeless restlessness.

Rumors circulated about the beautiful girl who had been seen with Herbert, and when they went to Belgrade the town was humming with gossip about the octogenarian and his young muse. Over the years Thomas had often looked at the framed photo of Tatiana, barely a woman yet, on his friend's desk. Once Herbert took it out of his hands and put it into a drawer. "I want to keep her to myself," he said. "If I let you meet her you'll just fall for her."

Thomas recognized her right away at his friend's funeral. Herbert hadn't wanted a church ceremony, and apart from Emma and their children only a handful of people attended. Even if he had never seen the picture of Tatiana he would have noticed her when she entered the chapel and sat down apart from the others. He thought of the stories he'd heard and it seemed as if the other mourners were thinking of them, too. Only Emma seemed unaffected. Was Tatiana really that beautiful? He couldn't make up his mind, as he glanced secretly at her pale, narrow face framed by unruly, swirling, chestnut-brown hair. She stared ahead of her, mechanically drying her eyes now and then with a handkerchief.

She stayed on beside the grave, a lonely figure in a long black coat. Herbert had asked to be buried in an unmarked grave. The gathering was on its way along the path when Thomas worked up his courage and went back. She raised her eyes as he approached and he noticed how unusually bright they were. "I know who you are," she said in a slight drawl. He didn't know how to reply and merely pressed her hand before turning to catch up with the others.

The last time he'd visited Herbert in hospital, he noticed that the photo of Tatiana was on the bedside table. When he was leaving, Herbert took his hand as he so often had. He smiled and looked at Thomas expectantly, as if he was curious himself to know what he might have to say. The skin hung loosely from his cheekbones, his smile was duller and the grip of his hand weaker, but the warmth was the same.

"You'll think I've given in completely," he croaked, "but I'm beginning to believe after all that it isn't the end when those things shut down." He made a feeble gesture in the direction of the machines attached to him by the tubes in his arm and nostrils. "Fancy that! And it isn't even for my own sake," he went on. "It's just hard to imagine, if there's someone you're really fond of, that you won't see them again." He dropped Thomas's hand and sank back on his pillows with a smile. "I'll be keeping an eye on you."

Tatiana was formal and reserved when she called on Thomas at the publishing house. She kept her coat on, the same coat he'd seen her wearing at the funeral. He had been thinking about her. He wondered how he could get in touch with her. Now that she was sitting across from him she seemed to know he'd been lying awake thinking about her. He could see she had been weeping. She asked him to read the material Herbert had left and to decide whether it was suitable for a book. She rose abruptly. Thomas asked for her phone number. She wrote it in the margin on the first page of the manuscript. When she offered her hand in farewell he held onto it, surprised at himself.

171

Her bright eyes studied him as he stood there with her hand in his, not at all surprised, merely expectant, before she withdrew it and left without saying good-bye.

A few days later when Thomas was leaving his office he decided to make a detour. As a rule he went straight home, in time to do the shopping while Sally fetched Magnus from school. He enjoyed strolling through the town as if he wasn't going anywhere. He tried not to think about it, but the idea kept imposing itself. He thought he might meet Tatiana in one of the streets in the city center. It was a childish thought but he couldn't stop it; and then suddenly he felt a hand in his as she suddenly appeared at his side.

She had recognized him from a distance. He hadn't seen her smile before but it was real enough, the humorously curled smile on her pale lips. An exotic smile, almost Cyrillic, he thought as they walked along hand in hand. She seemed amused at his nervous sideways glances. He suggested they should go into the gardens of the Royal Library. They sat and talked for a long time. He recalled Herbert when he'd seen him for the last time in hospital, weak and haggard, but with the same look in his eyes, the same warmth in that look, like a caress. He realized that it wouldn't be an affair unless it became something completely different from what it was. Still next to nothing. They were silent for a while, and he thought he still had time to get up, bid her a friendly farewell and leave before his life took a turn into the unknown.

This Thomas does have a weakness for royal parks, thinks Irene, and reproaches herself for the catty impulse. She tries to visualize Herbert's eye on them in the library garden and it helps. After all, she hasn't come to meet him again, she has come to bid him a decent farewell. Their first meeting suffered from a lack of symmetry, as did their parting, and she has come to say good-bye to a figment of her

172

imagination; to part, finally, with her cowardly longing. It was a mistake to see Thomas again, but she had to make it in order to understand. She must listen to whatever Thomas has to say about Tatiana, to understand what it is she has in common with Herbert Verhoeven.

Tatiana was born in Belgrade and came to Denmark with her parents as a little girl. When they divorced, she first lived with her mother, an intelligent, well-educated woman who supported herself and her daughter by taking a variety of underpaid jobs. She married a Swede, the father returned to Yugoslavia, and Tatiana lost contact with him. Herbert had met her mother at the home of a mutual friend and had had an affair with her. When her mother and the Swede moved to Stockholm, Tatiana stayed in Denmark. She attached herself to Herbert and lived for some years with him and Emma on Funen.

Their own children had long since left home, but he made up for his failings as a father by caring for his adoptive afterthought. He indulged her and took a keen interest in her schooling, and when she began to write he took her seriously and helped her to get her poems published in a newspaper. When he was away he left her with Emma. Now and then Tatiana accompanied him on his travels. He showed her the great European cities, she saw the renowned museums and sat in the famous concert halls. There was something old-fashioned about her education, and she was as ignorant of her contemporaries' concerns as she was well-versed in the classics.

"She seems to have walked out of a different era," Thomas explains. "A romantic world where the spirit of man hasn't been tamed. She isn't trendy, she dresses like someone from the turn of the century, and she laughs too loudly when we go out to eat. I often don't understand why. She has no idea how people look at her. She's instinctively feminine, she doesn't have to keep checking herself in the mirror all the time."

He looks at Irene uncertainly, surprised at her smile. She puts a hand over her mouth.

"Sorry...Do go on."

Thomas hesitates before he continues.

Gradually, Tatiana's relationship with Herbert grew more conspicuous. People talked about the mismatched pair and it culminated when they returned from Belgrade. Herbert was anxious about her reputation, and for once he gave some consideration to Emma. Over the years she had tolerated his affairs with silent dignity, but this time she'd had enough and she ordered him to break with his protégée. He replied that she was part of him in a way Emma would never be able to understand. It was Tatiana who decided the matter. She applied for a fellowship at an American university and spent the next few years in Boston, until Herbert fell ill.

When Thomas met Tatiana she was living in the attic apartment. She smiled her Cyrillic smile when he told her Herbert had stubbornly refused to introduce them. He had been hysterically jealous and when she came back from America she was subjected to a long interrogation. "He knew it," she said. "He knew what would happen."

It was one of the afternoons Thomas stole to visit her, before he went home to Sally and Magnus. They lay together in the twilight talking. He believed her when she told him there had never been anything between her and Herbert. She said it in a serious tone, which made him smile, but he regretted it immediately.

"He was a kindred spirit," she said quietly. "We loved each other. Not like a father and daughter, and not like man and woman. Not like anyone in the world. Not like anyone but us. The one he was. The one I am."

Thomas repeated what Herbert had said that last time they saw each other. He recalled Herbert's face when they parted. He knew his friend could see them from his hospital bed.

Nowhere is it written who is going to cross your path, thinks Irene, but it's not entirely unpredictable either. Out of all the chance encounters, some make a difference. There are just so many lines that must find each other in time and in space before it can happen.

It was too soon and too late as well when Thomas and Irene lay together wondering so much about these lives of theirs that wondering turned into the daydream of a different one. It was far more fateful when forty-one-year-old Thomas ran up the stairs to Tatiana, breathless with betrayal and desire, and she received him at the door, responding to his gaze.

He has found the place from which his life can be seen in its temporary wholeness, still open, still unsettled. This time he will not let his wonder abate into insufficiency, a feeling of something neglected or lost. When he lay beside Tatiana for the first time, he might have thought he had come halfway, and that from then on there would be more past than future in his life. But it felt as if he had always lain there waiting for himself to catch up.

The sunlight falls obliquely on the huge oil tanks. It's getting late, the plane from Stockholm will soon come gliding in over the sound to land. Irene feels his hand on hers, a cautious touch.

He was cautious, but not for long. Two weeks after their meeting in the library garden he went home from Tatiana one evening and told Sally he'd decided to leave her. She yelled at him; it somehow made it easier, and half an hour later he was out the door.

Irene slowly withdraws her hand.

They leave together and make their way into town alongside the harbor, past the Little Mermaid, sitting slightly forlorn as she has always done. A small verdigris-colored excuse for herself and the prerogatives of fairytale, after all. She takes his arm and he lets her, as they blend with the other strollers. Tourists snapping each other's photos, mothers with strollers, loving couples, and older ladies talking on the benches. A hollow note hovers above them and they watch the Oslo ferry as it departs from the quay and catches the low sunlight, dazzling white for a couple of seconds while the passengers stand along the rail and wave beneath the fluttering flag.

Thomas lives with Tatiana in the apartment where they met— the pair now walking arm in arm. Every night Thomas and Tatiana sit at Herbert's desk editing his posthumous papers from Belgrade. Once or twice a week Magnus comes to see them. A dejected adolescent bravely trying to understand that this is real. So different from what he knows, the reality of this city apartment where his father now lives. Tatiana is friendly toward him but she doesn't try to win him over.

Now and then Sally calls to weep or rage at him, vindictive and full of spite or desperate and imploring. Thomas hasn't been prepared for her fury and the vituperative power with which she wants to punish him. She listens greedily to anything people can tell her about Tatiana. She soothes her wounded heart with gossip.

"To her, there's nothing in between love and hate," he says. "What she's really saying is: Love me, and I will love you; fail to love me and I will hate you! As if she has nowhere inside herself to go back to, where she is the same regardless of whether I am in her life or not."

Irene thinks of what was said at Ursula's dinner party. There are at least two versions of the story about Thomas. In one of them he's the immature, overproblematizing shit swept away by lust. In the other he's the romantic hero who has followed his heart. The two sto-

176

ries are irreconcilable, thinks Irene, and equally untrue, taken separately. He can't embrace the latter without assimilating the former. He's done with the Jekyll and Hyde routine; he can no longer allow himself to falter, dizzy with emotion, unable to decide whether to be a hero or a shit.

She doesn't tell him that she, too, has heard Sally weep on the phone. Nor does she reveal what Sally's friend said about him. What good would that do? Anyway, it will soon be time to say good-bye, but they still have a little way to walk together beside the lurching blue-black waters of the harbor. They stop at the end of the quay, where the Oslo boat was moored a few minutes ago. Now it's no more than a shining white toy puffing clouds of black smoke out in the sound.

He looks at his watch. She smiles.

"You shouldn't think about the past so much, Thomas. Looking back only gives you a stiff neck."

He returns her smile, slightly delayed. She is surprised at what she's just said. She catches sight of a taxi and hails it. He stands looking at her as she climbs in. He places a hand on the window as the taxi moves off. She waves until he disappears.

She passes the house where she and Thomas used to meet in an apartment under the roof. She looks up when she hears the shrill cry of swifts above and shades her eyes with a hand, the better to see their flitting, circling forms. Little fluttering quotation marks in the evening sky.

III

On a raft in the lagoon

Autumn has begun to make itself known as a dryness along the edges of the leaves. The air is clear and there is still not a cloud in the sky when she passes Hamburg around noon. It has been many years since the last time she found herself in a car passing through Germany, and she has never driven this far alone. She listens to the same music on the journey, Bach's cello suites. Samuel is playing. She follows the vibrating threads of the music and their nodes, the logical distribution of the pattern, as she registers the big signs for one town after another. She tries to maintain a steady speed as she follows the pulse of the music, the same current hurrying through the steps and shifts of the scales. As she passes the exits for the northern and southern suburbs of the towns, the music reconciles her eyes to their chance ugliness, along with the September sunshine, its clear golden light falling on everything equally.

Samuel must have played that music countless times over the years. He is alive. That and an address in Vienna are all she has. She hasn't tried to contact him but she has started to draft several letters. She hesitated before going. She had finally booked a flight but at the last moment she decided to drive. She wants to take her time arriving. While she listens to Samuel it occurs to her that this slow arrival has been going on all her life. She just wasn't aware of it. She could not know what she was on the way to. She thought it was a place she would arrive at, a place in her life, as if there were a place in life where you could stay. The idea makes her smile.

The house was easy to sell and fetched enough for her to buy a small apartment in town and to give Josephine and Peter each a nice sum. She let them take whatever furniture they wanted and booked a second-hand dealer to take the rest. He asked if someone had died, and she said yes to avoid explaining. She took nothing with her, just as she had refused to take so much as a silver spoon from Vivian when she moved in with Martin. The apartment she found was in the district where she'd pictured Susanne living. Martin and Susanne live at the other end of town. She caught sight of them by chance one day in the street, but they didn't notice her in the crowd. Susanne isn't as young as Irene had assumed. She must be in her late thirties, maybe forty, an ordinary, nice-looking woman. They walked along laughing at something, but the pang Irene felt was not one of belated jealousy; it was a pang of joy for Martin's sake.

She let Peter furnish the new place and made a point of hiding how little it meant to her what it looked like. He was happy to make himself useful. She lingered on the threshold the first time she went home to her spruce, newly furnished pad. So this was how people lived these days. She felt alien in her new surroundings and that was how it should be, for it was not her home. She didn't want a home, only a pied-à-terre, temporary like all ports of call. It was situated in a side street along the wall of the old Jewish cemetery. The view was decisive, the trees covered with ivy and the tall grass between crumbling headstones. She played with the idea that Samuel's parents might have been buried down there beneath her windows, but made no effort to find out if in fact they had. It was summer before she tried to find out anything at all about Samuel.

She remained in town. Her colleagues were surprised that she didn't go on a vacation like everyone else. She could feel them thinking, but she had already trained herself to steer her thoughts away from imagining their ideas about her, whether they were sympathetic or worried. She didn't have much to do, but she still went to the office every morning, even during the couple of weeks when she was the only one there. She spent much of the time just sitting at her desk reading the paper and watching the light change on the walls of the courtyard. When she cycled home in the late afternoon the summer seemed an irrelevant event with its open-air jazz and scantily clad people in the sidewalk cafés and along the canal quays. She had bought a bicycle and enjoyed the wind in her hair when she pedaled across the Queen Louise Bridge.

Peter and Sandra tried several times to persuade her to go up to the cottage, which they had taken over. She said she needed to be alone, but actually it wasn't a question of need. She was alone whether she needed it or not, and she didn't want to disguise the fact. She babysat Emil and Amalie once or twice before they went to the country. She liked being with the children. Their eager little bodies and twittering voices evoked something in her, a dormant physical readiness and a sense of fun she had forgotten. She visited Vivian once a week. They sat on her balcony looking out at the pine trees as they had done before she was admitted to the hospital. The only sign of change between them was that Vivian talked even more frenetically, and that Irene let her talk without any sign of impatience.

Now and then Josephine paid a visit to the new apartment. At other times they gathered around the Provençal refectory table in its new home on Peter and Sandra's newly built veranda. Now it was Peter who sat at the head of the table, opened the wine, and swilled a little around in his mouth, distending his nostrils with the air of a connoisseur. She knew they also had Martin and Susanne over, but the subject was not touched upon. Peter had calmed down after his outburst, even more quickly than she had expected.

She began to accept dinner invitations from her friends, but she found it hard to tolerate the admiration in their eyes, their respect for how she was managing. Besides, it was a strain having to be diplomatically nonchalant about their hints that they kept in touch with Martin, too, mature and impartial as they were. She realized she was secretly on probation, and she refused to demonstrate a newfound serenity about feelings she had not felt. Feelings like bitterness and ignominy. It was just as stressful to be impartial with the impartial as it was to be in the company of Ursula, who continually urged her to let go of all the pent up bile that must be burning her up inside and which, in her friend's eyes, needed to be released. Ursula just looked at her with her black-lined eyes, expectant and empathetic, and Irene grew stubborn and refused to deliver. Her store of anger had been used up long ago, that store which according to Ursula—or rather according to her expectant face—it would have been so constructive to air.

Irene wasn't processing her grief. Even though grief was all she felt, she couldn't share it. And it wasn't that she wanted it all to herself, to suck greedily like the sticky licorice sweets that, as a child, she'd held in her mouth until the black saliva trickled from the corners of her lips. She didn't think about anything in particular when she was alone. She sat at the window smoking and listening to music in the evening sun as she looked down on the leaning headstones with their Hebrew inscriptions half obliterated by moss and fungi. She waited, and she knew what she was waiting for, and at the same time she felt she could sit like this forever.

She felt free and empty when she strolled through her neighborhood, shopped at the Turkish grocery and sat at a sidewalk café surrounded by young people. It occurred to her that she hadn't spent a summer in town since she and Martin were their age. She sat in the last rays of sunlight that fell between the houses and watched them skimming along on their bikes, the girls in light summer dresses. She watched them smile and heard them laugh and thought she knew what they were thinking and dreaming of and had coming to them like something they had no idea of, and it all felt so close and distant at the same time.

Ursula couldn't resist the subject of Bertel, and Irene guessed they must have been talking about her, but she kept a straight face. He called her a few times before finally giving up. When she spoke with him the idea crossed her mind for a moment, quite simply because it occurred to her, the idea of seeing him, being with him again. Initiating a relationship. It was not the idea that seemed grotesque but the words she used to express it. A relationship. But why should it seem grotesque? Both the idea and the words made her feel lonely when she wasn't otherwise lonely, merely alone, when she sat down late in the afternoon and looked down at the Jewish headstones. She was alone, and she had nothing to say to anyone.

She might seem like a person waiting for someone, well dressed, sunglasses pushed up, and legs crossed, sitting with her newspaper at one of the neighborhood's sidewalk cafés. She must have seemed something of an oddity; everyone around her was half her age, but in fact it was rare that anyone noticed her. Actually, she'd begun to notice it herself if one of the young men looked at her, even smiled, as he passed by. She'd begun to notice it because it happened so rarely, and because she was alone.

She thought of it during the telephone conversations with Bertel and she thought of it a month later when she met him again at another dinner party of Ursula's. As usual, the rest of the guests were new faces. He'd brought a woman his own age, pleasant and cultured like himself. Irene recalled what he had said in the car as he drove her home. How fortuitous it is whom you happen to meet, how exposed we are. She could have just jumped at it. He seemed relaxed when he introduced her to his new woman, and he drew them both into conversation so naturally that you would never believe he and Irene had made love to each other a couple of months earlier. Or was that the reason for their familiarity? Comfort sex. She had read the expression in the Sunday paper. That night it was harder than usual to go home, undress, lie down in the cool bedclothes, switch off the lamp, and look out at the bluish glow of the streetlights behind the curtain. It wasn't even that she wished Bertel was beside her, within reach. Or was it?

What was the matter with her?

She could understand, at a glance, how Vivian's life had been formed by the two men she had known, and by the void they'd left, one to be exchanged for another, the other to leave her by herself. What had Vivian been, apart from being Irene's mother? A lonely, powerless component of something so utterly absent that it was impossible to see what meaning her life could have after Irene had left home. It was a story you could find words for, but what about Irene?

And what about Sandra, who spent all her time fussing over her little chickens? What about Josephine, spending the summer in the south of France with her new guy? This time it was the real McCoy, she had said, and Irene answered that if Josephine herself believed it so did she. What was she supposed to say? What else could she allow herself to say to her grown-up daughter? Or should she have had another answer ready?

She'd never encountered opposition, far from it, back when she started as a law clerk, but she'd been aware that she had to be better than her trousered colleagues if she didn't want to be considered inferior even though she was their equal. She never forgot what Mrs. Frölich had said, not even when she herself started to wear pants. Of course pants were the latest trend, but there was something else as well. It was the fact that, in the years between her youth and her passage beyond it, gender-based differences had diminished considerably. But the equality that resulted was sexless and in the long run insipid, and in the end young women took to wearing skirts and high heels again. She understood why they painted their eyes and lips, she did so herself. Equality got boring, particularly when confused with uniformity. But although Irene had never quite grasped the political consequences of shaving your legs, when she watched the young women in the outdoor cafés she did sometimes wonder.

She had to ask herself if it was only her age and its envy that made her think in this way, but she didn't believe that. Yes, she had her hair dyed, but not in protest against age itself, only what age tries to wrest away from a woman. And she wasn't one to fix up her hair in every mirror she walked past. That was something she had cured herself of many years ago, when she first began to appear in court, trembling with fear in case she did not seem as competent and well prepared as she demonstrably was.

Perhaps it was only Martin's lasting, sustained adoration that had allowed her to forget her vanity, simply because he kept confirming it around the clock. Hadn't she astonished herself with the thought of what Bertel might think of her in a low-cut pink dress when they met for the first time? She watched the young women fix up their hair and listen with dreaming smiles to the young men talking to them. She could see they only listened with one ear, while the other listened to their own mute questions. Does he like me? Am I sexy enough?

At the same time the young men have become so feminine, Irene reflects, and they've been like this ever since I've been wearing pants. Strangely enough, they only became more effeminate, the men of my age, when they started growing beards. Martin never grew a beard; luckily I've never had to try and kiss a bearded man. But what happened? How did equality become so indifferent, unimportant, immaterial? Maybe it began when we stopped dancing properly. When Martin and I met we did the jitterbug, and he threw me around and grabbed me again, and my stomach was in a whirl. He made me feel like a woman when we danced or when he brought me flowers on Mondays. He never stopped buying me flowers, but we stopped jitterbugging, and I miss both, the flowers and the Chuck Berry, I have to admit. We never learned how to do the new dancing, to stand slopping around to the music on our own, equally disjointed in our corduroys whether he had a beard or not.

You can live without men opening the door for you, but look at the way they slouch. It doesn't matter that they're good at carpentry. Look at the feeble way they clutch their chins, like bashful children standing on their tiptoes. Listen to them, with their husky emotional voices, talking about female values, intimacy, how the children are the most important thing. Quality time. That's a new one—new to me anyway. They aren't out to conquer the world. They can't wait to get

185

home and have quality time with their overstimulated toddlers, frightened to teach them to eat with a fork and knife for fear of damaging the little geniuses' integrity.

It isn't that women have gained a foothold in the men's world. It's that society at large has turned into a nursery. Even the language whimpers around us. Words are like warm milk. Job security. Grief processes. Quality time. Trauma counseling. Even big, strong firefighters need trauma counseling when the heat's on. Excuse me, isn't that what they're trained to do? Put out fires? We've grown up in peace and security and we have everything, but we seem to forget there's a price. We still have soldiers, but they're not supposed to risk their lives. Even wars have been transformed into video games. Why should we sacrifice our well-fed boys for the primitive devils who are slitting each others' throats in our backyard? Hard to answer. Goodwill and righteous indignation just get so strangely abstract at an altitude of ten kilometers.

I'm losing myself, Irene thinks.

Perhaps I'm the only one who's not compatible. But I was born during the war, the last one we really experienced. We? I have no idea what I'm talking about. I didn't experience it myself, I was too young, but that was where my life began. And I saw the pictures, it's one of my first memories. Piles of naked matchstick men. Dead. Destroyed. The German towns I drive past in my expensive car. Only their names remain. And the pictures. Heaps of rubble and broken masonry that blend in with the gray and black grains. Here a gable, there a façade with holes gaping onto nothing, and on a path among the heaps, a tiny man carrying a suitcase. Or is it a bucket of water? I will never forget that picture.

I'm losing myself, and I feel lost. Out of contact.

Our wealth and security have turned into such a tall, dense briar patch. We gained so much, Martin and I, but we lost something too. Contact. Not just contact with each other. Although I could be wrong there. Has anyone had more contact with the rest of the world? Probably not, and we've probably been more sensitive than many were at the time, when everything was a struggle. But we were also more preoccupied with our own feelings than with anything else. We had plenty of sympathy for the poor wretches, the suffering and the miserable, at least for as long as they appeared on television, but we forgot them in the time it takes to change the channel. There was always some child being teased at school, or a car needing repair.

I have never talked to him about it. I don't think he'd understand me. There was always more reality in Martin than in me.

What is the matter with you, Irene?

The girls can't even fix their hair without you immediately criticizing them. And why shouldn't young fathers take an interest in their children? What's wrong with being absorbed in what's closest to you? Those you love? You can't love the whole world. If Peter and Sandra are doing things the right way, as you say, what's the problem? They donate to the Red Cross, don't they? Buy organic milk? Sort their recycling? Haven't they adopted two small orphaned Indians? What are you doing yourself to help the world? And what has the cruelty of the world got to do with women? Isn't your own corner of it more civilized since women have had a say? Where exactly are you heading?

Hannover, Hildesheim, Göttingen. She maintains her speed, follows the rhythm of the music through the cello's tonal register, now hoarse and dark, now crystal clear in its vibrations. The music marks out the way past power stations, industrial works, exit ramps, and sprawling urban developments, again succeeded by fields or forests, as the sun loses height. She pictures the ancient towns, their towers and spires, once surrounded by walls and open country where now they are besieged by the same suburbs, the same matter-of-fact, uniform modernity. Once they were less materialistic but also grimier places than now, more fantastic and dramatic, and more brutal. Razed to the ground and built up again, so that only the names and a few shipwrecked remnants survive the ravages of history.

In towns people circle around in harmony with the patterns of life. Out here on the autobahn one is always on one's way, one hour after another. Late in the afternoon she gets tired and turns off at a rest area with a service station, a café, and a motel. She doesn't know precisely where she is, but she has come a long way already. She thinks of everything she has left behind. Her situation. She stripped it off and left it in the rearview mirror, where it shrank until it had completely faded from sight.

Once more she is staying at a motel without anyone knowing where she is. She switches on the television and turns the volume down, just to see something move. She told Vivian and the children that she needed a vacation. Why not Vienna? She's never been to Vienna. Josephine thought it showed spunk to drive all the way. Peter gave her a road map when she went to see them a few days before. She spreads out the map on the bed. Europe. A multicolored, uneven link between Asia and the Atlantic. With a finger she traces the route she has taken. E45. She passed Kassel a good hour ago. When she approaches Würzburg she'll take E56 via Nuremberg and continue southeast.

Nuremberg. She remembers the pictures, rows of men, headphones. Ordinary men in ordinary suits. Samuel must have seen the same pictures. The pictures from Germany, Bach's Germany. He had been spared, he must have thought that. He'd escaped, her father, he could go on, free to play Bach's cello suites. She lights a cigarette and contemplates the silent pictures on the screen, new pictures all the time. News. A tropical storm whips huge waves over a coastal road and tears angrily at the palm trees. Statesmen drink fruit juice and smile. There are also pictures from the Balkans, minarets and ruined houses. Young men in track suits, older men in white felt caps. Mud, a hole, and something that resembles the remains of a human being. It is history already, but the history cannot be told yet. She is contemporaneous with it but she cannot fully absorb it, lying in a motel bed between Kassel and Nuremberg with an ashtray balanced on her stomach.

When she gets hungry she goes out to a shabby diner, but she can't face the ravioli the waitress heats up in the microwave and places before her with a resigned expression. She lights another cigarette. By the window a man in a down vest hunches over a mug of coffee. Probably a long-distance driver. He's left his family somewhere in the north to get into one of those trucks lined up in the lot and drive south. He spends most of his time at the wheel, on his way out or home, interrupted by cups of coffee at places like this. Any old place between towns. The sun is low outside, it blazes against the sides of the great trailers. She reads the names of trucking companies and the names of towns, Brindisi, Rostock, Ostende. The waitress stands with her arms folded over her polyester apron, looking out at the passing cars. Under her paper cap her hair is dark and curly. Maybe she comes from Brindisi or Tirana or Konya. Does she miss her home town, or does she prefer to be here, serving ravioli?

Irene goes back to her room. There are parrots on the waffled bedspread, and suddenly she can't see herself sleeping under it. She doesn't feel like lying in the dark listening to the traffic. She'll just rest for an hour. She'll buy water, cookies, and chocolate at the gas station vending machine and drive on as far as she can. As long as she's behind the wheel she is at least on the way.

No one disappears completely unless by express intention, but how could Samuel have known that someone would follow his covered tracks after so many years? He hadn't covered them himself, time had done that, but they were still there. Would he have done more to erase them if he'd known he would eventually be found? When he stood in the Botanical Gardens one Sunday after the war, he couldn't have known that it was his daughter in the stroller when his beloved and his friend passed, apparently without seeing him. And his daughter cannot know whether he will acknowledge her so many years later.

She had brushed it aside until late in the summer. Perhaps he'd died long ago. And if he was still alive? What good would it do half a century later? To disturb an old man and risk getting herself even more upset than she already was. She'd had a father. She'd felt deserted, found him again, and reconciled with him only to lay him in his grave. It wasn't a father she needed, not now. And yet she couldn't stop thinking of Samuel, the same questions kept recurring: Who was he? What kind of man had he been? She looked in the telephone book and found the number of the Danish Radio Symphony Orchestra. But what was she supposed to say? For once she had trouble expressing herself cogently. She didn't even know his surname. She wrote a letter instead.

The reply came some weeks later. They had found a cellist called Samuel Balkin in the personnel archive. He'd been engaged from August 1942 until he disappeared the following October. Since then nothing had been heard of him. They assumed he had escaped to Sweden like the other Jewish musicians in the orchestra, but an embarrassing detail attached itself to his disappearance. Samuel Balkin had been employed on a trial basis when the most renowned cellist in the orchestra fell ill and had to retire. In agreement with the older musician it had been decided that his young and unusually talented colleague should take over his cello. It was a rare and valuable instrument, a Ruggieri, built about 1680, and had been in the orchestra's possession for generations. Balkin had taken the cello with him when he fled. After the Liberation they'd tried to track him down, and the police had instituted a search for the cello through Interpol, to no avail.

Irene smiled when she read the letter. Her father, a thief.

According to Vivian's story Samuel had a younger sister. Irene contacted the synagogue in Copenhagen. It was some time before she received an answer. According to her information and the investigation they had undertaken, the sister could be identified as a Rosa Balkin, born in 1926 in St. Petersburg, then called Leningrad, who died in Copenhagen in 1998. She had been a widow and two of her three children had left the country, but the youngest, a son, still lived in Copenhagen.

He was in the phone book. Dennis Balkin, an auto mechanic. He had been there the whole time, her cousin. He sounded neither particularly surprised nor particularly forthcoming on the telephone. A day or two later Irene parked her car on a quiet road in a southern suburb of Copenhagen. She had trouble finding the way, she had never been in that part of town. His wife opened the door, a sturdy young woman in a sweatshirt and sweatpants with a baby on her arm. He hadn't come home yet.

The room was furnished with a dining table, a leather sectional, and a bookshelf with reference books and framed photos of the couple and their children. A boy lay on the floor in a corner, in front of a large television set. The woman picked up the remote control, still holding the baby, and turned down the volume. The boy yelled at her, she yelled back. From the living room there was a door opening onto a narrow garden with an inflatable pool and a swiveling clothesline hung with underpants, overalls, and socks. The boy went out and started spraying water on the lawn; a lake formed around the pool.

"Are you related to Dennis?"

The question was uttered without a smile and with no sign of interest in the reply, as if to pass the time. The woman hadn't introduced herself and had not offered her anything.

"Yes, in a way," Irene smiled politely.

"He called from the garage, he's on his way."

The woman pulled up her sweatshirt and bared a large breast. She took hold of it and guided the nipple to the baby's mouth. In a way, thought Irene, in a way she was related to the small red-faced being sucking away at its mother's white breast. In a completely fortuitous way. She was about to excuse herself and leave when a car stopped outside. The boy ran through the room and into the hall, the woman went into the kitchen adjoining the living room. In the space between the cupboards Irene could see her sweatsuited behind and the baby lying in a plastic chair on the kitchen table. It sounded as if she was chopping something. Irene could hear the boy's eager voice in the bathroom and the sound of water running into the sink. The smell of onions reached her.

Dennis Balkin was a quiet-voiced man in his forties with gray streaks in his vigorous black hair. The hand he gave her was still wet. He sat down opposite her, the boy crawled onto his lap and fixed Irene with a challenging look. Dennis Balkin's expression was neither challenging nor forthcoming.

"What do you want to know?"

"I'd like to know whether you have any contact with your uncle. As I said on the phone, I have reason to believe he's my father."

"Actually, I'd forgotten that I had an uncle." He smiled, almost scornfully, and put his head back as he turned to the kitchen alcove.

"Mona, did you know I had an uncle?" There was no answer. The boy slipped down off his lap and went into the garden again. Dennis leaned forward and rested his elbows on his knees. "Isn't he dead?"

"That's one of the things I want to find out."

"I'd really like to help you. You're almost a cousin." He smiled again, showing his teeth in a way that seemed somehow false.

"Your mother must have talked about him."

"She wasn't especially talkative."

"Do you think your siblings know anything?"

"They don't know nothing. He moved there, after the war. Israel, you know. Now I remember. But she hardly ever talked about him. I don't think they ever met again."

"You've never been to Israel?"

"What would I do there?" He looked at her and seemed to be taking pains not to blink.

"When did they come to Denmark?"

"Sometime in the thirties, I can't remember the exact year. Things were getting tough for Jews in the Soviet Union back then."

"What did your grandfather do?"

"At first he was a tailor, over there, but he doesn't seem to have been doing very well. Later he got into leather goods. Bags, belts—that sort of thing."

"Do you have a picture of your mother?"

"Of course."

He looked at her before rising and taking an album from the bookshelf. He opened it on the coffee table in front of her and pointed to one of the pictures. It had been taken in the garden, they were sitting side by side at a plastic table. A frail, elderly woman with white hair. She could have been anyone. He watched Irene as she studied the picture. It seemed meaningless.

"Wait a minute!"

He went out of the room. The snarling sound of a food processor came from the kitchen. It grew slower when Mona put something into the bowl. Mince, thought Irene. She'd risen to her feet when Dennis came back with a shoe box. He put it on the table, she sat down again.

194

"There isn't much left. We didn't have room. Old stuff, most of it, but have a look...."

She took the lid off the box. Some photographs and postcards, a yellowed document in Russian and a gilded Star of David on a chain. Dennis leaned forward and pointed with his chin.

"The postcards are from him."

One was black-and-white and showed an ancient city gate surmounted by a parapet and some figures in Arabic drapery. In one corner was written Jerusalem, Damascus Gate. The other card was a color photograph, artificially tinted, showing a view of the sea from above, framed by the outstretched branches of a lemon tree. In the middle of the scene rose a dome, covered with colored mosaics sparkling in the sun. She turned the card over and read the text printed in both Hebrew and English: Bahai Temple, Haifa. She couldn't read the few lines on the cards, but they were in the same irregular hand and both were signed with an intricate *S*.

"It's Yiddish," Dennis explained before she could ask.

"Do you read Yiddish?"

"Me?" He bared his teeth again and uttered a scornful sound. "It might as well be Swahili."

Irene tried to decipher the postmarks. One card had been sent in 1949, the other mark was illegible.

"That's all there is," said Dennis. "As you can see, he didn't have much to say."

She put the postcards on the table and picked up the photographs one by one. Dennis rose and left the room. They were ordinary family photos, small black-and-white prints with a white border. She recognized the young Rosa, photographed with her children, but saw no resemblance between the youngest child and the man who'd been sitting opposite her a few moments ago. There was also a wedding picture. She'd been beautiful once, pale, with black hair, dramatic eyebrows, and a full, bow-shaped upper lip. A mouth like the one Vivian had kissed?

One of the photographs was older and more worn than the others, taken on a bridge over a canal. On one side of the canal one could see a row of houses in classical style, in the other side of the picture was a tower with an onion dome. They were still children, the two standing together by the balustrade, though they were dressed as grown-ups, the little girl in a long coat, the adolescent boy in a dark suit, a hat in his hand. The picture was slightly blurred and the sunlight had blotted out their features, leaving little to see but their smiles and their eyebrows and eyes beneath their black hair. The boy's hair was combed back from his forehead.

"There he is."

She looked up. She hadn't heard Dennis come back. He passed her an old LP.

"I knew I had it somewhere."

A sizzling sound came from the kitchen as Mona put the rissoles in the frying pan. Dennis stood by the sofa as Irene studied the album cover. Under the angular Hebrew letters was a photo of a cellist, a dark silhouette bent over his instrument, cut off from the surrounding darkness by the spotlight, which cast a line around his profile and the curves of the cello. The cover was worn, and the edge of the record stood out in the dark of the concert hall like a white circle around the lone musician.

"Could we listen to it?" Irene looked up at Dennis.

He glanced toward the kitchen before turning to her. "We've converted to CDs. I could make you a tape if you like. A friend of mine has a turntable."

"Thank you. I'd like to borrow this picture, please."

196

He scratched his neck. "Could I send you a photocopy?"

He gathered up the postcards and pictures and packed them into the shoebox. She took her purse from her bag and gave him her card. He followed her outside.

"I'm sorry I can't help you," he said as she was getting into the car. "I've never met him, you know, and she didn't like to talk about him. For some reason or other."

"What?"

He rested a hand on the roof of the car and looked down the road. His son was running along toward them. "Who knows? I think she felt, well...how best to put it?...let down or something."

The boy came up to him and took his hand. Dennis rumpled his hair with an awkward gesture. She got into the car. He pointed a thumb at the windshield.

"You should replace those wipers."

"Yes, I must see to it."

She smiled and closed the door. He raised a hand and went into the house with the boy.

It is after midnight before she goes to bed in a motel room almost identical to the previous night's stop. She listens to the traffic and pictures the road and the signs rushing to meet her, the names of the towns and their distant lights in the dark. The next morning she sleeps late. It's well into the afternoon before she gets to Passau, the last town in Germany. She eats a late lunch and strolls through the old town center. She stands for a long time looking at where the Inn River meets the Danube. One stream is paler than the other before they blend and continue eastward.

When she stops at a red light on the way out of Passau, drumming her fingers impatiently on the wheel, she hears the clicking of her wedding ring. She must have heard it thousands of times in the past months without asking herself why she still puts on the ring every morning. She doesn't wear much jewellery. Has she worn it out of regard for Peter and Josephine? Or has she just been dulled by habit, not giving it a thought? She takes off the ring and puts it in the tray beside the gearshift. What have people been thinking? The question makes her smile as she listens to Samuel and Bach. After Linz, she turns onto E60 for Vienna. The tape faithfully reproduces every scratch and dust mote on the record's grooves. Their crackling blends with the changing voice of the cello, now singing, now trembling and hoarse.

She thought Dennis had forgotten her, but one day an envelope arrived containing the tape and two photocopies, one of the record cover, the other of the small picture of Samuel and his sister beside a canal in their home town. There was no letter, only a printed slip from Dennis Balkin Auto Repairs and Panelbeating Ltd., with a cross next to "by appointment" and an ornate, curly signature. She spent several afternoons listening to Samuel playing Bach on his stolen cello, as she looked down into the green jungle of the cemetery where Dennis's grandparents might be buried. She pinned the photocopies to the wall between the windows. A musician half turned away in the darkness of the concert hall, nothing but a shining corona around his shoulders, the high brow and hooked nose. Two young faces eclipsed by light, distorted beyond recognition in this copy of a copy, their trusting smiles all that remained.

The Israeli embassy helped her to fill in an inquiry form in Hebrew regarding missing persons. Later she made contact with an official at the Ministry of the Interior in Jerusalem. Her telephone bill went up five hundred percent that month, for although Mr. Czernowitz could be curt, he liked to elaborate his curtness with detailed explanation. She was amused at his grating accent, which made the words sound as if they scraped his throat. He grumbled when she phoned the second time. She must understand that she wasn't the only person searching for a relative in Israel. This kind of case took time, it wasn't done with a snap of the fingers. On the other hand, it wasn't impossible that he'd be able to help her himself; not at all, but she must be patient. Irene was not patient, but the first results of his quite exceptional and speedy investigation were negative. There was no Israeli citizen by the name of Samuel Balkin who met her description. The only one he could find was a twenty-seven-year-old American Jew living in a settlement outside Bethlehem. But he probably wouldn't be of much use to her?

Some weeks later, early one Sunday morning, Irene was woken by the telephone. Mr. Czernowitz sounded almost reproachful when she answered, confused and heavy with sleep. Only then did she remember that Sunday is a working day in Israel. Why hadn't she told him her father had changed his name? How was he supposed to find a Samuel Balkin who was no longer called Samuel Balkin? He'd hit on the bright idea of going through the list of name changes. He forgot to be brusque as he explained. At that time—that is, when the state was founded and during the years that followed—it had been common practice for immigrating Jews to assume a Hebrew version of their original name. It was part of the adventure. Coming back from the Diaspora, Jews were met with a Babylonian confusion of languages. The only tongue they had in common was a language that hadn't been spoken outside the synagogues for two thousand years. Did she see? New words, or new meanings of old ones, had to be found for everything from screwdrivers to garages. So what was more natural than finding new names for oneself and others as well?

Samuel Balkin must have arrived in Israel during the British mandate, but in 1948, the year when the state was instituted, it had been registered that a Samuel Balkin, born 1919 in Leningrad, had changed his name to Shmuel Bar Am, with an address in Tel Aviv. Irene found a ball pen and a newspaper and made notes in the margin. The same Shmuel Bar Am had since married a Hannah Mandelbaum, born 1923 in Krakow, died 1969 in Tel Aviv. The couple had had one son, Avi Bar Am, born 1949, died 1967.

Irene's pen came to a halt. There was a moment's silence, and in the silence she thought she heard other voices on the line, so distant they were hardly distinguishable from the faint buzz. "Many have died since then," said Mr. Czernowitz, clearing his throat. Avi Bar Am had been conscripted. That was about all. According to the latest information he had been able to obtain, Shmuel Bar Am took up residence in the USA in 1969. He had given an address in Manhattan to the Israeli consulate in New York. Irene made a note. The trail ended here. Mr. Czernowitz suggested that she contact the American authorities. She thanked him. He shrugged it off and grew almost warm. Had she ever been to Israel? She should think about a visit one day.

She took a bath, dressed, and had a cup of tea. She was unable to eat anything in the morning any more. It was quiet in the streets. She walked across the Queen Louise Bridge. Everything was bright and pastel colored: the clouds, the building fronts alongside the lakes, the blue film on the water. She thought of St. Petersburg, then Leningrad. Perhaps it had been a Sunday like this one, at the beginning of summer. They'd been out walking in their best clothes, and got the idea to have their picture taken by a street photographer. If it hadn't been for the photo they would have been bound to forget this Sunday, unable to tell it apart from all the other Sundays in this town where they'd been born, and where late in the spring you could see the ice floes gliding down the river. Perhaps they had forgotten that day, but the picture remained. Rosa had held onto it through the war and across the many years that had passed since Samuel left, until it ended up in a shoe box with the few other objects remaining after her death.

It wasn't far to the Botanical Gardens. Irene took one of the paths among the exotic plants; she was alone. She stopped beneath a cedar tree, a gray heron flew over it on wide wings. Were there any herons in the Botanical Gardens in 1945? Vivian had walked along this same path with the young doctor and the child that was not his, and up there on one of the benches by the greenhouse, she had caught sight of a familiar figure.

She went up the wide steps flanked by balustrades with cacti in vase-shaped pots. She sat on one of the benches with her back to the glass dome of the greenhouse. Maybe the same bench where Samuel had sat with Vivian fantasizing about New York and their future in the distant metropolis. About the child and the life they would have. About a place where no one minded where you came from. She could see the young couple as they came walking with the stroller along the path. In Haifa he had met a girl from Poland. A new life. A son. Another unknown brother who had seemingly vanished. It was beginning.

She contacted the American embassy. Another long wait before she received an answer to her inquiry. Shmuel Bar Am had indeed obtained permission, in 1969, to live and work as an orchestral musician in New York. He had left the country in 1976, and his green card had not been renewed. She found the orchestra on the Internet and sent an e-mail. The reply was discouraging, they had never had a cellist by that name. She wrote again and asked the secretary who had answered to look under the name Samuel Balkin. This time she was lucky, and the years were right. Samuel Balkin had played with the orchestra from 1969 until he resigned in April 1976. Irene wrote back asking if they could put her in touch with one of Samuel's former colleagues, who might know what had become of him. At the end of August she received a letter postmarked Fort Lauderdale, Florida.

It was typed. Some of the letters had jumped on the closely spaced airmail sheet, and it looked as if the ribbon hadn't been changed in a long time. It was probably impossible to buy color ribbons any more. Norman Roth had been a viola player and had retired shortly after Samuel left the orchestra. He was some years older than Sam. They had played chamber music together, sometimes in a string quartet Norman assembled from time to time, mostly for pleasure. They had given the odd concert, upstate and around New Jersey. They never became close friends. Sam was not a man you got intimate with, but Norman and his wife had taken a liking to him, and occasionally he came to dinner at their home in Brooklyn. He might sometimes have a lady friend with him, but it was seldom the same one twice in a row, and usually he came alone. Sam was something of a loner, quiet, almost secretive.

He spoke only briefly about his childhood in Russia and his family in Copenhagen, and never about his years in Israel. Norman had once seen an envelope on his music stand with his Israeli name on it. Sam explained that he had changed his name when he became an Israeli. So why had he changed it back again? Norman was puzzled by his reply and still remembered it. "Names are like clothes," Sam had said. "You dress for the occasion." Typical Sam. If you didn't know him you might think he was a cold, suspicious person, but that was only a façade, everyone who heard him play realized that. Sam was very proud of his cello, and no one was allowed to try it. He maintained that the sound would be ruined if anyone else played it. Musi-

202

cians could be like that, explained Norman Roth, and Sam had good reason to be sensitive about his instrument, for he played it like an angel. He could have gone a long way if he'd set his sights on a solo career, but he wasn't interested. He was an angel who'd burned his wings—that's what it had seemed like to Norman.

In the summer of the year before he left the orchestra they'd been on tour in Europe. One night they played in Amsterdam. They were to appear in Copenhagen the next night. After the performance in the Concertgebouw, Norman and Sam had a beer together—they often did that when they were on the road—but that night Sam was more reserved than usual. Norman thought no more about it before the next day in Copenhagen. They were to play in the Tivoli Gardens, and a few of them had arranged to eat there after the concert, but Sam went straight back to the hotel. He didn't reappear until they were about to leave next morning. In the bus on the way to the airport, Norman asked him if he'd been to see his family, but Sam replied that he had no family. Norman was about to say that didn't match with what he'd told them earlier, but Sam's expression made him keep quiet.

Since then they hadn't seen much of each other in private. Six months later Sam told him he'd applied for a position in Vienna, and he left suddenly. Irene was to send regards from Iris and Norman Roth if she found him. She was always welcome if she ever came to Florida.

The Bräunerhof is a dark place. Daylight manages to filter in only as a faint, diminished reflection in the sheen of walls covered with old posters and narrow mirrors, above sofas upholstered in fleecy brown cloth. The stagnant air is heavy with tobacco smoke and the smell of fried food, and the silence is only disturbed by the infrequent tinkle of a teaspoon on a saucer or a brief rustling when one of the few guests turns the page of a newspaper. Samuel could have chosen a more inviting haunt, but this is where he comes every morning, nodding briefly to the waiter before he picks up the *Neue Zürcher Zeitung* from the newspaper rack and seats himself in his favorite corner. Irene is surprised at how small he is. Soon, the waiter brings a cup of black coffee and a glass of water. Until then she has not heard them exchange one word. It can't be long before his white-haired, stooping profile passes across the yellowed curtain that half shades the room from the street outside. He is punctual, and his habits seem to be ingrained.

For two mornings running, from her seat by the window, Irene has watched the elderly gentleman who punctiliously takes a case from his inner pocket and puts his glasses on his nose before immersing himself in what the *Neue Zürcher Zeitung* has to report from the world beyond the dimly lit café. He keeps his coat on. It's hard to know whether he has noticed her. Most of the time his face is hidden behind the neat columns of the sparsely illustrated newspaper. Only when he turns a page or folds the paper in half does she have a chance to form an impression of her father's face. He is eighty-one, and looks it. The deep furrows in his forehead and on each side of his flared nostrils, along with the drooping corners of his mouth, divide the loose pale skin into bulges. Like the narrow clefts between mountain ridges, thinks Irene, sipping her strong coffee. He has bushy eyebrows, which would benefit from a trim, but otherwise he is always clean shaven, and every day he wears a fresh, well-pressed shirt and a tie, olive green or burgundy, under his tweed jacket. She is relieved to see that he is so impeccably groomed.

She had felt paralyzed the day after her arrival. As long as she was in the car, meeting Samuel was nothing but an idea. She had found herself between two realities, the one she had left behind and the one she could not imagine. The autobahn and the landscapes along the way had not been real, but Vienna was all too real. The hotel where she had reserved a room turned out to be some distance from the city center, in Schönbrunn. It was a lush nightmare of fake antiques and fleur-de-lis patterned velvety wallpaper, embellished with gold-framed hunting scenes. She stayed in her room until late in the day, when she went for a walk in the castle park. As she sat on a bench in the sun, staring vacantly at the luxuriant rose beds, she realized that she hadn't a clear idea of what to do next. Wasn't it meaningless? As she sat breathing the heavy scent of roses, what she most felt like was to get into her car again and drive north.

When she returned to the hotel and started to unpack she found a fat letter at the bottom of her overnight bag. It was from Thomas, she had not yet opened it. She hadn't given it a thought since she'd bundled some clothes and toiletries into the bag early in the morning two days ago and carried it down to the car. One afternoon, after shopping in the neighborhood, she was on her way back when she'd seen him sitting in the sidewalk café where she often spent half an hour before going home. She hadn't spoken to him since their lunch beside the harbor at Langelinie Pavilion. He almost hit his head on the awning as he shot up out of his chair to wave. He smiled enthusiastically as she approached, and in the slightly awkward transition before she reached him she caught a first impression of the woman beside him, dark haired, with a narrow, slightly foreign-looking face, and long suntanned legs. It was true, what he'd said, her eyes were unusually bright.

The awkwardness would not quite disappear, although Thomas did his best to get a conversation going. Irene could not gauge, as she met Tatiana's eyes now and then, how much he had said. There was no coolness in them, but the usual social approach was not there either. Interested, thought Irene. Tatiana looked as if she was studying her with sincere interest. She couldn't be very young, at any rate not as young as the gossip at Ursula's table had made her; perhaps thirty, perhaps older. Nor did she look like the scandalous tramp she had been touted as. She wore sandals, although it was a cool day, and a simple dress in a subdued dark red shade. Her long hair glowed in the sun. There was something serious about her presence but not her expression as she made the occasional remark in her droll accent.

206

Irene tried to remember the framed photo of a very young girl on the desk in Herbert Verhoeven's attic apartment. Thomas asked what she was doing at the moment. She couldn't help smiling at the hackneyed question.

"I'm searching for my father."

The words fell out of her mouth before she could stop them. Apart from Dennis Balkin, Mr. Czernowitz, and the other officials she had contacted, she hadn't told anyone about her search.

"Has he disappeared?" asked Tatiana.

"He left the country when I was a child. I haven't seen him or heard of him since."

She couldn't bring herself to say "never." The word was too comprehensive, impossible to discuss, at least at a café table in the afternoon sun.

"Aren't you afraid of finding him, then?"

"Afraid?"

Tatiana must have seen that the question took her by surprise. Thomas looked attentively from one to the other, relieved to be superfluous for a moment.

"I have had the same kind of experience," she went on. "My father lives in Belgrade. I had not seen him for years, either. I have never really known him. But I would have preferred not to see him again."

"Were you disappointed?"

"Not just disappointed. How can I explain?... It was wrong. It disturbed me, it still disturbs me."

"How?"

"As if I ought to have been someone different. As if...," Tatiana searched for words. "Oh, well, never mind."

"I don't think so."

Tatiana looked her in the eyes.

"I mean it," insisted Irene.

Tatiana smiled. Thomas regarded her lovingly.

Someone called him, he turned abruptly. The smile vanished from Tatiana's mouth and she dropped her eyes. A woman in tight jeans and a red baseball cap stopped her bicycle beside their table. She wore the same color lipstick, bright red. She had pulled her ponytail through the strap at the back of the cap. She could be anywhere between twenty-five and forty. Even her smile was painted, thought Irene, and she talked through her bright red smile, now and then glancing at Tatiana. Sweat broke out on Thomas's upper lip as he answered the woman's empty questions about how things were in a slightly befuddled way. She asked about Magnus, too. Thomas reddened. Tatiana's bright eyes fixed on a distant point at the end of the street, apparently lost in thought, as she was sized up. After less than a minute, the woman was gone. One of Sally's friends, mumbled Thomas. The conversation came to a halt. Irene gathered up her bags and rose. Tatiana stretched out her hand and looked at her. Thomas rose, too, and kissed her on the cheek, a little too formally.

As she walked on down the street she pictured them at the café table. Exposed, she thought. Alone with the simple but significant fact that they were together. Thomas had told her how he had come to feel like a social outcast, whether because friends were standoffish or because of his own innate, almost nervous, shyness, increased a hundredfold by a bad conscience. Some of them condemned him, he knew—Sally hadn't neglected to let him know. Others seemed to be waiting, as if they were not quite certain whether they still knew him. As if he had been inseparable from the life he'd betrayed, almost inconceivable as a person outside the frame he had broken free from. Irene thought of the woman with the red cap. She would like to have stayed, and she would like to have heard what Tatiana had to say about her reunion with her father. She'd been surprised to hear herself come out with what she would otherwise hide from those around her, but something in Tatiana's expression had made it possible. An unexpected contact.

As Irene sat in her car opposite the anonymous apartment building in a side street off the Ringstrasse, she thought of what Tatiana had said. She wasn't afraid of being disappointed, but she was afraid, and not knowing what she might have to be afraid of didn't help. It was still early in the morning, but she had been waiting for nearly an hour. She had seen some of the residents coming out, well-dressed women and men ready for another day at the office. She had slipped into the lobby with the postman and found Samuel's name on one of the mailboxes. Perhaps he wasn't at home, perhaps he seldom went out. The idea of climbing the stairs and ringing his bell seemed as unlikely as walking on the moon. A laundry van parked at the curb, obscuring her view of the entrance. She got out and stood behind a tree. Soon afterward the laundry man returned with a canvas sack over his shoulder, and she got back into the car.

She hadn't been able to sleep the night before. The long drive had left her with a buzzing in her body, but fatigue would not turn into sleep. She didn't feel like watching television. She lay in the dark, listening to the ceaseless hum of the ventilation system in the hotel courtyard. The sound joined with the buzzing inside her in an enervating way. When she turned on the light she caught sight of Thomas's letter. The big envelope contained a postcard and a handful of photocopied typed pages. Thomas and Tatiana had been glad to meet her. He wrote "we." As she'd probably noticed, it was a difficult time, not the least for Tatiana. The enclosed pages were from Herbert's posthumous manuscript. They had come far enough to see there was insufficient material for a book after all, but Tatiana had asked him to send her this extract. When she read it she'd understand why. They wished her luck.

The postcard depicted a blank, white oval with a small peg in the middle. There was no mistaking it, even though the head, according to the caption on the back of the card, was several thousand years old. A human head and yet merely a little bud in space. Although it had no eyes, it seemed to be looking at her. She tried to remember Tatiana's features as she read Herbert Verhoeven's notes from Belgrade.

The student demonstrations against Milosevic had been going on for a couple of months. Herbert and Tatiana are staying at the Hotel Moscow. When they return at the end of the day they sit in the hotel café. Brown plush and liver-colored marble. A sleepy little orchestra, a violinist with dyed hair and bags under his eyes. Herbert has not been here since Tito's palmy days, and Tatiana hasn't been here since she was so little she can't remember it. But the Hotel Moscow hasn't changed.

He has come to write about the demonstrations, Tatiana to meet her father. She acts as his interpreter when they mingle with the crowd in the procession that sets out every day from the square in front of the philosophy department, a run-down concrete building like all the rest in this grimy town, where even the snow is gray. Rock music plays from a car stereo—Mick Jagger—it's like a carnival. Mick Jagger in Belgrade. A breath of hope in the raw cold, or is it just normal, irrepressible youth? One blends into the other on the way through the gray streets, echoing with the wild, shrill notes of thirty thousand penny whistles. Flags are flying everywhere, flags from all over the world, mostly for the sake of their colors, it seems. Carnival in Belgrade.

Tatiana translates what her contemporaries say in response to Herbert's many questions. She is frightened of the shoving, jostling wave of people, and Herbert is frightened at the responses. Their parents' and grandparents' stories seem closer to him than their own. Stories of the Ustashi, of the massacres of World War II, bad blood, but old. When the talk turns to Sarajevo or Srebrenica, there's always a "but." Are they angry with Milosevic for starting the war, or are they angry because he lost it? One question flows into the other.

One evening at the Hotel Moscow Tatiana sits quietly studying the red veins in the marble columns. What is she thinking? She thinks about what she is. What to reply if she's asked. Not Yugoslav, because there is no Yugoslavia anymore. Nor Serbian. Certainly not that.

Irene puts down the pages and looks at the postcard with the anonymous Cycladic head. A blind face, lifted and listening in silence as the hotel kitchen's exhaust fan hums mechanically.

She waited for an hour and a half in front of Samuel's entrance before he finally appeared. It had to be him. She got out of the car and followed the little man with white hair and a beige raincoat. He stopped to wait for a trolley at the Ringstrasse; luckily, other people were there. She didn't dare look at him in the streetcar, and when he got off the doors almost closed before she followed.

Soon she was sitting at a window table in the Bräunerhof, glancing at the man reading the newspaper, supposedly her father. Supposing she was wrong? She knew that wasn't so, and her stomach churned at the thought of addressing him. What language should she use? What should she say? He was her father, but he might just as well not be, after all those years. What could they have to say to each other?

The same thing happened two days in a row. She waited in the car in front of his entrance until he appeared. Today she went straight to the Bräunerhof. He arrives, nods to the waiter, picks up the paper, unbuttons his coat, sits down in his corner, and takes out his eyeglass case, hardly noticing the waiter serving him his coffee. If he recognizes her from the previous days he doesn't show it. Presumably he hasn't seen her at all. He might just as well be the only morning guest at the Bräunerhof. She might just as well be sitting in her office at home in Copenhagen, looking out at the chestnut tree in the courtyard, the clusters of soft, woolly leaves. They could just as well have gone on, each in their circle, each in their town, unknown to each other, but she has already risen to make her way across the room to him.

She stops, and he looks up as her figure blocks the scant daylight that reaches his table. She lifts the unlit cigarette she holds in her fingers, the oldest, worst excuse, and asks in English if he has a match. He looks at her blankly over his reading glasses, obviously still immersed in an article. Then he half turns towards the counter at the back of the room and calls the waiter, who immediately appears. She tries to catch his eye but he doesn't notice. He asks the waiter in German if he can assist the young lady with a match, and is already deep in his paper again as Irene gets her light.

She says thank you, in confusion, almost chokes on the smoke and returns to her place. "Young lady," what is he thinking of! Was he being gallant or rude? One thing blends into the other. Her coffee is cold. It's hopeless, the Bräunerhof is a blind alley. You don't walk up to a gentleman deep in his paper, introduce yourself, and say "Excuse me, Sir, but I believe you're my father." As on the two previous days, Samuel gets up when he's finished the paper, nods to the waiter, and leaves. He doesn't look in her direction, no doubt he's forgotten all

212

about her, and once more Irene watches his profile passing the window in the opposite direction.

She goes back to the hotel. In the afternoon she sits in the rose garden behind the castle. That's all she has seen of Vienna up to now: Schönbrunn, the Bräunerhof, and Samuel's street. She doesn't feel like seeing Vienna. She looks at the brightly colored roses as people stroll past, at ease with where they've come from and what they'll return to after this walk at Schönbrunn on an ordinary September day. She decides to write a letter. The evening sun glows red behind the curtain when she lowers her pen to the last sheet of hotel stationery. The rejected attempts lie about her on the carpet.

She writes:

Dear Mr. Balkin,
You may have noticed me at the Bräunerhof the last couple of days. I don't know how to introduce myself. You once knew my mother. This was during the war, before you and your family fled to Sweden. The night of your escape, you spent a few hours with her in her parents' house. I am the result of that last encounter. I will be at the Bräunerhof tomorrow.
Irene Beckman

At the front desk they promise the letter will arrive the next day. She leaves it with the concierge and takes the elevator up to her room. What if he doesn't come? At least he knows where he can find her. She wakes up late in the evening, relieved, buoyed by the thought that no one else knows exactly where she is. Vienna is a big city, and when Peter asked her she pretended she didn't know where she would stay. The hotel restaurant is closed, she orders a sandwich. The roll crumbles like dust in her mouth and she can't swallow a single mouthful. She

213

finds a small bottle of whiskey in the minibar, lights a cigarette, and sits down on the bed with Herbert Verhoeven's manuscript. She pictures Tatiana, her pale, calm, interested gaze.

One evening, Tatiana goes to see her father. Herbert is observing a demonstration at the Republike. Some of the protestors hold three fingers up in the air, the Serbian sign for victory. Herbert studies the middle-aged men and women; several of them have penny whistles hung from their necks like the young people. Is it indignation or just humiliation he sees in their faces? What do they think about Srebrenica, about Dayton? What do they hope for? A better world, a better car?

A nightclub, loud music, the ubiquitous whistles around the neck. Young people dancing close in the half darkness, just like everywhere else in the world. The revolution is one way to meet girls, writes Herbert. He chats up the bartender, who is a little older than Tatiana, broad-shouldered, even his face has muscles. Called up in '92. For the first week at the front he tried to aim off target. They were contemporaries, the Croats, comrades from the Yugoslav army. The next week he aimed to hit. So as not to get hit himself. He pours out slivovitz, on the house. Doesn't want to die for anyone or anything. Herbert persists. Again the same innocent smile in the eyes. All wars bring civilian casualties.

Herbert is almost asleep when Tatiana knocks. She lights a cigarette and sits down on his bed, tells him about the taxi driver who brought her back. The stubble on his shaven pate, the tattoo on his thick neck. Barbed wire or a crown of thorns?

It had been her grandmother's apartment, but she couldn't remember it, even though it didn't look as if it had changed in years. She describes it: glaring lighting, faded wallpaper, tattered furnishings. She could hardly recognize her father. He'd been drinking before she arrived. He embraced her, almost a stranger. There was a woman there, too, peroxide hair and plucked eyebrows. She talked intimately with him but didn't eat with them. Tatiana didn't find out whether she was just a lodger, as her father claimed. He asked about her mother, and she steered around the pitfalls; the conversation was sluggish. She didn't tell him about Herbert and Emma.

Herbert asks why. She shrugs and reaches for the brandy bottle on his bedside table. He's never seen a woman drink brandy out of the bottle before. Tatiana is freezing, the radiators at the Hotel Moscow are not even lukewarm, she gets into his bed, so only her face shows above the blanket. He's sitting in the armchair.

Her father went on and on about her mother in Stockholm. At one point he had to brush away a tear with the back of his hand. She found him pitiful, his sallow, flabby face; she felt nothing more, and it made her feel ashamed. Of him and of herself. The conversation kept threatening to grind to a halt. The bleach-blond woman sat at the other end of the apartment watching television. He obviously didn't know what to ask Tatiana, and Tatiana didn't know what to tell him. She asked why he had come back. What had there actually been to come back to? He looked aggrieved. It was his home, he was a Serb. She was not a Serb, she said. Yes, she was! His fist came down on the tablecloth. She should be proud of being a Serb, but she had lived too long in the West. He shouldn't have come home without her, that was his own fault. She'd been brainwashed with lies about the Serbs.

She asked whether Srebrenica was a lie. He rose and walked over to the window. Did she know what they'd done to her grandfather? He turned and drew a finger across his throat. She could find nothing but coarseness in his sodden face. She stood up. He went to embrace her, she fetched her coat. He rummaged in a drawer and took

215

out something that was wrapped in a scarf. She didn't look back as she went downstairs. It was a little figurine he had given her. She sat in the taxi studying Mary's masklike features to avoid looking at the driver's neck and the shabby, dismal town. She left the statuette on the back seat.

She shouldn't have come to Belgrade with Herbert. It would have been better if she'd contented herself with the idea of her father and the place she'd come from. It shouldn't be here. It shouldn't be him. Why is it so important anyway, who your father is?

Herbert repeats her question. She turns onto her back and looks up at the ceiling. She looks like a sick princess, her hair loosened on his pillow. It had made her feel removed, but also as if she had some kind of secret, unused capital, that she came from a different place. That she did not belong. Her remarkable name alone was a sort of mantra or jewel. Tatiana Pogorelic. It wasn't just that she was teased at school! She smiles at herself in the girlish self-effacing way Herbert can remember from when he first met her, a silent, confused fourteen year old. Long ago, he notes. Yet something in her humorous grimace is not the same as it was then. More feminine and more cynical at the same time. She has never felt she belonged, he writes. Some people don't, and if they are lucky they find each other. Is that something one of them says, or just something he thinks of in the armchair at the Hotel Moscow or later, bent over his portable typewriter?

She closes her eyes and curls up on her side. Why aren't you my father? That's the last thing she says, hoarse with fatigue and cigarettes, before she falls asleep. Her hair covers the part of her face that isn't buried in the pillow. A black-stockinged foot sticks out from the blanket. He thinks of all the times she has lain on the couch in his study reading or just watching him work. It didn't disturb him when she came, without a word, into the room with her blanket. Like a cat.

Far from it, he grew almost dependent on her presence nearby. He felt closer to her than to his own children, and he'd felt she understood him even when she was still a child. Not necessarily what he said, but who he was. He brought her up, he showed her the world, and she gave him her curiosity. He felt recognized, despite the years between them. As she gradually grew into adulthood he became accustomed to their easy mutual understanding, but for the first time he felt lonely in her company.

He feels an urge to caress her foot, its arch, but stays seated where he is. Something inside him has been dislocated, and only now does he understand it. He watched her grow beside him, saw her features maturing around the same eyes she had ever since he took her into his home on impulse. An old lover's lost, intractable child. There was a mute question in her gray-blue eyes, and he discovers it has become a question in himself. Why isn't he a different, younger man? He falls asleep in the armchair. When he wakes up, the winter sky is visible behind the curtain. She's not there. He goes back to bed, relieved, and in the pillow breathes the scent of an unknown young woman.

The letter was a mistake. She should have known that. Samuel did not turn up at the Bräunerhof the following day, nor the next. After she'd waited for an hour or two she drove to his street. The gate was open. She hesitated at the bottom of the stairs before walking up, but she could wait no longer. If he slammed the door on her she would simply go home. She rang the bell several times and had already turned around to leave when the door was opened a crack. A small woman in her sixties looked up at her suspiciously. She wore a pale blue apron and felt slippers. Herr Balkin had gone away. Irene had trouble understanding her florid Viennese accent. When? This morning.

217

She explained, embarrassed by her lack of fluency. She felt she sounded like a dull-witted schoolgirl. His daughter, really? The little woman smiled and invited her in. Herr Balkin had never mentioned that he had a daughter. Irene told her she was passing through and had tried to telephone. What a shame! The housekeeper looked at her, head to one side. She looked like her father, no mistake. Irene asked where he'd gone. She threw out her arms and smiled mischievously. It was hard to keep track of Herr Balkin. Irene asked if she could leave a message. Of course. She was shown to a desk by the window in the first room. She must take all the time she wanted. A vacuum cleaner started up in the next room.

She sat down at the desk. Around the walls were bookcases and old copperplate engravings, prospects of towns, portraits of composers. The floor was covered with dark green carpeting. Apart from the desk, there were a wingbacked armchair, a standard lamp, and a small octagonal Moroccan table inlaid with mother of pearl. The window was hung with two sets of curtains and daylight only infiltrated like a faded glow on the gold tooling of the picture frames and books. She spotted her own handwriting on the envelope pushed into a corner of the worn blotting pad. She pulled out the drawer. Writing paper, a bottle of ink, a pack of playing cards, the concert program for the autumn season of the Musikverein.

When she leaned back and stretched out her legs under the table, she happened to upset a cane wastepaper basket. She picked it up and caught sight of a scrunched-up envelope. She unfolded it. The name and address of a tourist office was printed on one corner. It had been postmarked in Vienna the previous day. The envelope contained a bill, with the lower part torn off where the payment slip had been. Samuel had bought a flight to Ljubljana. She picked up the telephone and dialed the office number. A Viennese waltz played as she waited to get through. She was lucky. They had made reservations at a hotel in Ljubljana for Herr Balkin. She noted "Grand Union Hotel" on the back of the envelope.

One hour later she leaves Vienna and drives due south on E59 to Zagreb. When she passes Graz the sun is disappearing behind the mountains. It's dark when she crosses the border, she can't see the landscape that was once part of Yugoslavia. She has a meal at a restaurant on the outskirts of Maribor and follows E57 southwest. The warm, crisp notes of the cello accompany her through the Slovenian night.

He won't get away, she won't let him off before he has looked her in the eye and uttered her name. She pictures his stooping figure, glasses resting on his nose, immersed in his daily newspaper at the Bräunerhof. He could be any elderly man. There's nothing for him to fear. They may not have much to say to each other, but it isn't a father she's after. It is the simple fact that he is her father. That he is her father whether or not she discovers a bond of sympathy. The simple, in itself meaningless, reality. It is reality that has fled yet again, escaped from her hands, and which she intends to corner at long last. It is not something neglected that she is trying to catch up with on the road between Maribor and Ljubljana. It is a departure that has been postponed for a long time, much too long. A leave-taking she has never arrived at.

After midnight she drives through the suburbs of Ljubljana, anonymous concrete in the sharp orange lights over the avenues. The Grand Union Hotel is a white building near the river. The receptionist speaks fluent English. Has Mr. Balkin arrived? He looks at his screen. Yes. Mr. Balkin arrived yesterday. Does she wish to leave a message? Irene shakes her head and asks for a wake-up call. She carries her bag up to the room herself. A glass door leads out to a small balcony. Behind the façade on the other side of the street, she glimpses a steep, tree-covered mountain crest. It is a clear, starry night, and the traffic has quieted down. The street runs out into a square farther away, and from the square three bridges lead across the river. There is hardly any space between the bridges, their white balustrades blend into each other from this perspective. On the shore between two of them, a group of poplars look like feathers in a hatband.

She wakes up of her own accord. Her voice is hoarse when she answers the call from the receptionist. She stays in bed for a little while looking out at the blank sky before taking a quick bath and getting dressed. In the bar adjoining the lobby, she finds a table from which she can see who goes in and out of the elevator. There's no one else in the bar. The walls are mint green; a fat little woman in a maid's uniform serves coffee. Irene has forgotten to put on her watch, she doesn't know how long she has been sitting here while the hotel guests come out of the elevator and pass across her field of vision. She listens to the voices around her speaking various languages. She picks up a newspaper from the neighboring table and studies the incomprehensible headlines and black-and-white pictures. Nevertheless, she must have been inattentive, for when she looks up again he's standing beside her table, newly shaven, with his lightweight coat over his arm.

"Will you allow me?"

He doesn't wait for an answer, lays his coat over the back of a chair and sits down opposite her, bent over and stooping. He rests his elbows on the arms of his chair, folds his wrinkled hands, and regards her wryly. He speaks Danish with an old-fashioned, educated diction that tempers his heavy accent.

"You are an obstinate young lady."

His deadpan look makes her smile. He turns to the bar, conscious that she is looking at him as he waits to make eye contact with the waitress, and with a little nod indicates that he wants to order. There is a touch of the cosmopolitan in his punctiliousness, as he asks in German which teas they serve, and after a fastidious pondering decides on Darjeeling. He could be any elderly man. What difference does it make, actually, who he is?

He turns toward her again.

"Do you live in Copenhagen?" He straightens a pleat in his trousers. "I must admit your letter perplexed me a little. Your mother, is she still alive?"

Irene nods.

"She doesn't know I am here."

"Sounds mysterious."

Irene tells him about Vivian's hip operation and the notebook from Lago Maggiore. He sips his tea, holding the saucer beneath the cup. She tells him about her childhood, about her stillborn twin brother, about Vivian's life. He brushes a speck of dust from his knee and puts down his cup.

"Do you have children?"

"They are grown up now. Peter and Josephine."

He nods, as if acknowledging the choice of names.

"And their father?"

"We've just been divorced."

He nods again. They sit for a while without saying anything. She was not prepared to be interrogated.

"It is long ago," he says. "Incidentally, you are a good-looking girl."

She can feel herself blushing.

"I'm sorry I embarrassed you."

221

Again he shoots her a mischievous glance.

"It is a bit late to have a daughter."

He looks out the window. Neither says anything. There is activity going on around them, the coffee machine churns, and the voices reverberate between the marble floor and the high ceiling. The sun is shining outside as if it were summer.

"Iris and Norman Roth said to say hello."

He looks at her again. "You have been busy."

"I took a long time to get started."

He makes a gesture with his wrinkled, liver-spotted hand. As if it is life he lacks the words for, at once frail and old in his freshly pressed trousers, with his newly ironed shirt and meticulously knotted tie.

"Do you know Ljubljana?"

She shakes her head.

"Good little town. I have performed here often. Perhaps we could take a short walk?"

It takes him a long time to get his arms into his coat sleeves, but she doesn't dare help him. She is a head and a half taller than he is; he notices it with a droll face. When they are outside he offers her his arm.

"It's a nice day, isn't it?"

They go on down the street, arm in arm; she adjusts her speed to his. When he can't find a word in Danish he falls back on English or German. They near the square with the three bridges. Up on the mountain there is a walled castle. Its rough-hewn stone gives it a forbiddingly medieval air.

He had forgotten the picture of himself and Rosa beside a canal in their home town, but he remembers his suit, the first one he ever had, with navy blue pinstripes. He couldn't have been more than fifteen. His father had tailored the suit for him with the last bolt of English worsted he had left. Slightly too big so there was room for growing into it. Stout woollen cloth, as good as impossible to wear out. There was a waistcoat to match. The blue garment accompanied him through the years in Denmark and Sweden, all the way to Haifa. When he arrived it was all he had, but of course it was too warm for the sub-tropical climate, and besides, the sleeves were getting shiny, even English wool had a shelf life.

Irene tries to picture Samuel in Haifa. A sweating young man in English wool with a cello case in his hand. She doesn't know how to imagine Haifa. A scent of oranges?

Not that the Jews in Leningrad were worse off than so many others in the years after the October Revolution, but it certainly wasn't easy. Anti-Semitism was forbidden, Samuel says with a crooked smile, but it was also forbidden to be a Jew. Perhaps not downright forbidden, but frowned upon. Newspapers were available in Yiddish, even poetry books, but the poems in them were all about tractors. They were hard times for a tailor, customers were scarce, and his father had to go to work in a textile factory. Bread, land, and peace, Lenin had promised. Samuel cannot remember whether it was in that precise order, but he remembers his father's horror and indignation when the Jews were encouraged to go to the Crimea and settle there as farmers. Did they want him to exchange his needle for a ploughshare?

Samuel had not given much thought to the fact that he was Jewish, even though his family kept the Sabbath and ate kosher. He had regarded his bar mitzvah as a formality. As a child he thought everyone was Jewish, and on the street of small merchants and workshops where they lived, most people were; but it was nothing to do with him. You could be a Jew, an Abkhasian, or a spiritualist, you could take your stand on the flight into Egypt, the dictatorship of the proletariat, or levitating tables, the music was the same, and to him music was everything. He practiced diligently when he was not at school, and his parents saved to pay his music teacher. Two evenings a week he sat in an unheated gymnasium playing in the Komsomol orchestra. He had already aroused notice. He had played the violin since he was six but when, at the age of eleven, he put his bow to a cello for the first time, his future was sealed. It was the contact, he explained, the vibrations that were transmitted to his chest and on through the whole of his body. You hold a violin away from you; it is more virtuous, platonic, as it were. Pure, sparkling spirit. With the cello you enter into a different physical relation, you play with your body.

From then on he thought of nothing but music, even when his contemporaries started to think about girls. Apart from his mother and his sister, the cello was the only being in his life resembling a woman. A chaste embrace, and yet melodiously filled with all the impulsiveness and idealism of his youthful nature. He was unusually gifted, and he knew it. His first teacher had already taught him what he could, and he'd started taking lessons with a noted soloist when the first shock changed his life.

He had gradually separated himself from family life, although his mother and sister were always around in the cramped apartment. They were mere shadows, like cows grazing in a meadow when you pass by deep in thought, and he entrenched himself for hours with his cello in his parents' small bedroom. They spoke in low voices behind the door and refrained from making any noise; his mother went so far as to spread straw in the courtyard where a milkman stabled his horses. Their respect for his talent was only surpassed by their anxiety when he forgot to eat dinner and joined them late in the evening, with hair on end. Estranged, although they themselves had created him. Like a golem.

When a distant uncle in Copenhagen offered his father a partnership in his uniform factory his parents decided to leave. Samuel does not remember that, he didn't take part in the preparations—as usual completely lost in his music. The family traveled to Copenhagen via Helsinki. As he remembers it, he became an adult when he first encountered the strange town. He had lived in a state of childish innocence, immersed in music, but he'd been able to forget everything about his surroundings only because they were so reassuringly familiar. Here he felt naked and exposed as never before, reduced to stammering like a two year old in a new language. It soon became clear that the uncle had promised them better things than he could guarantee, and Samuel's father was obliged to start from scratch in a basement shop. They lived in a ground floor apartment, three cramped rooms over the shop, and for the first time Samuel realized they were poor.

He thought about that when he walked through the strange, glittering town, past the shops where you could gratify your deepest wishes providing you had the money. He felt shabby, although he looked respectable in his dark blue suit, which he filled out perfectly now. But the suit made him feel like a spy in disguise when he saw the elegant people on the main shopping streets and observed their self-assured manner, as if everything good in the world was naturally theirs. He didn't notice that there were others besides his family who were also relegated to a dingy, miserable existence. He only saw the sunny, carefree life that seemed beyond his reach, and when he went home to the dark side street it was with a feeling that this was where he belonged, in the shadows. In Leningrad he had merely shrugged his shoulders and acknowledged he was a Jew, but in Copenhagen he came to equate Jewishness with poverty. It didn't help that, on the rare occasions he allowed himself to be persuaded to go to synagogue with his father, he realized that there were also rich Jews. Their sleek courtesy seemed assumed, like another luxury they allowed themselves, and he thought that he and his father were nothing but Jews of the Jews.

But unlike his father, Samuel did not have to start all over again. He was accepted at the Academy of Music and was even allowed to skip the first two years. Again he sought refuge in music, not like a dreaming child confidently turning his back on his secure environment, but like a young man doggedly confronting a strange and possibly hostile world with the only weapon he knew how to master.

The cello, a weapon?

He smiles at her question. They've stopped midway across one of the three white bridges extending from the same point on one bank. He leans against the balustrade looking down at the river, as if trying to fix a whirlpool with his gaze. Irene thinks of the young man in the dark suit, his face in the photograph from Leningrad erased, so that only the smile is left. Is it really the same man who stands on a bridge in Ljubljana leaning over the river, the same one who once walked the streets of Copenhagen? Those streets she knows so well.

Yes, he replies, a weapon. He thought only of shining, making them submit, those strangers who belonged here, his slightly older fellow students and amazed teachers—any of those cool, low-voiced, and controlled natives, smiling and slippery as soap. When he was on the trolley he was merely a stocky, swarthy Jew-boy who was barely tolerated if he was noticed at all, and he didn't know which was worse. But when he played he could make even the chilliest Danes clap like passionate gypsies. Although he was still at the academy he'd begun to give concerts, and for years his mother kept a newspaper clipping with a picture of him bent over the cello. She never learned to read what the caption said.

At nineteen he was an acrobat on his instrument. His playing was supreme, dazzling, and heartless. It was a true master, perhaps the greatest of all, who made him see the limitations of his apparently un-limited freedom. Pablo Casals visited the academy as a visiting pro-fessor and gave a series of concerts. It was the first time Samuel had heard Bach's cello suites. Before Casals began to play them they had long been regarded as tedious academic exercises. He told the young cellists how he'd found the music in an antiquarian shop in Barcelona, when he was looking for some short pieces for his repertoire as a café musician. He had the students play one of the suites, and when Samuel had presented his virtuoso interpretation, Casals laid a kindly hand on his shoulder. "Who are you playing for?" he asked in French. Confused, Samuel looked into his olive green eyes. "You are playing for yourself," the Spaniard continued with a quiet smile. "Follow the music," he said, "you don't have to force it."

The bald maestro put his bow to the instrument and played a few bars of the piece Samuel had whirled through. The master followed the music, opened himself to it, and allowed it to flow unhindered. Samuel felt Bach's gamut of notes transmitted as if they were communicating vessels, the old German, the little magician from Barcelona, the Jew from Leningrad, and his Danish fellow students. It dawned on him that he had been concentrating all his practice and effort on mastering the music and making it his own instead of accepting it and sharing it with others. In those few bars, before Casals lowered his bow and smiled at them, he understood that music is not a message but a gift. That it is not a matter of revealing and expressing one's precious self, but of giving way to it, losing oneself and becoming one with something more comprehensive and universal. From that day, he would keep returning to the cello suites. Their blend of poetry and mathematics became a lifelong spiritual exercise. The cello suites were the core of Bach, and Bach was the core of music.

He was not only becoming a better musician, he himself was changing. Until then he had kept to himself and regarded the other students as a necessary evil. He had despised them because his mastery of the cello was so much greater than theirs, and he imagined they envied him, but his imaginings proved to be a defense against his own envy. A superfluous defense. He learned their language, and he discovered that they wanted to talk to him. Music had opened up for him, but it had also opened the door onto another world. A brighter, easier life than the one he had known. He began to believe this life could be his, as he cycled along the coastal road with his new friends and lay in the sun smoking cigarettes, watching girls, and dreaming of the future.

The war disturbed him in the middle of a cello suite by Bach, in the midst of his surrender to the lightness. He looked up at the alien airplanes in amazement, when they roared overhead one spring morning in heavily droning formations. They were not his concern, and for a long time he almost succeeded in ignoring both the German soldiers and the growing anxiety of his parents. He refused to be affected by the rumors that ran from home to home among the Danish Jews, his life had nothing to do with theirs. He left the academy, his debut concert aroused attention, he was engaged by the National Radio Orchestra, and he fell in love.

There had been other girls in the light summer nights, but none of them meant more than a pleasant, vapid tingle, and none of them could compete with the cello. Ironically enough, he met Vivian at the same time as he met the instrument that was to be his only lasting life companion.

He closes his eyes in the glimmering light on the river. His combed-back hair shines white in the September sun. The breeze shakes the yellowing leaves. They are sitting at one of the little cafés under the bay windows and galleries; around them people are talking. Neither he nor Irene can understand what they say. She observes his pronounced features, the folds of skin and rays of wrinkles around his screwed-up eyes. It is warm, he has taken off his coat and hung it loosely over his shoulders. He turns to her as if he recognizes her anew with a surprised smile.

It was an honor, greater than any other distinction, to play that cello, one of the most precious treasures of the orchestra. A Ruggieri. She pretends never to have heard the name before. It was red as a pomegranate under the old varnish, and when he put his bow to the

229

strings and felt the finely crafted poplar transmitting its vibrations to his chest, he knew he had found his soul mate. "It was the same feeling," he says, slipping the lump of sugar he has dunked in his coffee into his mouth, "the same joy as when I embraced your mother for the first time."

Behind him, Irene can see the three white bridges and the poplars on the river bank rising between the balustrades. The moon is just visible, wasted and frayed in the empty blueness above the pine-clad slope.

Ljubljana. What a long way they have come for their meeting.

Ruggieri was one of the most eminent instrument makers in the world and one of the first to develop the model upon which no one has ever been able to improve. After a while, the instrument molded itself to Samuel's playing, until they became one, resounding with music.

"Perhaps the same thing could have happened to your mother and me." He lowers his eyes and catches the sunlight in the little concave mirror of the teaspoon.

Old instruments have a soul of their own, he explains, and string instruments wear better than human beings. There are cellos in existence that have been broken and put back together again, and the sound is still the same.

Vivian sounded something similar in him, a string deep inside him, which he had never heard before. She was the most beautiful girl he had ever seen, and he could only stand and stare in a corner of the garden where he saw her for the first time. It was on a summer evening north of the town, he had been invited along by a friend. Her future husband, as it later turned out. He casts a brief glance at Irene. Otherwise he didn't know any of the elegant young people gathered in festive groups by the rose bushes between the garden and the shore.

It was the sort of evening that never gets dark; rather like the white nights of his home town, when you feel you are hovering weightlessly.

He dared not speak to her; it was Vivian who suddenly met his eye, went up to him, and asked who he was. He was ashamed of his accent and his too-dark, too-heavy woollen suit, but she merely smiled, self-assured yet approachable, the one an enviable prerequisite for the other. She even encouraged him, beaming with the goodwill of the affluent, as he stood there mumbling his clownish words. He fell in love on the spot, and before the evening was over he had declared his love for her. Where did he find the courage? Not in her upper-class smile, nor in the knotted heart of the Jew-boy that had swung so drastically between arrogance and inferiority. But where else? They were down by the jetty, alone at last. The water was calm and smooth and the lights of Sweden, where there was no war, sparkled across the sound. First she was smiling, then she grew serious, and he hastened to kiss her before she could run away.

It lasted for about a year. The happiest of his life.

Irene can see them standing on the jetty beside the sound, the young Samuel and Vivian, but she needs the help of the pictures. The blurred photo of Samuel and his sister, the one of Vivian at the edge of the sea, smiling and pregnant. A wonder, she thinks, that the two pictures have ever touched one another. What if Vivian hadn't gone to meet him with a smile beside the roses? A chance impulse like so many others, thinks Irene. She never would have been born. Her life, her own children, her will and her insufficiency. Another man, another child could have been in her place, if Vivian had ignored the unknown guest on that summer night.

When, hesitant and a little surprised, she returned his kiss or just let him put an arm around her shoulders when they were out walking, she made him feel like a man. Not a Jew-boy from the back

231

streets with shiny, worn sleeves, not a solitary, dogged genius, just a young man. Indistinguishable from the other young men walking in the sunshine with an arm around a girl's slim shoulders. She admired his talent and his knowledge, the extraordinary education, but she was also remarkably passive. When the weather was good they sometimes went out to the Deer Park and lay hidden in the tall grass. He caressed her as she gazed dreamily up at the clouds, but it was like caressing a marble goddess. A Greek goddess, breathing, yes, warm and soft, far from cold and impervious to him, yet seeming not to notice the adoration of his wandering hands.

If you can't say yes, sometimes it's because it is just as hard to say no. Irene thinks of another girl who once stayed at a villa outside Nice, allowing another young man to fumble his way to her. Another girl, but the same hesitation. The same passive wonder that an insistent young man wanted her with such determination, precisely this one and no other.

It was a dream he awoke from one autumn night when he kissed her farewell and was ferried over to Sweden with his family and the other Jews packed together beneath the deck of a cutter smelling of fish. But despite the drama he did not know he was awake. He dreamed of the girl day and night, the girl he had left on the other side of the sound.

Perhaps it had been a dream from the start. Young women can be so silent, and their silence can seem so mysterious, he says with a smile. It can so easily make young men dream of more reality than a young woman's life can hold.

Irene smiles back. For the most part, he was the one who talked. He had even succeeded in persuading himself not to take account of her anxiety, or what it might make her think in secret. Young women can be so romantic, but they can also be very sensible, much more sensible than a young man can be.

He had noticed that she was afraid of what her parents thought. He noticed it chiefly from the faraway look in her eyes when he fantasized about their shared future. That only made him fantasize himself even further away from what she knew and was capable of imagining, making him feel like a passing guest. As if he could talk himself out of the fact that he was the son of a Jewish tailor from Russia. No one must know they were meeting, she said. That should have made him think, but he was only too glad to have her to himself.

He thought about Vivian when he was practicing, and he thought of her when he wasn't. He'd been unable to let go of the cello; he and it had become one. Every single fiber in its body of ancient poplar and spruce had adapted itself to him. Every cell in his young body had learned to oscillate with its most imperceptible vibrations, and he couldn't bear the thought of anyone else distorting its voice. The cello's register corresponds to that of the human voice, he explains. The tone of the Ruggieri had become as intimate as the sound of his own voice.

He comes to a stop and suddenly looks at her stiffly, chin raised. Irene is taken aback at his expression, until it dawns on her that she is meeting the defiant look of a young man. It is the young Samuel behind the old man's cultured mask who looks her in the eye. There is something hard, almost ruthless in his face, and she realizes her father must have been a street fighter.

"My daughter, the lawyer, probably thinks I ought to have duly returned my cello when the war was over."

His accent and cracked voice make her laugh.

"Yes, I am a common thief, if you like. I kidnapped it. Others would say I liberated it." He rests an elbow on the café table and stretches out his fingers. "You can count them on one hand, the musicians who would have deserved to play it, I'll be modest and say in Europe. Just Europe. And in all modesty I must confess to being one of them. And I can't conceive how such a magnificent example could have gotten lost in that absurd afterthought of a country. I mean, the orchestra... It was like playing with monkeys. Their string section, God help me, they might as well have been playing the saw. I released Ruggieri from his prison."

"I've heard you play."

He raises his eyebrows.

"When?"

"On the way here."

She tells him about Dennis and the record he copied.

"I've never been satisfied with that recording. But that is not Ruggieri's fault." He smiles a sly, boyish smile and empties his coffee cup. "I don't have the certificate, I don't know who played it before me, but sometimes I try to picture its journey from Cremona up through the centuries, around Europe, through the salons of princely courts and the concert halls of ancient towns until it ended up in my arms on a fishing boat bound for Sweden."

They were interned in a camp, but he could not endure walking around in circles surrounded by frustrated Jews complaining about the food and passing the time quarreling over what the future might bring. He, who had allowed himself to forget what he had been and where he had come from. He had dreamed of carving his own destiny out of music and love and nothing else. He found a clump of fir trees a little way from the camp. He sat there playing, sitting on a block of granite among the rustling spruces.

He became a Zionist out of heartache.

When he returned after the Liberation, he heard Vivian had married and had had a child with his friend. He felt no bitterness, strangely enough. One Sunday, as he stood in the Botanical Gardens watching them with the stroller, he realized that his love had been a dream. He had no one but himself to blame for not having woken from it before. Walking with their child in the gardens, they looked like they belonged together. The picture was complete. It was he who didn't belong in it. That Sunday marked the end of his youth, but something else had happened as well. He could not stay in Copenhagen. He had become a Jew again and it was no longer a question of what he allowed himself to forget, what he chose to acknowledge or defy.

The young couple with the stroller couldn't help the fact that he was a Jew. His friend had even introduced his family to some courageous people who saw to it that they were taken away to safety, now that the only thing to do with Jews was to help them escape. But he never wanted to be taken to safety by courageous people again.

He heard what they had been doing to the Jews as he sat on his stone in Sweden playing Bach's cello suites. He knew why he'd been taken to safety, but just as he felt no bitterness toward his kindhearted friend and successor, he saw no need to feel grateful either. True, his former friend couldn't help the fact that Samuel was a Jew, but nor could Samuel himself help it. And he didn't want to be a victim or possible victim once again because of something he couldn't change.

He arrived in Palestine in August 1945, on one of the illegal refugee ships, with Jews from the English and American zones in Germany. He arranged passage on a freighter from La Spezia; the Italian harbor authorities shut their eyes, but there was no certainty of arriving successfully. Palestine was still a British mandate, and the British had blocked Jewish immigration. Most of the ships were intercepted by the British fleet, and stories circulated of Jewish immigrants interned in Cyprus, kept behind barbed wire in the blazing sun with no water. But he was lucky, and one morning before sunrise he was put ashore on a beach near Haifa with his fellow passengers. Irene pictures them, the exhausted, bewildered flock in the gray morning light on a beach in the Middle East. What kind of life awaited them there?

During the voyage he had listened to survivors' tales of the death camps. He looked at them, tradesmen, officials, dentists, or musicians like himself. Some had lived in villages in Poland, Hungary, or Romania, surrounded by other Jews, some had lived in Berlin, Prague, or Vienna without taking much interest in their background. But regardless of the differences between them and what had interested them or not, they had been Jewish the whole time. Condemned to annihilation. It wasn't thanks to some reprieve that they'd set out across the Mediterranean in a rusty ship heading for a place they knew only from the Bible.

He pauses and looks at Irene as if to apologize for his sharp tone. For the first time since she read Vivian's notebook, it occurs to her that she must be part Jewish herself. Although she once heard that one's mother must be a Jew for it to count. Does it mean anything? She can choose for herself, but Samuel couldn't choose. What does it mean? It would have meant nothing to him if he hadn't been disturbed in the middle of Bach and Vivian, and forced to flee. When all he wanted was to turn his back on everything he knew and everything that lay behind him. To be nothing but what he aspired to be. Something more comprehensive and universal.

He met Hannah in '48, the year Israel came into being. He had taken part in the war of independence, had been wounded in the battles of the Negev Desert against the Egyptian army, and had to spend a month in a camp hospital. She was a nurse, a gentle, slightly

236

plump girl from Krakow. When she changed his bandages he could see the number on her arm. An odd number in the sequence, rather indistinct, deeply ingrained in her pale skin. One of the other nurses told him her parents and siblings had disappeared at Auschwitz. She often sat with him when she wasn't busy.

They spoke Yiddish together, and later on Hebrew—as a symbolic gesture to begin with, like two industrious schoolchildren. They told each other where they had come from, stories about Leningrad and Krakow. Their new country was surrounded by enemies, but it was childhood they talked about in the brief fragmentary exchanges that broke their calm silence. He felt at ease in her company; he didn't know why. Every afternoon he lay waiting for her to appear and he discovered, to his surprise, that he was disappointed if she didn't come. She was the one to whom his circling thoughts returned like a reassuring center in the whirl of violent events in which he sometimes felt he was about to drown.

He felt guilty in a wordless way at the thought of the number on her arm and the vigor of her body in the nurse's uniform. A week after he had been discharged he stood waiting outside the camp hospital. It didn't seem as if she'd expected to see him again. They went for a long walk and she took him home. She squeezed orange juice for him, they listened to the radio, he told her about music. That night he became her lover. He felt he could get what he wanted from her. She submitted at once to his gentle advances on the divan in her little room, surprised but acquiescent.

She had no one but him. For a while they lived on a kibbutz in Galilee. She thrived, but he was unable to reconcile himself to putting down his cello every day and getting up on a tractor. It was bad enough that once a year, like all the men, he was called up for a stint in the reserves. They settled in Tel Aviv, he was hired by the Israel Philharmonic, she became pregnant. It was a busy life, but simple. He often traveled with the orchestra, she worked in a hospital and looked after the boy. When he was on tour he sent postcards. Not that he had much to say, but he felt an unwonted peace and warmth when he wrote her name and address under yet another foreign stamp. It had become his home, an apartment in a new building in Tel Aviv, near the sea.

A home. A woman and a man, a child. Irene finds herself thinking of Vivian and the young intern, their small apartment near the Municipal Hospital and the Botanical Gardens. She also thinks of the building in the leafy suburb where she and Martin lived during Peter's early years. She thinks of her new apartment with its view of the Jewish cemetery and of Samuel's room in Vienna with its wing-backed chair and the octagonal Moroccan table. A home is only a temporary place to stay, though one seldom gives that a thought.

Hannah was a quiet woman. There was a vulnerability in her eyes, strangely at odds with her comfortable figure and assured, confident way of moving and acclimating. She was practical and not very introspective, merely quiet, and he felt safe at her side. They kept to themselves, and even as time went by he never spoke of his family in Denmark, afraid of reminding her that she had no family. He was on tour in America when he received the news of his father's death. When his mother died a few years later Hannah was ill, and he chose to stay at home to look after the boy. Later he lost touch with Rosa; but actually, did they ever have anything to say to each other? Music had always come between them, and to him it had always come first. Vivian had been the only exception. The exception that proved the rule. He lived for music and for the child, in that order, and Hannah seemed to find it natural.

He made a couple of recordings with chamber ensembles, but did not feel the urge to launch out into a solo career. He was content to be an anonymous member of the orchestra, content with his peaceful life, the three of them sitting over their supper on the balcony or walking beside the sea on Saturdays. He had never been in love with her. Copenhagen already felt very distant. He was quite simply bound to her, and not only on account of the child. It was the mute, unguarded tenderness in her eyes. It could make him rise to go over and embrace her and clasp her tightly in his arms. She didn't push him away, her arms held him lightly around the waist until he released her and let her get on with what he had interrupted.

Samuel takes out his wallet and hands her a black-and-white photo.

"I still have it."

Irene studies the woman in the picture. Hannah Mandelbaum. An attractive, plump young woman with short black curly hair, smiling at the photographer.

"Where was it taken?"

"Dizengoff, Tel Aviv."

She stands under an awning, her pale face reflecting the strong sunlight on the asphalt. She wears a dark dress with white dots. They look like snowflakes drifting down from the shadow beneath the awning to land around her feet. She smiles with her head on one side, slightly forced, almost apologetic, as if wondering why it's taking Samuel so long to focus. A handbag hangs from one bent arm, she keeps the other behind her back, awkwardly. It makes Irene think of the number on her arm. She doesn't want that in the picture, doesn't want to have it stamped into the grains of film that will capture her features. All that will remain of this sunny day in Dizengoff.

"She's two months pregnant. There's nothing to see yet."

Irene gives him back the picture. He glances at it, returns it to his wallet, and puts it in his inside pocket. They sit for a while in silence.

"I always wanted a brother."

He leans forward in his chair and looks down at the cobbles and his shiny toe caps.

"Tell me about Avi," she says.

He looks at her.

"You know his name."

He leans back again and closes his eyes, as if he is just sitting by himself, enjoying the sun like any other elderly gentleman.

"What shall I tell you?"

"Tell me about when he was a child. What did you do on a day like this?"

He gazes at the river and the trees, and for a moment she doesn't know if he has heard her.

"In September we could still swim. If it's a Saturday we would certainly be at the beach. Hannah didn't like lying on the beach, so she stayed at home. We would always get a drink first from the lemonade man who parked his van under a palm tree. Sometimes you could get balloons, too. Avi liked the red ones best."

He never kept them for long, they always flew away from him. He cried, and it didn't help when he burned his feet on the hot sand. Samuel had to carry him to the edge of the sea. They stood in the waves, hand in hand. His little one was sticky and rough from the lemonade and sand. He screamed and laughed when the waves came in, forgetting he'd lost his balloon. They discussed where it might have flown. A tiny red dot high above. That's how they would pass a Saturday.

Irene and Samuel follow the river to the marketplace where the vendors are packing up their wares. Pumpkins and corncobs, long pointed paprika in bunches, brown mushrooms the size of a child's head. A dog comes up and wags its tail, sniffing at Samuel's coattails. He bends down to pet it, stiffly, and pulls gently at its loose-skinned neck. They walk through a terraced arcade where other old men sit on folding chairs chatting. Samuel looks down at the river and tries to catch sight of something.

They saw each other for the last time one Saturday night in the spring of '67, at the bus station in Tel Aviv. Samuel wanted to buy some fruit. Avi was shuffling his feet, a broad-shouldered, short-haired young man in a green uniform with a rifle over his shoulder. He'd been home on leave and was going back to camp. Eighteen and embarrassed by his fussy father, determined to buy him bananas. Maybe he left them behind in the bus that rumbled up through the cypress-covered hills. Soon they would be indistinguishable from the darkness. It gets dark so quickly in the Middle East. Maybe he gave his father's bananas to a pasty-faced Hassidic Jew with a fur cap and ringlets. Or did he eat them after all?

They had known for a long time that another war was on the way. The Syrians shelled Galilee from the Golan Heights and Nasser was deploying troops in the Sinai Peninsula and Gaza. The army mobilized and Samuel was called up to active duty. At the end of May the streets were empty and the towns quiet at night. Everyone held their breath, waiting. It broke out at the beginning of June. Six days later Israel had triumphed on all fronts and taken Sinai, East Jerusalem, the West Bank, and Golan.

"He died on the 9th of June. During the offensive on Golan. But he was never involved in any fighting, it was an accident."

"An accident?"

Samuel hesitates before meeting her eyes.

"A bulldozer. They used bulldozers to force their way up the heights toward the Syrian positions. A frontal attack, a crazy stunt, but it worked."

They sat by the radio in silence, Hannah and Samuel, when it was all over. They listened to the radio a lot, the familiar silence between them had become unbearable. He called in sick and stayed at home with her during the time that followed. They were lost for words, their new language was too intractable, could not contain them. All he could do was lie beside her in bed and hold her close.

Two years later he was called to the telephone during a rehearsal. Hannah had been found at the bottom of their stairwell, she'd broken her neck. They lived on the top floor, she had carefully locked the door behind her before she climbed over the banister and jumped. He can't remember anything from that day or the days just before. They'd had breakfast, he'd read the paper. They'd talked a bit before he left. She hadn't seemed any different, everything was as usual. An ordinary day.

They walk along an avenue of villas through patches of sunlight under the gold leaves. Samuel points out the opera house, a small but stately building with Greek columns. He searches for words in Irene's language, unused since his youth. They have kept a place for themselves though, the words, stored in a distant fold of his memory. He speaks more slowly, with longer pauses, but without a trace of grief or nostalgia. He merely relates. It's all so long ago. Irene was only a child when he started a family in his new country, still a young woman when he lost it again.

He asks if she's hungry, and smiles at her puzzled expression when he points to a villa behind a latticed gate, whitewashed and modern in an outdated style. There's a restaurant on the top floor. They sit on the terrace. A tall pine tree shades them from the sun, and Irene can see a distant mountain ridge covered with spruce trees. He orders mushrooms in olive oil, garlic, and parsley. They're good here, he tells her, the mushrooms, they grow on the mountain slopes. Sometimes you can get air-cured bear meat. There are still bears in the forests. He's cosmopolitan again as he pours white wine into her glass with a slightly shaky hand. She thinks of Hannah and Avi. The quiet woman who had seen her family vanish in a cloud of smoke over Auschwitz. The boy who loved lemonade and red balloons.

It seems as if he can read her mind. He speaks quietly, clearing his throat now and then before continuing, hesitantly, in his rusty voice and mangled accent. There is so much one does not remember. You have to make do with the bits and pieces that are left. Do they amount to an explanation? He doesn't know. He cannot know.

Once, he had lured her down to the beach. It was a splendid, boiling hot day, and there were crowds of people. They rented a beach umbrella; she sat under it with a long-sleeved blouse over her swimsuit, he lay in the sun. It was the year before Avi was born. They still didn't really know each other. He isn't sure he ever got to know her. She was always friendly, always patient and helpful to others, but he could seldom get any insight into what she was thinking. Her thoughts remained a mystery, he only felt them, but he grew familiar with her nature. The shyness and what she shielded with her reserved manner. He was in the dark about her. He never managed to get through to the real person and had to be content with feeling her presence, recognizing her with his fumbling hands. Only at night would she open up to him, wordlessly, with a sudden, swift passion.

He has never forgotten that summer day by the sea. He kept encouraging her to lie in the sun, she was so white, but she preferred to sit in the shade. He teased her, she laughed good-naturedly, and in the end he tickled her and she rolled around like a puppy. She was very ticklish. In the midst of their mock fight he managed to pull off her blouse. She threw herself on top of him and grabbed desperately at the blouse, it wasn't fun any more. He was amazed at her frantic rage. When he let go she pulled the shirt over her head and jerked down the sleeves feverishly, beside herself. She had tears in her eyes. He tried to dry them, and stroked her back to soothe her, but she was inconsolable, just sat looking out at the waves, knees drawn up under her and arms firmly crossed.

In the end, he left her alone and went for a walk on the beach. He thought it might calm her down if he bought her an ice cream. As he looked around at the suntanned people playing with beach balls or lying on their towels, he suddenly realized what had happened. He passed a man standing at the water's edge gazing out over the sea, fat as a barrel, and as the man shielded his eyes from the sun with a hand, he glimpsed the little row of numbers branded on his arm. If you kept a lookout you would be sure to find more people like Hannah and the fat man on a summer day like this on the beach at Tel Aviv, but they were absorbed into the bigger picture. It resembled every other beach in the Mediterranean, an ordinary beach full of ordinary people enjoying the sun and the sea, yet this was not a beach like all the others, the bigger picture was misleading.

It was a defiant exception, the picture of relaxed, suntanned people in bathing suits. This was a hard-won piece of land, wrenched from a fate that had intended something different. Only a stubborn act of will had made it possible for the branded Jews here to be able to mix with those who had not been branded, play with beach balls, gambol in the waves, or bask in the sun. Whether they had a number printed on their flesh or, like him, had escaped that thanks to luck and kindhearted people, the beach at Tel Aviv would never be like the fashionable beaches on the other side of the sea, like Nice or

Cannes, where no one would ever have any reason to question their natural right to sprawl around so unself-consciously.

Hannah soon regained her composure when they were eating their ice cream under the parasol, but he understood that he'd unwittingly exposed something that she, with her reticent nature, tried to keep hidden. Something more than the dark number on her white arm. It increased his urge to protect her, and it made him feel lonely. At that time he couldn't have found the words to explain this, either to himself or to her. The subject never arose, they never spoke of the indefinable something that lived its own life in the silence between their affectionate, everyday exchanges.

The silence was noticeable in a new way when Avi was no longer there. Many years later he asked himself if it was simply the silence that had spread behind her pale, shy face and so undermined her that the day came when she could no longer keep her feet—only fall in a long, floating moment, until the silent void within her became one with the silent emptiness at the bottom of a Tel Aviv stairwell.

She was ashamed of her branded arm, even though others had suffered the same experience. To her, there was no mitigation in that community of fate. It wouldn't have been enough to defy the wordlessness; perhaps she was too shy. To begin with, he thought it must be the brooding shame of the survivor confronted with the thought of those who had not survived. He knew it, too, but as a shame directed at both dead and living. He couldn't meet a healthy, well-fed person like the fat, suntanned man by the sea and see what the man made no attempt to hide without feeling strangely ashamed. As if Samuel could help having been merely grazed by history. As if he was responsible for his good fortune. But for Hannah it must be another, deeper shame. Not just the question of whether one of the disappeared had deserved to survive in her place. Who could know that? Who does not deserve to live? If there was an answer, only God would know it, and if God held the answer, Samuel would have nothing to do with him.

He didn't believe Hannah was ashamed in the face of the dead. She was ashamed in the face of the living. She was ashamed of what they had done to her, as if she was responsible for her bad luck, and Samuel came to share her shame. He had no words for it as yet. He didn't find the words until it had been too late for quite some time, but the silence had been collusive, he realized afterward. Her silence and his own. And there is something he still lacks the words for. Words like harm, and endless, lonely horror are not enough for the nameless thing he noticed in Hannah when she clung to him at night. There are things one doesn't try to find an explanation for.

He was embarrassed by her shame. Perhaps it had more to do with humiliation. He came to feel embarrassed by the humiliation she had suffered, and he was ashamed because she hadn't managed to recover from that humiliation. It already sounds so unreasonable, doesn't it? So unreasonably hard to understand.

Could he have saved Hannah if, together, they had found words for what is worse? Only God knows that, but he doesn't believe in God. There was in any case a mute shame in the fact that, although she'd been luckier than others, she was one of those who were suited for victimhood. There was a kind of modesty in concealing the fact that you belonged to those who had not deserved to live. She was changed by the knowledge that human beings had wanted her dead and had taken such painstakingly elaborate measures to achieve their aim. People like herself and everyone else. It left behind it a question she hadn't the strength to answer, even after she'd been rescued. That's the difference between a woman like Irene and a woman like Hannah. It is also the difference between Nice and Tel Aviv, even if the palm trees are the same.

She didn't lack courage, though, and when Samuel saw her with the newborn Avi on her strong, young, numbered arm, he himself came to believe that life, the small life in her embrace, would prove stronger than all the muteness, all the shame and horror. A life like everyone else's. They came to believe it. They came to a belief that one day Avi would meet a girl, a sabra like himself, and have children who would still be around when they were no longer there. Like everyone else, they managed to believe, too, that their new country would one day be an ordinary one and not a defiant exception. For eighteen years they trusted this. Long enough to overestimate the viability of faith in a country won through defiance.

They lost faith. Others did not, others who, like her, had lost everything in advance. Others who, like him, had only been grazed. Others who, like them, had lost a son. The others endured, doggedly and bravely, despite war, despite the rockets that fell on Galilee, despite the armed men who landed on the beaches at night, seeking to kill whomever they could. The others merely grew more staunchly hardened in the faith that they were entitled to this foothold of land, but there was one thought he could neither think aloud nor stop thinking: he could not stop thinking of his new homeland as a land for the shamefully unwanted, armed to the teeth with their ugly, lonely ruthlessness. He knew that Hannah and he were not the only ones to lie awake at night, but none of them could share their grief with the others, wordless as they were in the silence that spread among them.

The waiter pours the last of their wine and removes their plates. They gaze at the Slovenian mountains and the pine trees below the terrace. Irene pictures Hannah, the woman in the picture from Dizengoff, still young, with Avi on her arm. It's not difficult. She thinks of Peter and Josephine, of their early childhood, when she could carry them and hold one of their small feet in her hand. Hannah had known the same feeling of a perfectly formed but tiny foot against the palm of her hand. A child's foot like any other. Both Hannah and Vivian—and Irene and Peter—had held such a little foot in their hand, and they must have felt the same. The same courage. We don't know each other, she thought, but the feel of a child's foot is the same, and in brief moments of synchronicity all stories are one.

In the months after Avi's death, he took up his cello now and again. He sat by the open balcony door with his bow raised and the cello's body resting against his breast. He looked out at the buildings between their apartment and the sea. Ordinary residential buildings like theirs, where life went on as theirs did. It was quiet in the room, usually Hannah was resting after getting home from work. He would like to have played for her, now that words were no longer adequate, but each time he put the cello back in its case.

He felt worried about leaving her alone when he had to go away on tour, yet he did go. She didn't ask him to stay home. It was his job to play with the string section in one town or another, on one or another continent. The music was the same, the towns and the concert halls only the changing framework for its free flow. He didn't think of anything or anyone when he played—he merely went along with the music, and it carried him along until it didn't matter who was playing and who was listening. As long as the music kept streaming through him he forgot Hannah and Avi, and he forgot himself. All that was left was the feeling, not its faces, melting together in the current of the music.

He played in towns all over the world without seeing much of them besides their concert halls and hotels. Sometimes he slept with other women. He avoids Irene's eyes as he tells her about the women. It wasn't so much a matter of desire, he says. It was the relief of not knowing anything and knowing they knew nothing about him. When there was nothing but a strange body and an unknown face before him, without words, without history, he felt for a moment that he was entirely anonymous. He never fell asleep with them, and after they had gone he sat by the window waiting for dawn. He imagined that Avi was somewhere behind him in the room, with his closely cropped hair and green uniform like the last time they were together. He imagined that the silence in the anonymous hotel room was merely one of the pauses that can arise in a conversation when neither one nor the other partner has anything to say. Not an awkward or embarrassing pause, merely a pause in which you breathe together in the soft gray light of a morning hour.

"He would have been fifty-one next month. Strange, isn't it?"

Samuel clenches his hand on the armrest of his chair and gazes at the forested ridge on the other side of the valley. Irene reaches for the back of his liver-spotted hand but he quickly removes it, ostensibly to brush off a few breadcrumbs. He looks at her.

"Dessert?"

She shakes her head. He makes a sign to the waiter and they sit in silence waiting for the bill.

"The Philharmonic is putting on a concert this evening. They're playing Mozart. Now that you have heard me play Bach, perhaps we ought to finish off with Mozart. He's the only one who compares with Bach."

Samuel pays the bill, and they rise. His face stiffens in pain and he supports himself against the table edge for a moment.

"It's my knee. I ought to get myself a new one."

He smiles apologetically but rejects her proffered arm, not unfriendly, but firm. He looks at her for a moment.

"To think I have a daughter."

Then he looks away.

They walk slowly downstairs and along the avenue. He speaks more slowly and stops at times, either to rest or to search for words.

He didn't know what to do with himself the evenings he didn't have a concert. He was used to the afternoons alone in the apartment before Hannah got home from work, but the evenings grew intolerable after the sun had set beyond the sea and she hadn't come home. Not until darkness was falling would he fully realize that she was never coming home again. He started going out for drives. He couldn't fall asleep anyway, and he found it necessary to keep moving. He followed the coast north toward Haifa as it grew dark, sometimes all the way to Nahariya near the Lebanese border. He would sit alone at one of the small restaurants beside the sea or just eat a falafel sandwich on the street in one of the towns he drove through.

At other times he drove through the mountains up to Jerusalem. He strolled around the labyrinth of covered alleyways in the Arab quarter that had only recently become a part of his country. He drank Turkish coffee in cafés where men wearing Bedouin head scarves sat smoking water pipes and playing backgammon, scowling at him. It didn't concern him. They were right, it wasn't his country—not anymore. Like any other tourist, he could stand gazing at the golden cupola of the mosque above the Temple Wall, where the orthodox Jews prayed, rocking back and forth with their faces turned to the weathered stones. It had nothing to do with him. He looked at the dry grass growing in cracks between the stonework, and felt nothing. Next year in Jerusalem. For centuries that had been the Jews' promise to each other, an end beyond all hardships and alienation, like a sense of direction in the world.

Six months before Hannah died, they had visited the reunified Jerusalem. They laid a stone on Avi's grave and went for a walk through the part of town that, until his death, had been inaccessible to Jews. Al Quds. How could that be their town? He had booked a room at the King David Hotel, she'd never stayed at a luxury hotel before. She hadn't been in a bathtub since she was a girl in Krakow. He massaged her tired feet as she lay submerged in foam so that only her sweet round face showed above it. During the night he woke to the sound of her shouting in her sleep. He tried to wake her, but she looked at him wild-eyed and yelled at him in Polish, not recognizing him. When he tried to hold her she struck his face with clenched fists. In the morning, he found her wrapped in a blanket by the window, in front of the view of the citadel and the old town, gray and barren like the mountains. Neither of them spoke as they stood there together listening to the muezzin's call blend with the barking of dogs.

Last year in Jerusalem. It was already long ago, he thought, when he stood once more on Temple Square one evening, watching the Hassidic Jews flitting by in their long black coats. It was on one of those occasions that he decided to leave. Several times in the past he'd been offered a position in New York, but each time had refused it on account of Hannah and Avi. At the age of fifty he finally settled in the city he'd fantasized about when he sat with Vivian in the Botanical Gardens in Copenhagen.

New York did not set him free, but it was a relief to live in a city where everyone came from somewhere else. Rather like Israel, he says, but in a different way—no one came to New York with the feeling of coming home. He rented a room from a widow who lived in a spacious townhouse near Central Park. He liked sitting in the park looking at the dark rocks and the gray squirrels. He tried to imagine the distant past, when Manhattan had been covered by a primeval forest, only accessible by the Indian trail that later came to be known as Broadway.

Now and then he visited a Russian tailor who had a shop between Broadway and Seventh Avenue. Saul Meyer was also from St. Petersburg, as the town was still called when his family emigrated. He was a good deal older than Samuel, but maintained that their fathers had known each other. They sat at the big work table in the back room among the shelves that held bolts of cloth, drinking vodka and exchanging stories about the Jews from their home town. Meyer was not usually nostalgic. Samuel ought to find himself a woman while he was still good-looking. He himself had married a second wife, a Latin American woman of forty, a shiksa. He lived life without a rearview mirror, as he said, puffing away at one of his big cigars. Now he could look forward to dying of a heart attack rather than lung cancer. But it was to be cancer. Samuel went to see him in the hospital. One day Meyer asked him to buy a box of cigars for him. It wasn't because he intended to smoke them. He just wanted to look at them and smell them. Even he was ending up in Nostalgia Corner, he said, with a glint in his eye behind the thick horn-rimmed spectacles.

Life was peaceful again. Samuel did his best to follow Meyer's advice, but he couldn't reconcile himself to the idea of a new marriage, and he couldn't bear women who badgered him to tell them his story. He glances at Irene with a quaint expression that makes her smile. He couldn't stand the exchange of life stories made into the mutual embroidery that transformed a chance meeting into a pattern of significant coincidences. The succession of women and the chaotic, motley life of the city remained peripheral disturbances. Music was the only thing that made the days coalesce and turn into months and years. It streamed on, throbbing in the cello's old body as it sent its vibrations back through him like an echo of everything that had passed. Perhaps the music sang on in those who had listened, but he himself was as empty as his instrument, hidden away in its lined case when he sat in a bus after the concert looking out at New York's moving mosaic of light. Nothing else was left, not a thought, not a sound.

When his contract was up for renewal, he chose to leave. There were too many Jews in New York. Some of them were friendly just because he had lived in Israel, others were sceptical, he could feel, because he'd left again, and he didn't know which was worse. He started looking for a position in Vienna, the Vienna of Hitler and Mozart. They had both had a decisive influence on his destiny, and it seemed a suitable choice. He was no lonelier than so many others. Occasionally, a woman would pass through his life, just as in New York, but inside he was as hollow and slippery as varnished spruce and poplar. That's how it was with the women, and it lasted so long and no more, like music. As always, he became secretive when they asked about his past, afraid of their sympathy but also afraid of something else. Again and again he saw Hannah's small figure beneath an umbrella on the beach in Tel Aviv or by a window in the King David, with its view of the holy city. Lost, out of reach, even when he held her in his arms.

He was only in his fifties, he still could have started anew. A year or two before he left New York he had a relationship with an Italian woman and was rash enough to visit her in Verona. She lived in a red-washed villa on the far side of the river and was somewhat younger, but with grown children. Divorced, beautiful, intelligent, and in love, believe it or not. In love with him—of all the middle-aged cellists in the world. He could have lived in that villa and lain down every night next to her warm, beautiful body, opened the shutters every morning to the view over the mountains and the tiled spires of the towers.

Throwing caution recklessly to the wind one afternoon, he told her about his life as they strolled in the Giardino Giusti. Maybe he only did so because she had never asked. She listened, gazing at the

254

marble figures and splashing fountains. It was a friendly, understanding silence, and in an unexpected way it made him feel close to her as they walked side by side past the row of cypresses. Two adults, each with their irreparable history.

She had a habit of closing her eyes when he kissed her; it seemed like a game. "Where are you?" she would ask, waiting for his kiss. She repeated the question one evening at a restaurant at the Piazza dei Signori. He had been gazing at the statue of Dante and the heavy, lofty medieval façades on the other side of the square. Where are you? she asked, and took his hand. Here, he replied, slightly embarrassed at his lack of attention. Where? she repeated, looking him in the eyes. Here, in Verona, he replied. She gave him a long look and shook her head.

He really did want to be there. He tried hard to convince her, had almost begun to believe it himself when he arrived in Verona on the train from Milan a few months later. He spotted her on the platform among the other people waiting, but he stayed in his seat. He hid himself behind a newspaper while people came in and out. An hour later the train was crossing the embankment between the mainland and Venice and he remembered something he had once heard about the old instrument makers of the city on the lagoon.

He recalls it again as he and Irene are walking back to the hotel. When it was calm, he says, they sailed out on the Adriatic, right out to where there was no dust or insects. Only out there in the clear, clean air could the smoothly polished instruments be lacquered without the risk of even a single mote of dust settling in the varnish and impairing their tone.

"I don't know if it's just a story…" He stops in the middle of the avenue of golden trees. "But since then I have thought that must be the place where I belong. Only there." He looks at her with a tired air, as if the loose, wrinkled skin around his eyes could barely carry their weight. "Under an awning, on a raft out in the lagoon."

She walks aimlessly while he takes an afternoon nap. She thinks of Vivian. Maybe she's sitting on her balcony looking out at the lawn and the pine trees. Perhaps they will never come to talk about Irene's journey to Ljubljana, the two of them separated and yet bound together by the same secret. She doesn't know where she's going, she just walks on as if his story is leading her. She's not a part of that story and yet she feels surrounded by it.

She hasn't come to find a father. She came because she had to look into his eyes before she could say good-bye to him. She can't share his story, she's not a Jew. She is an unknown, unexpected tangent to his life, the accidental result of a chance meeting. Like everyone else. But in her case the difference lies in the story, Samuel's own and the one that has been hurling him around for half a lifetime. Which says most about him? That he is a Jew, or that he once tried to avoid a designation he had not himself chosen? In the long run, he could only escape through music, opening him up to something more comprehensive, but also more forgetful.

She cannot share his story, and yet it is a part of her own. The unknown part of her story. What she had behind her has been just as unknown as what awaited her. She, the fugitive, the daughter of a refugee.

She can't share his story, and he couldn't share Hannah's. He had no access to the darkness inside her, which ended by sucking her into itself. But they have the question in common, Irene and Samuel. Which is most telling? What you cannot run away from, what you once reached out for, or what you have lost? In his story one flows into the other. And in hers? The same question unites and divides them. To her the question is still open. She can still reach out, as she turns her back on everything that she knows, and that lies behind her.

She walks among the shadowed façades and the silhouettes of cars and pedestrians. Ljubljana. It could be any town at all. And she? The low sun is warm on her face, and she fancies it is the future shining on her. An altered light. She is only visible, she thinks, in the glimmer of what has not yet shown itself. That which she has not yet reached nor overtaken, not yet arrived at.

An hour later, when she stands outside the small concert hall watching Samuel approach from the square, he is merely an elderly, stooping gentleman, just as when she first saw him in Vienna a few days ago. A strange, slightly limping elderly gentleman who happens to be her father. The feeling persists as he recognizes her and raises his hand in a frail, old-fashioned manner.

"Mozart makes you feel young again," he says as they walk through the foyer. "Deep inside you are still the same, just as Mozart is. He died young, and the music is the same forever. It's still there, and within the music you are still the one you were."

He stops to look at the other concertgoers standing in groups, speaking their language. Dusk has fallen among the trees, although the sky is still blue.

"You don't change. It is the world that's different. Mozart's world and the one you've known yourself. But deep inside it is still the same beginning. What nonsense I talk."

Irene smiles and takes his arm. This time he doesn't brush her away. They go in to find their seats. The same beginning, she thinks. The same original wonder.

There is complete silence, the last cough has died down. The musicians sit slightly hunched over, intently watching the conductor. Their coat tails hang behind them like swifts' wings, ready to take flight. The conductor raises his arms, and it is silence itself the strings touch softly with their bows, subdued, calm but resilient as they follow each other in the stepped rising of the theme, answered by the waving and bobbing of the woodwinds. An old song and yet new.

Who are you? I wonder who you can be?

Inside, Samuel is still the young man who stood on the deck of a cutter, watching the dark water grow wider between himself and the coast where Vivian lay in one of the houses waiting, he thought, for him to come back. Inside Samuel, Hannah is forever the pale, shy woman who sat under a beach umbrella looking out at the sea, and Avi is a young soldier standing at the bus station in Tel Aviv, shuffling his feet impatiently while his father buys bananas.

And Irene?

Deep within her there's a sleeper car. The thought makes her smile in the darkness of the concert hall. A compartment on its way through the darkness, dimly lit by a nightlight, where she lies listening to the rhythm of the wheels on the rails. On the way to Paris and an altered life, completely different from anything she could have imagined.

Samuel's hand finds hers, and their hands close around each other.

When they get back to the hotel he asks her up to his room. He lays his jacket on the back of a chair and bends over the worn instrument case that rests on the bed. He fumbles with the catches before he gets the lid open. It's true, it is red and shining like a pomegranate. He lifts the cello out of the case, it seems to weigh nothing. Slowly he gets himself seated on the edge of an armchair. He seems suddenly very old, as he sits there in his shirtsleeves, small and emaciated, with the cello resting against his left shoulder. She closes the instrument

258

case and places it on the floor. It has left a hollow in the bedspread, round like a woman's torso. She sits on the bed, he looks at her.

"Perhaps you think I'm going to play for you?"

She shrugs her shoulders.

"Too late, my dear." He stretches out his hands. "Arthritis." Only now does she notice his bony, deformed knuckles. "I always keep it with me even though it's been a long time since I've played it."

He strokes the curved sides of the cello with his palms and looks down its smooth, arched surface. They sit there for a long moment. Then she knows the time has come. She rises.

"Father...," She will probably never speak that word again. "I'll go now."

"Irene..."

He utters her name in a low voice, as if it was a thought. It's the first time he's spoken her name. He lifts his face and looks at her again.

"Will you do something for me?"

"Of course."

"Take it with you. It's time I gave it back."

"What shall I say?"

"Well, you can send my regards and say thank you for lending it to me." He plucks the strings with a thumb. One or two crisp, subdued notes. "It has been an unusual day," he says, laying the cello on its side.

"Will you take care of yourself?"

He attempts an arch smile, but it only results in a twisted grimace of pain as he struggles up out of his chair.

"Perhaps. Perhaps I can."

"If you can't say yes, you have already said no."

He puts the instrument case on the bed.

259

"Who says that?"

"You do."

He gives her a brief look from beneath his bushy eyebrows before opening the case and fitting the cello into its velvety nest.

"I have never said that," he mumbles.

He glances once more at the instrument, takes in the wave-grained pattern one last time before closing the lid, snapping the catches shut and passing her the case. It is surprisingly light.

They stand awkwardly, facing each other. She would like to embrace him but doesn't know how to go about it. She removes a hair from his shoulder. He takes her free hand and goes out with her. When she is out in the hallway she turns round. He nods and watches her in the diminishing crack between the door and the frame.

She rose early the next morning. Her car was waiting for her outside the hotel when she went down with her bag and the instrument case. She paid for her room, put the bag in the trunk, and strapped the cello to the back seat with one of the seat belts. An hour and a half later she reached the Austrian border. She stopped at a rest area a few hundred meters short of the Slovenian checkpoint and went into the cafeteria for a cup of coffee. As she was on her way back across the empty parking lot she caught sight of a young man standing near the exit with a bag over his shoulder. She got into the car and started up, and as she approached he stuck out his thumb. His bag was made of plaited plastic thread. The rustic luggage made an amusing contrast with his suit, dark brown with pale stripes, double-breasted, and slightly too large.

The young man's eyes were squinted against the slanting morning sun. He was so thin he almost disappeared inside the dusty jacket.
His hair was dark, and his brown face was long and narrow. She had
barely stopped before he opened the door and got in beside her. He
repeated the same sentence several times in his strange language. She
pointed to the seat belt. He fumbled a little before managing to fas-
ten it. She couldn't understand a word he said.

He gazed stiffly ahead, clutching his bag as they approached the
border. His hands were still darker than his face. The Slovenian border guard waved them through, and on the Austrian side the guards
were too busy chatting to notice Irene and her passenger. He relaxed
his hold on the knots of his bag when they'd gone through, but otherwise he sat motionless, without expression, as if he wanted to confine
his presence in the car to an absolute minimum. She put on a CD
that Samuel had given her the previous evening. Mozart's 40th Symphony. The last recording he made before retiring. Her passenger
didn't react to the well-known theme of the first movement. "It
sounds so light," Samuel had said, "and it should be light. Lighter
than nothing at all. But you only need listen to the first few bars to
know whether the conductor can play Mozart. He's not as easy as he
sounds. Compared with Haydn he is almost frivolous, and compared
with Brahms he is as pure and innocent as a Franciscan. But he is
never pedantic and boring, as Haydn can be, never unctuous and
bourgeois, as Brahms can be. He is as light as a butterfly. A butterfly
with a shadow image on his wings."

Had Samuel guessed she would follow him to Ljubljana? Was that
why he'd taken Mozart and Ruggieri with him? She never managed
to ask. There was so much she hadn't managed to ask. She listened
to the strings' playful, lightly flowing, and almost waltzlike theme, answered the next moment by the whole orchestra, triumphant, dra-

matic, passionate. "That music embraces everything," Samuel had said. "Everything a human being can hold, everything one can long for, and everything one cannot bear."

She followed E55 north toward Salzburg as she listened to the music with her anonymous passenger. Samuel must have arrived some time ago, he might be already on his way into Vienna from the airport. While she was in her car thinking of him he could be walking upstairs to his front door. At this moment he might be sitting at his table in the apartment, with the sun slanting in, still in his overcoat. Perhaps he could vaguely see his own reflection in the glass of one of the framed engravings of old towns with towers and spires behind their enclosing walls. Perhaps he was thinking of his daughter and his son, of Vivian and of Hannah, before he rose laboriously to go into the hall and hang up his coat.

Music was between them, thought Irene. It parted and united them, the same time, musical time, the same bars he had so often played. She could not hear him and yet he was somewhere in the orchestra, bent over his cello among the other cellists. Concentrated, completely present, as the music vibrated through him, and everything that had passed flowed together and vanished in its throbbing stream.

At first it felt odd to have a stranger in the car, and it seemed even weirder that they couldn't talk to each other, only sit. She with her hands on the wheel, he clutching the bag between his bent knees. She hardly knew what he looked like, but she didn't dare even glance at him. The traffic was denser here, and the thought of meeting his eye seemed insurmountable. She had only a vague recollection of a narrow, reddish brown face, even though he was sitting right next to her.

Gradually, she grew accustomed to his silent, motionless presence. He was her witness, it occurred to her. He was her witness, without knowing what he was witnessing. Her thoughts. He wouldn't have understood her even if she had thought aloud. But he was there. Just beside her, this noon on E55 one day in September. We are each other's witnesses, she thinks. But in most cases you have no idea what you are a witness to. She is a witness as well, to this stranger's story, without knowing what set him down temporarily with his bag, at a rest area on the border between Slovenia and Austria.

Suddenly she realizes she's not frightened. Should she be? It had never even occurred to her when she stopped and let him get in. The idea of fear seems remote, as she follows the regular stream of traffic. She keeps to the same speed, as if following the music, the changing tones and the shifting sequences of notes, further, constantly further. They can't talk to each other but the music is there between them. It parts and unites them, just like the road ahead, squeezing its way through the mountains and taking them closer to their separate destinations. Unknown witnesses to each other.

Who are you? Who can you be, I wonder?

We don't know each other. We shall never get to know each other, but I'm already used to you sitting beside me with your bag. I don't know where you've come from or what you imagine you're on the way to. An altered life? A better life than the one you've known? Perhaps you wouldn't be able to describe it more closely even if you had words for it that I could understand. Perhaps it was only a wordless, vague idea that made you break away. Maybe the only thing you knew was that you must leave, that you couldn't stay.

Was it too crowded, too cramped; or was there too much space around everything you hold in your dusty suit? All your will, belief, and doubt? You look as if you left with everything you own, in your best clothes, to try your luck. You can only try, can't you? To find out whether a crack, a narrow passage, will open up between the un-known world and your own innermost hope.

How strange it is to sit here together while my car drives us on through life, your life and mine. My guesses about where you come from are as vague, I imagine, as your ideas about where you're going. What do we ever see ahead of us? Something from television and something we imagine ourselves in. Flimsy, fleeting images. Perhaps you come from a village in Albania or the Carpathians, perhaps from as far away as the Anatolian Plateau. Perhaps you grew up in a city, Bucharest or Ankara, Sofia or Tirana. I've never been there, they're just names to me. Like Leningrad and Al Quds, Timbuktu and Atlantis. Is it the same for you?

Yet it must make a difference whether you leave because your be-lief and will are stifled, or make the break because it's too empty, too lonely around your innermost self. So empty and lonely that you lose sight of it. I think you know what you want. Where will is concerned I think you're like Martin. He was never in doubt. As for me, in the end I felt ashamed of how my will fumbled around, bemused, in the void that swirled around everything within its reach, dividing people from each other and me from all of it.

I think that's the difference between the two of us, my friend. You probably desire everything I have had, and you're right in your con-jectures about the rich lady who has taken you into her expensive car. You wouldn't mind a car like this, would you? You're right. I have had everything I could wish for, everything you dream of. But you know what? I have been too inept, too shortsighted, to interpret my inner-most hope. For years I felt my innermost self only as an insufficiency dulled by the familiarity of habit. A bewildered hesitation on the way from the door to the table to the bed.

You're going to be surprised by the diffuse melancholy of the rich. If they don't manage to catch you and throw you out because your papers aren't in order, that is. But they wouldn't change places with you all the same—even though, like me, they may have forgotten the name of their most precious hope, abandoned it somewhere between names like Mozart and Mercedes. Music is too abstract and the world too concrete, and it hurts when you fall against it, whether you fumble in bemusement or stand at the roadside, like you, with your bag over your shoulder, without possessions, unwanted.

You remind me of my father. The young man my father once was, in pinstriped English wool. But it's not just your shabby, shiny suit. It was something in your narrow face, which I caught a glimpse of earlier. Your frailty, your raised hand. Something vulnerable, exposed. I didn't understand what you said, but it was obvious what you wanted. It was clear because of the will in your foreign voice. You wanted to get going, to get away, as far away as possible from what you've left behind. That's all I know, of course, and I keep my eyes on the road. It would also be too strange to look into your eyes, boxed in with you in my car, unable to exchange a single word.

Now and then I feel your eyes on me, but to me your face is no more than a narrow oval with a peg in the middle. The idea of a face. The picture of someone unknown. You squeezed your eyes up against the sun, and the sharp light erased your features. Perhaps it was just something in the tilt of your face that seemed so expressive. What should I call it? Something chaste, but tense. An innocence without naivety.

So here we are, both of us on our way. I, too, am a long way from what I left behind. A life, a home. We make it ourselves, and we pick it apart ourselves. Maybe a tornado comes and blows it down, maybe it will collapse from lack of maintenance. Every life has its faults and lacks. Hidden cracks that open up a frightful endlessness when you lie awake at night, invisible to each other. Just like the two of us as we sit here, moving along in our separate stories.

How much have you left behind? How many wishes have you left unfulfilled? Maybe I'm wrong about your unknown will. Maybe you're lucky. Maybe you'll be a happy man with a lovely wife and a nice car in the garage. Maybe you've only made the break in order to return one day with your bag full of money to build a house in your village, larger than all the others, with rooms for your children and their grandparents. Maybe you're in no doubt about where you belong.

All the same, you reminded me of Samuel when you stood at the roadside, stranded between yesterday and tomorrow. With nothing to hold onto but your bag. Suddenly conscious of how shabby and absurd you look in your pinstriped suit.

Regardless of where you're going, you'll always be a stranger. You will walk like a shadow past the brilliant shop windows, stealing a glance at the well-dressed figures who belong in the strange town, and asking yourself if their life could someday be yours. You'll have nothing but your indomitable will, and you don't even have a cello to make your fortune with. Unless you've got a harmonica in your bag? Will you stand, for lack of anything better, on a cold, sparkling street in Frankfurt, playing the wistful melodies of your homeland? No work without papers, and without work no papers.

Samuel was luckier than you, he had a cello and talent, and he acquired the papers. But the country that gave him the papers wasn't one where he could feel at home in the long run. It's hard to feel at home in a country where you've lost everything. You'll be luckier than he was if you do manage to find work, with or without papers, so that one day you can go home to your village with a bulging bag. You're luckier than he was if you think you have a place to go home to.

267

I, on the other hand, am rich, my papers are in order, and I am legally entitled to live in a country my children have no need to die for. Where no one has been designated to die and supplied, for the sake of order, with a number imprinted on their flesh. I ought to feel at home. My homelessness is only a dizzy feeling of insufficiency, of something missing, neglected. Like a dream you try in vain to remember, before you pull yourself together and get up because you can't go on lying about like that.

The crack—do you know it? The crack through which you feel the coldness of endless space. That was what opened up in Samuel and allowed the music to flow freely. It was his luck, knowing how to make the void resonate. It was the only place where he felt at home, in the sound that throbbed through him when he put his bow to the strings. Was music a refuge or was he abducted by it, while his life changed direction, unforeseen and beyond the reach of his will?

To begin with, he had still only been grazed by history, not marked by it like Hannah, not swallowed up by it like Hannah and Avi, but even a touch can be enough to throw you off track. Each time he was on the verge of finding a foothold, the world suddenly changed shape. The world as he'd known it. Only the music was the same, but music is abstract, you vanish into it.

Three times life turned out to be different from what he'd imagined.

When he stood beside a canal with his sister one summer day in Leningrad being photographed, he couldn't imagine that his home town would fade into a dim memory, an inaccessible place.

On a cutter one autumn night, as he watched the coast fade away into the dark, he imagined that a life awaited him with Vivian on the other side of the war. A life, a child, a home.

The third time he believed in earnest that he had finally arrived. At Dizengoff in Tel Aviv taking a photograph of Hannah, pregnant and shy, with her branded arm behind her back and a smile that became stiff as he focused.

Only the music unites the three images, but music is blind, it unites them by erasing their contours. In the end, only the music remained. For he didn't know that his young, immature dream had germinated that October night during the war. Just as I couldn't know that for eighteen years I had a brother instead of the brother I never had.

Samuel can never be my father. Music is blind, but it unites our stories, divided as they are. I cannot be his daughter, but his story throbs through mine. I may never see him again, but we shall meet in music, for the music is the same. It is our witness, blind and meaningless, indomitable in its flow.

After they have passed Salzburg and are approaching the German border, Irene's passenger starts to grow restless. His eyes are dark and fearful, they seem unnaturally large in his bony face. His face is so narrow that it is little more than an extension of his curved, prominent nose. He is like a desperate bird imprisoned in the car. He keeps repeating the same thing in his strange language. She thinks she understands him and pulls into a rest area beside a spruce forest. He gets out. The cars race past, very close. He moves into the half darkness among the columns of trees, watching her, with his bag over his shoulder, as she herself gets out and walks around the car.

She opens the trunk, gets out her bag, and waits for a pause in the shoals of passing cars and trucks. He reacts to her beckoning too late, and she has to make a sign to him to stop when yet another group of vehicles approaches from behind. She gazes straight at the point where the three tracks converge on the bend behind the dark green spires of the trees. When the road is clear again she waves him over to her. This time he reacts quickly. She manages to meet his eyes before she closes the trunk on his huddled figure, bent over his bag with his knees drawn up beneath him. She puts her bag on the seat where he's been sitting, walks round the car, waits until yet another line of cars has passed, then gets in again. It's half a kilometer to the border.

Excuse me, Irene Beckman; what are you up to?

I don't know. I really don't know, but you mustn't distract me just now. I don't know what I'm doing, nor do I know what I should have done. He is my witness. We don't know each other, but we are each other's witness, as long as it lasts.

She turns Mozart up as she approaches the covered bay of the Austrian border crossing. A few minutes later she's driving through no man's land. A fifty-six-year-old woman with a stolen cello on the back seat, an unknown passenger in the trunk, and a father in Vienna she got to know far too late. She follows the music. It is her innermost self the strings are touching with their bows. Subdued, supple, they follow each other up the steps of the theme, where the woodwinds wave and bob. He, too, must be able to hear them in the dark back there.

It's Mozart, he died young. He was still on his way. You are never anything else, whether you're on a cutter with the lanterns extinguished or at a border crossing with everything you own in a bag. We are both on our way, you and I. For you, everything is still undecided; for me, it's already late. And for Samuel? Never say never. There is no such thing as never, as long as the music is flowing, and tomorrow he'll be at the Bräunerhof again reading his paper.

It is still the same beginning. Life is ceaselessly altering, and there isn't a place in the world where we belong. Beginnings have no arrival, no final destination. Hope is homeless, but indomitable, flowing beneath an awning between glinting spots of light on the calm surface of the water. Bare and finely cut, shining with moist resin. A heart of poplar and spruce, light and thin enough to vibrate and resonate with everything that passes.

Printed in the United States
133233LV00002B/7/A

9 780151 010431